THE RACHEL PAPERS

MARTIN AMIS

HARMONY BOOKS / NEW YORK

for Gully

Published in the United States in 1988 by Harmony Books, a division of Crown Publishers, Inc., 225 Park Avenue South, New York, New York 10003

Originally published in Great Britain in 1973 by Jonathan Cape Limited

HARMONY and colophon are trademarks of Crown Publishers, Inc.

Manufactured in the United States of America

Cover art by Robert Risko

Library of Congress Cataloging-in-Publication Data

Amis, Martin.

   The Rachel papers.

   I. Title.

PR6051.M5R33   1988   823'.914   87-30638

ISBN 0-517-56777-6 (pbk.)

10 9 8 7 6 5 4 3 2 1

First Harmony Paperback Edition, 1988

Seven o'clock: Oxford

My name is Charles Highway, though you wouldn't think it to look at me. It's such a rangy, well-travelled, big-cocked name and, to look at, I am none of these. I wear glasses for a start, have done since I was nine. And my medium-length, arseless waistless figure, corrugated ribcage and bandy legs gang up to dispel any hint of aplomb. (On no account, by the way, should this particular model be confused with the springy frames so popular among my contemporaries. They're quite different. I remember I used to have to fold the bands of my trousers almost double, and bulk out the seats with shirts intended for grown men. I dress more thoughtfully now, though, not so much with taste as with insight.) But I *have* got one of those fashionable reedy voices, the ones with the habitual ironic twang, excellent for the promotion of oldster unease. And I imagine there's something oddly daunting about my face, too. It's angular, yet delicate; thin long nose, wide thin mouth – and the eyes: richly lashed, dark ochre with a twinkle of singed auburn ... ah, how inadequate these words seem.

The main thing about me, however, is that I am nineteen years of age, and twenty tomorrow.

Twenty, of course, is the real turning-point. Sixteen, eighteen, twenty-one: these are arbitrary milestones, enabling you only to get arrested for H.P.-payment evasion, get married, buggered, executed, and so on: external things. – Naturally, one avoids like the plague such mischievous doctrines as 'you're as young as you feel,' which have doubtless resulted in so many trim fifty-year-olds flopping down dead in their tracksuits, haggard hippies checking out on overdoses, precarious queers getting their caps and crowns stomped in by bestial hitch-hikers. Twenty may not be the start of maturity but, in all conscience, it's the end of youth.

To achieve, at once, dramatic edge and thematic symmetry I elect to place my time of birth on the stroke of midnight. In fact, mother's was a prolix and generally rather inelegant parturition; she went into labour about now (i.e., about seven p.m., December 5th, twenty years ago), not to come out of it again until past twelve, the result being a moist four-pound waif that had to be taken to hospital for a fortnight's priming. My father had intended – Christ knows why – to watch the whole thing, but got browned off after a couple of hours. I have long been sure that there is great significance in this anecdote, although I have never been able to track it down. Perhaps I'll find the answer at the moment at which, two decades earlier, I first sniffed the air.

I confess that I've been looking forward to tonight for months. I thought when Rachel turned up about half an hour ago that she was going to ruin it all, but she left in time. I need to make the transition decorously, officially, and to re-experience the tail-end of my youth. Because something has definitely happened to me, and I'm very keen to know what it is. So : if I run through, let's say, the last three months, and if I try to sort out all my precocity and childishness, my sixth-form cleverness and fifth-form nastiness, all the self-consciousness and self-disgust and self-infatuation and self- ... you name it, perhaps I'll be able to locate my *hamartia* and see what kind of grown-up I shall make. Or not, as the case may be. Anyway, it ought to be good fun.

Now it's – let me see – just gone seven. Five hours of teen-age to go. Five hours; then I wander into that noisome Brobdingnagian world the child sees as adulthood.

I snap open my dinky black suitcase and up-end it on the bed; folders, note-pads, files, bulging manilla envelopes, wads of paper trussed in string, letters, carbons, diaries, the marginalia of my youth, cover the patchwork quilt. I jostle the papers into makeshift stacks. Ought they to be arranged chronologically, by subject, or by theme? Patently, some rigorous clerking will have to be done tonight. At random I pick up a diary, cross the room, and lean against the bookcase, which creaks. I sip my wine and turn the page.

The second weekend of September. At that point I had only a couple more days of home to endure before going down to London. It was on the Thursday that my father, drinking spirits for the first time in years, had wondered why I didn't 'have a crack' at getting into Oxford and I had nodded back at him, wondering why not, too. I was going to have a year off before university anyway. My English master had always impressed upon me how fucking clever I was. I didn't particularly want to go anywhere else. It seemed logical.

Mother got all bustly the next morning (fixing everything up) but came on vague and spiritual over lunch and resolved to take an afternoon nap. When I asked her what there was left to do she free-associated, until it became clear, as a jigsaw becomes clear, that she had succeeded only in telling my sister that I would be coming to stay and also (one assumes) giving her the usual half-hour rundown on the perils of the late menopause, and other such female smut.

'So,' I said, 'I ring the Oxford Admissions and U C C A *and* the Tutors.'

Mother left the kitchen with one hand flat on her forehead and the other suspended in the air behind her. 'Yes, dear,' she called.

It took about an hour because I am surprisingly ineffective on the telephone. I spoke to key tarts in the University Administration complex and finally got on to the Tutors, where a shifty dotard told me that it wasn't for him personally to say but he was fairly sure they would be able to fit me in. I realized then that I was half hoping for some insurmountable snag, like entrance dates. Yet it all seemed to be going forward.

I didn't know why I hoped this. Oxford meant more work, of course, but that was no problem. It meant more exams, but, again, I rather like having definite horizons, foreseeable crunches, to focus my anxieties on. Perhaps, as a person inclined to think structurally about his life, I had planned the next few months with my twentieth birthday in mind. There were several teenage things still to be done: get a job, preferably a menial, egalitarian one; have a first love, or at least sleep with an Older Woman; write a few more callow, brittle poems, thus completing my 'Adolescent Monologue' sequence; and, well, just marshal my childhood.

There is a less precious explanation. My family lives near Oxford, so if I went there I should have to spend more time at home. Furthermore, I dislike the town. Sorry: too many butterfly trendies, upper-class cunts, regional yobs with faces like gravy dinners. And the streets there are so affectedly narrow.

It is a Highway tradition that on Sunday afternoons, between the hours of four and five, any family representative can approach its senior member in what he calls his 'study' and there discuss matters, or crave assistance, or air grievances. One simply knocks and enters.

A small and rather hunted-looking figure now, my father said hello and asked what he could do for me, leaning over to empty the two-pint jug of real orange-juice, his daily ration, which he usually tucked away before eleven a.m. His eyes bulged warily over the discoloured glass as I told him that everything was fixed. There was a pause, and it occurred to me that he had forgotten the whole thing. But he soon roused himself. His hostile levity went like this:

'Super. I'm driving down tomorrow morning, I suppose I can take you along without too much trouble, so long as you don't bring all your worldly goods with you, that is. And don't worry yourself about Oxford. It's only the icing on the cake.'

'Sorry?'

'I mean it's just an extra.'

'Oh, absolutely. Thanks for the offer, by the way, but I think I'll take the train down. See you at dinner.'

I made myself some coffee in the kitchen and browsed through those Sunday papers that weren't draped over my mother's tent-like bulk on the sitting-room sofa. I wore a tired smirk. What did you expect? I thought. Outside, the sky was already beginning to turn shadowy mackerel. How soon would it get dark? I decided to leave for London straightway, while there was still time.

I suppose I really ought to explain.

The thing is that I am a member of that sad, ever-dwindling minority ... the child of an unbroken home. I have carried this albatross since the age of eleven, when I started at grammar school. Not a day would pass without somebody I knew turning out to be adopted or illegitimate, or to have mothers who were about to hare off with some bloke, or to have dead fathers and shabby stepfathers. What busy lives they led. How I envied their excuses for introspection, their ear-marked receptacles for every just antagonism and noble loyalty.

Once, last year, when we were all sixth-forming round the school coffee-bar (everyone else had to be in class), I was boringly reproached by a friend for 'actually hating' my father, who wasn't villainous or despotic, after all, merely dismissible. My friend quietly pointed out that he 'had no feelings of hatred' for *his* father, although he (the father) apparently spent most days with one fist down his wife's throat and the other up the au pair's bum. Precisely, I thought. I tipped my chair back against the wall and replied (somewhat high-mindedly, having that week read a selection of D. H. Lawrence's essays):

'Not at all, Pete, you miss the point. Hatred is the only emotionally educated reaction to a sterile family environment. It's a destructive and ... painful emotion, perhaps, but I think I must not deny it if I am to keep my family alive in my imagination and my viscera, if not in my heart.'

Cor, I thought, and so did they. Pete looked at me now with moody respect, like a sceptic at a successful séance – which, of course, was exactly how I looked; there it was, morally intelligible at last.

Not that there aren't, in my view, plenty of urgent reasons

for hating him; it's just that he constitutes such a puny objective correlative, never does anything glamorously unpleasant. And, good Lord, in this day and age a kid has to have something to get worked up about, skimpy though his material may be. So the emotion that walks like a burglar through our house trying all the doors has found mine the only one unlocked, indeed wide open: for there are no valuables inside.

Now I kneel, take from the bed the largest stack of papers, and fan it out on the floor.

It's strange; although my father is probably the most fully documented character in my files, he doesn't merit a note-pad to himself, let alone a folder. Mother, of course, has her own portfolio, and my brothers and sisters each have the usual quarto booklet (excepting the rather inconsequential Samantha, who gets only a 3p Smith's Memorandum). Why nothing for my father? Is this a way of getting back at him?

At the top left-hand corner of every page in which he features, I write 'F'.

My father has in all sired six children. I used to suspect that he had had so many just to show the catholicity of his tastes, to bolster his image as tolerant patriarch, to inform the world that his loins were rich in sons. There are in fact four boys, and he has given us progressively trendy names: Mark (twenty-six), Charles himself (pushing twenty), Sebastian (fifteen) and Valentine (nine). As against two girls. I sometimes wish I had been born female, if only to rectify this bias.

The most unattractive thing about him, or at any rate one of the most unattractive things about him, is that he gets fitter as he gets older. The minute he started to get rich (a mysterious process this, dating back some eight or nine years) he started also to take an increasingly lively interest in his health. He played tennis at weekends and squash three times a week at the Hurlingham. He gave up smoking and abstained from whisky and other harmful liquors. I correctly took this as a vulgar admission on my father's part that now he was richer he had every intention of living longer. A few months ago I caught the old turd doing press-ups in his room.

He looks sweaty, too. Due no doubt to delayed shock, his hair began pouring out soon after the money began pouring in. For a while he tried things like combing the seaweed curls forward, practically from the nape of his neck, to form a Brylcreemed cap which any sudden movement would gash with etiolated scalp. But eventually he realized it wasn't on and let his hair go its own way, which it did, teasing itself into two grey-coloured wiry wings on either side of his else hair-free head. It was a great improvement, I'm sorry to say, combining with his large, pointed face and short-shanked body to give him a certain ferrety sexual presence.

For some time now, his ferrety favours have been the preserve of his mistress, as I was assured at the age of thirteen by my elder brother. Mark was raffishly mature about it and had no patience with my falsetto disgust. Gordon Highway, he explained, was still a healthy and vigorous man; his wife, on the other hand, was – well, look for yourself.

And I looked. What a heap. The skin had shrunken over her skull, to accentuate her jaw and to provide commodious cellarage for the gloomy pools that were her eyes; her breasts had long forsaken their native home and now flanked her navel; and her buttocks, when she wore stretch-slacks, would dance behind her knees like punch-balls. The gnomic literature she was reading empowered her to give up on her appearance. Off came her hair, on came the butch jeans and fisherman's jerseys. In her gardening clothes she resembled a *slightly* effeminate, though perfectly lusty, farm labourer.

Anyhow I rampaged enthusiastically about all this, largely I think as a reaction against my brother's greasy permissiveness. Also, I had never thought of my father as being particularly vigorous nor of mother as being particularly unattractive or of either of them as being anything but quietly, and asexually, content with each other. And I didn't want to see them this way, in sexual terms. I was too young.

13

Even this, though, you see, even this failed to put any bite, any real *spunk*, into family life.

The Highway kitchen, nine o'clock, any Monday morning:

'Are you off now, dear?'

My father pushes his grapefruit aside, swipes his mouth with a napkin. 'In a minute.'

'Shall I be able to reach you at the flat, or at the Kensington number?'

'Uh, the flat tonight and,' narrowing his eyes, 'I *think* on Wednesday. So the Kensington number Tuesday and probably' – flexing his forehead – '*probably* Thursday. If in doubt, ring the office.'

I always tried to avoid these exchanges and felt like peeing in my trousers whenever I accidentally witnessed one. But in fairness it wasn't the sort of thing you could actually get yourself into a state about. If only mother minded more. Surely, I felt, she must spend *some* time wondering when he would start arriving on Saturday morning instead of Friday night, start leaving on Sunday night instead of Monday morning, when his weekend with the family would suddenly and irreversibly become his day with the children.

I packed – crucial juvenilia, plenty of paperbacks, and some clothes – then looked round the house for people to say goodbye to.

Mother was still asleep, and Samantha had gone to stay with a friend of hers. The study was empty so I wandered through the dusky passages calling out to my father, but there was no reply. Sebastian, being fifteen, was probably making eyes at his bedroom ceiling. There remained one brother.

Valentine was in the attic playroom, knee-deep in a metropolis of Scalextric, dicing model sports-cars. I said I was going and told him to give my love to everyone, but he couldn't hear me. I left a note on the hall table, and crept off.

Seven twenty: London

Now I look round my room and it seems a companionable place to be – what with the two wine bottles, the subdued lighting, the listless but reassuring presence of paper and books. *Highway's London*, one of my note-pads, has it that I found the room 'oppressive, sulky with the past, crouching in wan defiance as I turned to look at it' on that September Sunday. My word. I suppose I was just moodier then, or more respectful of my moods, more inclined to think they were worth anything.

Of course, if Philip Larkin is anyone to go by, we all hate home and having to be there.

It was certainly nice to get out of the house and, come to think of it, I did feel quite braced and manly walking the nut-strewn lane to the village. The Oxford bus wasn't due to leave for another quarter of an hour, so I had a well-earned-half at the pub and chatted with the landlord and his wrecky wife, Mr and Mrs Bladderby. (Interestingly, Mrs Bladderby had an even wreckier mother, who was eighty and had, moreover, during a recent outing, got her left leg slurped into a dreadful piece of agricultural machinery; she was far too ga-ga to die of shock, had indeed never mentioned the fateful picnic since. Now Mrs Lockhart resided in the room above the saloon, clubbing the floor with a warped bar-billiards cue whenever she needed attention.) As Mrs Bladderby disappeared to answer just such a summons, Mr Bladderby wagged his head at my suitcases and asked whether I was off on holiday again.

I stalled until the lady returned and then settled down to making it clear that, chinless elitist and bratty whey-faced lordling that I most unquestionably was, my move to London had nothing to do with any antipathy towards themselves, nor

15

towards the village – far less did it symptomize a disillusionment with the rustic pieties, etc., etc. I gave two reasons. The first was 'to study', earning a look of grim approval from Mr Bladderby; the second was 'to see my sister', earning a glare of congeniality from his wife. When I finished my drink and glanced at my wristwatch they appeared to be really sorry to see me go, and two of the unemployable old locals looked up and said goodbye. Carefully closing the door after me, I was in no doubt whatever that one of them would now be saying: 'That Charles, you know – he's a fucking nice boy'; and then: 'Yes, I agree – a *fucking* nice boy.'

And quite right too. Thinking back, actually, 'self-infatuation' strikes me as a rather ill-chosen word. It isn't so much that I like or love myself. Rather, I'm sentimental about myself. (I say, is this normal for someone my age?) What do I think of Charles Highway? I think: 'Charles Highway? Oh, I like him. Yes, I've got a soft spot for old Charles. He's all right is Charlie. Chuck's ... *okay*.'

The bus was good, too. I sat up the front, to admire the chubby, unsmiling driver, whose combination of snake-eyed intentness and natural flair made quite good viewing. Elation was gathering on me like a drug – I smiled at my fellow-passengers, gazed interestedly out of the window, and was polite and deferential to the transport operative, producing the correct money and enunciating my destination clearly.

Nor was it as if this was an obviously epoch-making journey. Perhaps it was simply that I had rung this girl Gloria before I left.

At any rate, Oxford station, recently modernized so as to resemble a complex of Wimpy Bars, was sobering enough. The newsagents was closed so I looked out a paperback from my suitcase. Seated appropriately far from the window, *A Room with a View* lay unopened beside me all the way there.

London is where people go in order to come back from it sadder and wiser. But I had already been there – returned from it only three weeks before, in fact.

When my A-Level results came through my father beefily gave me seventy-five pounds with which to 'get the hell out of England and have a good time'. It was suggested that I go to a warm healthy country, and stay there some while; otherwise I was given a free hand. A boy I knew was going to Spain the next week so I gave him a newsy letter addressed to my parents for him to post when he got there. Then, with Geoffrey (a like-minded friend), I headed for Fat City.

We holed up for a month in the Belsize Park flat of a Miss Lizzie Lewis, Geoffrey's actress sister, who was away doing a summer season of panto at a holiday camp in Port Talbot. It was a month I always think of with a certain pimply lyricism. It was a month of plonk and coffee-bars, pinball arcades and party-hunts, of looking for girls and wet daydreams, white smell of sweat and dusty afternoons, of getting burnt by ghoulish hippies, of such mind-expanding drug experiences as pork-chop vomiting and consommé diarrhoea. It ended one mid-August morning when I happened to glance down at the undulating area between my stomach and the stomach of a girl I just so happened to be poking at the time (in a sweaty, hungover state, I might add). What I saw there were worms of dirt – as when a working man, his day done, strides home rubbing his toil-hardened hands together, causing the excess grit to wriggle up into tiny black strings, which he soon brushes impatiently from his palms. Only these were on our stomachs and therefore much bigger: like baby eels.

I was back in Oxford for lunch that same day, with feverish stories about its having been Spain's worst summer since the war – hence the pallor. My parents informed me, however, that I had 'been seen' on the Portobello Road in the last week of July. I denied this and silenced them by pretending to be far iller than I was, not that they need much silencing. (There was also the question of a little going-away present from the young lady – my partner in grime – which is another story.)

The train got into Paddington about eight thirty. The station, empty for what was a Bank Holiday weekend, seemed vast, echoic, etc., and I hoped that it wasn't going to come on all uncanny and Hemingway-esque on me. Curious (no?) how clearly I remember this: far more clearly than the events of the last couple of weeks.

I decided in the end to take a cab, arguing that it was an indirect economy because I then couldn't afford to take Gloria out and the evening would cost no more than a level teaspoonful of my sister's instant coffee. Furthermore, it was far, far too late to go on the tube without getting denounced by drunkards or, alternatively, castrated by skinheads. As the taxi swept up the ramp into the city, I unwound in the back, quietly rehearsing lower-middle-class accents for the benefit of my brother-in-law. Behind the darkened windows I peered at the many purple-T-shirted and Afghan-fur-waistcoated girls who lined the throughways of Paddington and Notting Hill Gate.

I had met Norman Entwistle, my sister's terrifying husband, on only two occasions. I saw him now, for the third time, as I walked up the sloping approach to his Campden Hill Square home. If it hadn't been for all the noise he was making I might have missed him altogether.

Norman was up in the tree that stood alone in the middle of the slender front garden. He looked rather as though he were trying to saw himself in half – an activity that on his previous showings I wouldn't have put past him. Both his legs and one of his arms were wrapped round a branch. Using his free hand in a piston-like action, he was attempting to sever it at its base. The branch, which was obviously dead, hung about six feet from the ground.

I halted. 'When you cut through the branch,' I pointed out to him, 'you'll fall down.' Norman ignored me. I could just make out some of his face; it was stretched in murderous concentration.

'To the ground,' I explained.

I went on watching him for a few seconds, then walked up to the front door and rang the bell. The door was about to open when I heard a wrenching noise – as of the splitting of wood – followed by a loud crash. I turned round. Norman was already on his feet, brushing himself down like someone covered in lice.

'Christmas,' said Jennifer Entwistle, my sister.

We kissed, blushing, as we always did when we kissed, and on the way into the kitchen Jenny gave me a formulaic ballocking for not alerting her of my premature arrival.

'What's Norman up to?' I then asked.

'Oh, just sawing down a dead branch.'

I assumed I was interrupting the denouement of some kind of row. Probably Jenny had wondered out loud when Norman was going to get round to cutting down the dead branch and Norman had raced out and cut it down straightway, thus putting her in the wrong. There you go.

I sat not being a nuisance at the kitchen table, put on my glasses and watched her make tea. She looked all right. In the role of elder sister she had seemed to me merely graceless and sulky. None of my friends (for instance) had ever asked to be told what her tits were like. Even on her vacation visits from Bristol, when I was especially sensitive to this sort of thing, I never masturbated about her once. However, I *did* masturbate about her – electrically – all through last Christmas holidays. That voluptuous languor, those invigorating, slow, easy movements: what a transformation, real physical deliverance. To quote my elder brother Mark, who sports-carred up on Christmas Eve and down again on Boxing Day, she looked 'spunk-drunk'. And it was evidently Norman's she was carousing on, because she never went back to Bristol to complete her B. Litt., and by April they were married.

Now, she seemed somewhat hungover, but wholesome enough. In particular, her hair was long, shiny, and quite thick for a Highway; and, remarkably, even though she was mousy-blonde, big-boned, full-breasted, wide-hipped and generally slightly sallow, there was no reason to believe that with her clothes off she would smell of boiled eggs and dead babies.

Norman himself came in now. He nodded in my direction

and sat down opposite me at the table, briskly flattening a dog-eared *Sunday Mirror* on to its artificial surface. He read with concentration, his nose perhaps six inches above the page, mouthwashing with tea from a pint-sized mug which Jenny had time and again to refill. She stood by her husband, one hand resting awkwardly on his shoulder, as she and I chatted about home, and my plans.

Norman spoke only once on that occasion. I mentioned that Gloria would probably be stopping by later on.

Jenny had asked, 'Will she be wanting dinner?'

'Oh no,' I said, 'she won't be here till about nine, nine thirty.'

Norman looked up from his paper and said, with scorn but without disapproval:

'Fuck and coffee, is it? Just fuck and coffee.'

After tea I went to unpack. My bedroom was in the front basement, commanding a view of the dustbins and redundant coalshed. Jen had clearly done some work on it: matching curtain and bedcover, Expo '59 coffee-table, serviceable desk and chair. I lowered myself on to the bed before starting to unpack. The room wouldn't, after all, need much preparation for Gloria – record-sleeves scattered negligently about the room, certain low-brow paperbacks displayed advantageously on table and desk, and the colour supplements, open at suitable pages, on the floor. Gloria probably had no very fixed conception of me so there wasn't much point in going into detail.

I wondered if there were any important lies I had told her which it would be worth reacquainting myself with, but could think of none. But ... ah yes, I was twenty-three and an adopted orphan, that was all. (She was an undemanding girl.) Instead, I got out a note-pad and drafted a short list of topics with which to amuse her for the duration of the walk back from the station and the pre-pass half-hour. I could enlarge on my guardians busting me about last summer, which she would enjoy, and thereby explain why I hadn't contacted her for a month. Also, there was the continuing story of Gloria's driving lessons (given by her father, a twenty-stone carpet-layer), of which she would certainly welcome the chance to keep me abreast. Otherwise, there was always pop-music. – Which reminded me; there was another lie: I was friendly with Mick Jagger. But before I did anything else I went up-stairs to make a telephone call. Not to Gloria; to Rachel.

In fact I lost my nerve after six digits, hung up, took deep breaths, redialled; her Continental mother answered, I hung up again.

On my way to the bathroom I glimpsed Jenny and Norman standing by the cooker. They were enjoying a kiss – well, more of a snog really. It didn't look half as extraordinary as one might have thought.

But you should have seen my parents, when they got the news.

The Highway breakfast-table, once again, the Saturday before Easter :

'My God,' cries mother, 'Jenny's going to be married.'

Gordon Highway : 'Jenny?'

'Jennifer. To a businessman. Thirtyish. "Norman Entwistle".'

'What kind of businessman?'

'Household "appliances".' She reads on. 'Second-hand appli-ances.'

'My God.'

'In a fortnight. She's giving up Bristol.'

My father leans over. 'To whom is that letter addressed?'

'Both of us. I opened it because –'

'I see. Well, she's twenty-four' (actually she's twenty-three), 'legally an adult. I see no point in forcing the issue.' He sighs. 'There'll be some sort of reception to arrange ... ?'

'Jenny says she realizes it's short notice. She says she rather thinks a small dinner-party. At his house.'

My father looks up meanly from his newspaper. 'Well. That's something.'

The following weekend the young couple motored down for tea. I diluted it. My Valium-ed mother fluttered between them on the sofa. My father paced the hearth. When Norman gave voice to such idioms as 'settee', 'pardon?', and at one point 'toilet', my father could be seen to wince as a man who is in pain will wince. He was a bit thrown by the opulence of Norman's car and accoutrements – but he wasn't a man to be gulled by the mere tokens of privilege. (Furthermore, my father was so very much shorter than Norman that Norman had had to go down practically on his haunches to be introduced.)

While my mother and sister convened their teach-in on babies, honeymoons and pre-menstrual tension, I gave Norman a game of backgammon – later abandoned for pontoon. We seemed to get on quite well.

'It could conceivably be worse, I suppose,' my father supposed when they'd gone.

Gloria and I had just reached an impasse on the subject of is there, or is there not – excluding, for the purposes of argument, the Tamla-Motown genre – a legitimate place for brass accompaniment in the current pop scene, when I counted down from ten in my head and glided forward in her direction, eyes half closed, lips pursed, arms spread wide.

Sitting comfortably? In fact, that was a direct quote from *Conquests and Techniques: a Synthesis*, a folder of mine. Most of the stuff here is in note form, with the odd diagram; but when I get a good idea, or a detail worth elaborating on, then I turn it into a full-dress sentence (and circle it with red ink). The section entitled, simply, 'Gloria', I now see, is done in a rather pompous mock-heroic style, like Fielding's descriptions of pub brawls – the sort of writing I usually have little time for. But there is a sense in which this style is suited to the subject, so I'll let it pass. That evening had something inimitably teenage about it and, after all, I shall never see its like again.

Firstly, I assume I'm right in saying that teenage sex is quite different from post-teenage sex? It's not something you do, just something you get done. The over-twenties, I grant you, must see it largely as a matter of obligation, too: but obligation to the partner, not to oneself, like us. Take a look at the scaly witches round your local shopping centre, many of them with children. Grim enough with their clothes on. Imagine them naked! Snatches that yo-yo between their knees, breasts so flaccid you could tie them in a knot. One would have to be literally galvanized on Spanish Fly even to consider it. Yet it gets done somehow. Look at the kids. – The teenager may be more spontaneous, doglike, etc., but it's generally only another name on the list, only another notch on the cock ... Perhaps there's some kind of plateau during one's twenties and very early thirties. I might well give statistical weight to these filthy speculations by going down to the village tomorrow morning, twenty years of age, and finding out. (I could easily pull the village idiotess, who in any case, one windless summer night, had wanked Geoffrey and me off through the school railings, simultaneously; we stood there clutching the bars, like prisoners.)

Anyway: Gloria. I imagine that the older man thinks it's going to be hell and is often agreeably surprised to find that it's not quite, not *quite*, as bad as he had such excellent reasons to fear. With the youngster the very reverse is true. Gloria and I undressed like lifeguards, and without actually separating. I always forgot the full drama of the change that came over her the minute she was underway. In normal circumstances, with her embarrassment in any kind of pre-coital conversation, her unassumingly pretty face, the stiff-limbed movements: you were a plaything of her unease. Once underway, though, Gloria would have been able to detect few noteworthy points of contrast between sexual arousal and rabies.

It wasn't that bad, as I remember, not significantly worse than usual. Fifteen, maybe twenty minutes trying not to come, with a beady dread of what was going to happen when I did; a decent (i.e. perceptible) orgasm; a further two or three minutes in garrotted detumescence. Cock attains regulation minimum and is supplanted by well-manicured thumb; Gloria has another ... five? orgasms; and so it ends. I roll over. My thumb looks as though it has been for a four-hour swim: grey, puffy, dappled where I've eaten bits of it in the past. My alarm clock claims it's only ten fifteen. I wish I were back in Oxford.

A remarkable phenomenon, students of the human condition gather round. While thinking about this, while leafing through my notes, I have a shirty erection. I am jealous of myself. If Gloria came through the door now – I'd do it again. She is a fine-looking girl, certainly: excellent middle-weight figure, costly red hair, huge mouth, a judicious number of freckles, and, paradoxically, she does look very becoming with her clothes off. But such attractions shouldn't becloud (let alone obliterate) an elementary correlation of pleasure and pain. Can it just be experience we're after?

Restored by a cigarette, Gloria beguiled the following hour in an attempt to actualize my full nineteen-year-old potential. *Conquests and Techniques: a Synthesis*: 'Now she wheedled and tugged at my snaily genitalia, now scoured my ears with her tongue, now patrolled my ankles and shoulder-blades for uncharted erogenous zones. After our second coupling I go as far as *faking* a third orgasm. My gurgles of pain are taken for cries of virile delight.' That sort of thing.

'Wow,' I then said. 'That really was something. Well – have you got enough pillow there? – night night, sleep well. Until the morning.'

Gloria looked at me oddly.

Front to the wall I feigned sleep ... the odd incoherent murmur ... two or three tentative snores ... a certain amount of involuntary twitching. But the sheets whispered beside me. I felt a hand traverse the lower areas of my back. In seconds – radar-tracked by my whisker-sensitive pubic hairs – it was treading air above my groin. And my groin, in its youthful way, said: 'I'm game.'

During the long pre-copulative session I glanced downwards – and what should I see but Gloria, practising the perversion known as fellatio. Unaccountably, she was doing this with great rigour and enthusiasm, circling her head so that her long plush hair skimmed and glided over my hips, thighs and

24

stomach. Visually, it was most appealing, but all I could feel was a remote, irrelevant numbness – plus, in my legs, cramp and pins-and-needles respectively. Have I come already, perhaps? I asked myself.

Gloria didn't think so. She swooped up, said 'I only do that for boys I like,' planted a fizzy kiss in my mouth, and hoisted me on top of her.

I recall turning at one point from the section of wallpaper I was perusing to check on Gloria's face (just for the files): and impressively atavistic it was too. Accordingly, her orgasm came with clenched teeth, bull-whip shuddering, yelps of dismay; mine came (or did it?) with back pains, bronchitic gasping, with everything all caving in. When I withdraw, it occurred to me, I shall surely get blood over Jenny's nice room.

Gloria lay back, her race run. After a while she folded up and went to sleep. And I watched the ceiling, breathless with envy.

Quarter to eight: the Costa Brava

On average I get through seven diaries a year; no matter how big the pages are, and no matter how pithy and austere I try to be, my days always run into weeks. These early sections are embarrassingly full of teenage largesse. But now I glance down the closely written columns and I smile, dear Charles, at your past holidays.

'I see. So you've already got in.'

'To Sussex, yes, but not Oxford.'

'I see. Then you'll be wanting to take the scholarship exam this – November?'

'Yes' (you stupid bitch, you dull clit), I said. 'And I'll need Use of English and General Paper.' Shouldn't she know all this? 'And Latin O Level.' I grinned across the table at my future Directress of Studies. She was most unpleasant to look at. I won't go into it, but she was about thirty-five, had eyebrows as big as teddy-boy quiffs, and her teeth bucked out from her gums at right-angles.

'I *see*. So you'll only be taking the three subjects with us. and they are ... ?'

I repeated them. 'And Oxford Entrance,' I added, as if it were not necessarily relevant but perhaps of interest in its own right.

Glancing again at my newly compiled dossier she read out in an incantatory honk: 'A-Level passes: English, grade A, Biology, grade A, Logic, grade A.' Her chins settled on her throat. 'Curious subjects ... but, yes, I don't think we'll have much trouble getting you through your ... O Levels. Um ...' She cocked her head in decorous misgiving. 'You're a bit old to be going up to Cambridge, aren't you?'

'Oxford. Only nineteen,' I said.

*

When I awoke that morning the bedroom was a rhino pen, the sheets hot straitjackets. Gloria had insisted on sealing the window and keeping the gas fire on – for the purpose, one imagines, of simulating jungle conditions. There appeared to be a seam of sweaty mist all over the floor, as in student productions of *Macbeth*. My head came up like a periscope, on the look-out for air.

I inched out of the bed, without waking Gloria, and stalked upstairs dressed only in my duffle-coat. No one seemed to be up. I made two cups of tea and – for the lady – two slices of energy-giving Hovis, after some thought spreading them with Marmite, which I hoped would help create a Bacchic after-breakfast atmosphere.

'Good morning,' I said, putting the tray down beside Gloria's cracked smile. I drew the curtains back an inch or two. A gash of sunlight fell athwart the bed, causing a token shriek from the compromised Gloria, who was sitting up and well into her second round of toast. I watched her finish. She wiped her mouth with freckly knuckles, lay back with a grunt and lit a cigarette. Her breasts were exposed; they looked very white now. What did I feel for her? Ambiguous lust, genial condescension, and gratitude. It didn't *seem* enough.

She was so much better in the morning – in fact there was no comparison – because one knew that it couldn't go on all night. I slipped in beside her, tricked out with a bladder-filled erection. Why, the reechiness of the bed began to strike me as rather stimulating. Gloria was evidently bucked by her breakfast, and we rolled about hugging and tickling each other, and laughing, in an evasive cross-fire of bad breath, before coming together cautiously for the first kiss of the day. In my limited experience, this is nearly always tolerable if one is wholehearted about it and almost invariably emetic if one isn't. I was wholehearted about it, what with adulthood pending.

Tragically, though, Gloria was 'too sore'. Normally, of course, I would have been greatly relieved. Normally, of course, this would have been one of the most bewitching things she could possibly be : *too sore.*

Gloria looked actually ashamed. 'Don't worry,' I told her. 'It's quite flattering really.'

I went into a long routine of being good about being good about it, gently reproaching her for being so attractive, suggesting that there might just possibly be ways of getting round this problem: all in a diverting, twinkly-eyed manner which Gloria found vastly entertaining. She said things like 'Oh, Charles, you are terrible,' and 'It's not *my* fault,' and '*Ow*, that hurts.' Eventually I pointed out that she could, you know, always sort of, well, *I* don't know, perhaps, I mean ... She laughed uproariously at these antics before moving softly on top of me and downwards so that her head lay in the vault of shifting, sunlit dust. It was divine.

Gloria held the assistant pet-food saleswomanship in, handily, a Shepherds Bush emporium. I walked her there, then came back up the Bayswater Road to the Tutors, which was barely half a mile from Campden Hill Square.

Mrs Noreen Tauber, B.A. (Aberdeen), went on to bore me some more about dates and things. Then, with a frowsy sigh, she offered to take me on a tour of the school, probably with nothing more ambitious in mind than to show me that it wasn't a workhouse or blacking-factory after all, We walked up a corridor, admired two identical classrooms, and walked back down it again, over wobbly parquet, past farting radiators. The pace was relaxed, donnish; the conversation general, discursive; we tried, in our small way, to make the place seem nicer than it was.

Legless buskers cavorted outside Holland Park Underground. I bought some newspapers (Fleet Street's big two, in fact, the *Sun* and the *Mirror*), leftily dropped ten pence into the musicians' bowler hat and stood there reading the headlines, tapping my foot to a trilled-up version of 'Oh, You Beautiful Doll'. I was about to aim up to Notting Hill for a coffee at the Costa Brava when a hook-nosed queen with flat hair appeared from behind the curtains of the station photograph booth. He asked if I knew the time. I said what it was, referring him to the large clock attached to the wall opposite. He thanked me and inquired if I ever went down the Catacombs club in Earls Court.

'I don't *think* so,' I said, flattered.

It was being a good September, quite warm in the sun, so I took my time, glancing through the papers, occasionally halting mid-stride to mull over a joke or the better to marvel at a pin-up.

I was a queer, too, once upon a time.

The point is worth elaborating.

For possibly the most glamorous thing about me is that I am, actually, a delicate child – or as near to one as you can well get nowadays.

I got bronchitis – absolutely spontaneously – at the age of thirteen.

The night after it was diagnosed I crept down and looked it up in the encyclopedia. There it was, 'acute bronchitis', which was what the doctor said I had. Better still, though, was 'chronic' bronchitis: you got that at least once a year. I asked old Cyril Miller, our GP, whether there was any chance that I might develop, or acquire, the chronic kind. Praising recent scientific breakthroughs and modern drug techniques, he said this was unlikely. *Chronic* bronco was reserved for nicotined oldsters with suede-shoe lungs.

Yet, if you want a couple of weeks in bed (as I did, bi-annually), and if you have indolent and credulous parents, it's amazing what a few packs of French cigarettes will do.

Besides, there were plenty of other things to keep me going. Take, for example, my mouth – literally a shambles. My milk-teeth wouldn't go away, they just curdled, although politely moving over to accommodate my grown-up ones. At the age of ten I must have had more teeth in my head than the average dentist's waiting-room. Soon, I used to think, they'll be coming out of my nose. Then months of high-powered surgery involving metal strips, nuts, clips, bolts ... you name it. For two years I went about the place with a mouth like a Meccano set.

The diseases you're supposed to get only once I got twice. My bones were the consistency of fresh marzipan. I nurtured seasonal asthma.

Patently, it was all right by me. Dozy afternoons slugging on opiate cough mixtures, sleeping-draughts dropped at noon, stolen handfuls of Valium, a sheet of aspirins before breakfast. I read every readable book in the house, and also most of the unreadable ones. I wrote two epic poems: an heroicall romance in twenty-four cantos entitled 'The Tryst' (© 1968), and an asthmatic, six-thousand-line *Waste Land* called 'Only the Serpent Smiles' (© 1970), some parts of which reappear in the aforementioned 'Adolescent Monologue' sonnet sequence. I wrote cameos of everyone I had ever met. I recorded all I saw, felt, thought. I had myself a time.

About my queer period.

I was being a bit roguish (for dramatic purposes) when I suggested to my friend Peter in the sixth-form coffee-bar that I hated *all* my family. I don't really mind the women in it. This bias officially dawned on me towards the end of my second bedridden winter. I concluded that it was merely rather trustingly Godfrey Winn of me, nothing more sinister. My age? Fourteen.

However, one afternoon, in a doped half-state, I read a Chunky Paperback on Sigmund Freud.

I spent the night in a state of mild, run-of-the-mill delirium, sweating quietly as my mind wobbled and raced and swerved: and with morning, came the unshakable, indeed serene, conviction that I was a homosexual. It all added up: I had had, it was true, one queer experience (a smegmatic handful of queer experience in my primary-school cricket pavilion); I was a *soprano*, a *first* soprano, often taking descants, in the choir; I was as yet a virgin, and had to lie my unpimpled head off to my friends about how I wanked as often, and with as much piston-wristed savagery, as they said they did. Clearly, the minute I was off my arse I'd be getting it on the bus to Oxford and hawking it there to the friendly under-graduates at Magdalen. In puzzled preparation I read the col-lected works of Oscar Wilde, Gerard Manley Hopkins, A. E. Housman, and (for what little it was worth) E. M. Forster.

Next, exploring my powerhouse elder brother's desk I came across a body-building mag, called *Tensio-Dynamism* or some-thing, one of the ones that explains to you how to kick the shit out of anyone who bugs you at the seaside. Resignedly I went back to my room, curled up in bed with it, started turn-ing the pages, waiting equably for an erection. No way. Idiot faces glaring in pinhead conceit, ghastly all-out-of-control ten-ements of beef-cake. Never felt less sexy in my life: it beat me how *females* could fancy them. These gentlemen were, I real-ized, unrepresentative – but even so.

Luckily, I had, and still have, a mind like a bear-trap; as soon as one idea wriggles free I'm sprung and tensed for the next unwary paw. As with most people who pass for sensi-tive, obsessive types, I simply can't get enough of things to get worked up about – an interest. Now I was keen to know why all woman weren't dikes. Anyway, that summer I had a formative heterosexual experience. I'll go into it later. Let me say only that as a direct result I got my first decent pimple, a fine double-yolker, and that that pimple flourished over the weeks, to become the object of much silent envy when I re-turned to school in September.

To be fair, there weren't all that many maniacs in the Costa, and hardly more than a smattering of blinkies.

Sipping on my coffee I tackled the *Mirror* crossword. If I completed it I would fuck Rachel within ... three weeks. Put-ting in a couple of clues I decided I would ring her when I got back. It would be intelligent to do it while I still felt tolerably spermy and Joycean after my night with Gloria. In my mind I saw young Charles leaning against Jenny's passage wall and smiling into the telephone. I couldn't hear what he was saying, but his eyes were bright and his face pleasantly animated. 'Hi,

Rachel? This is Cha – ... *Great* – thanks – how're you? Whoah, baby. Yeah, sure, tonight's fine.'

I ordered another coffee. An old woman passed by surreptitiously dropping paper-wrapped sugar-lumps on to the chair opposite. 'Hello. Good afternoon. I should like to speak to Rachel Noyes, if I may. I wonder whether this would possibly ...? *Thank* you. So kind. Hello, Rachel Noyes? Rachel *Francette* Noyes? Good afternoon. You probably don't remember me (why should you?) but in fact we met at the party in August? August 9th? I was wearing ... '

We met at the party in August. It was a wine and lights flashing and everyone jumping up and down party, as opposed, say, to a lie on the dank carpet cradling empty Pipkins wishing there was more than one girl there party, or, again, to a smoke hash and eat syphcakes while Charles Manson, Esq., pats the bongoes and recites scabrous prose poems party. It was the very best kind of party.

Geoffrey and I had got wind of it from a young (quite posh) hippie in the Marble Arch Okeefenokee Pancake House. He wouldn't tell us the address until Geoffrey offered him a hallucinogen (in fact an asthma pill of mine he had momentarily immersed in a bottle of blue-black Quink).

'It's LDH,' Geoffrey had whispered to him, 'just over from the States. Better than acid. Stronger than MDA. Chas?'

'Oh – any day.'

'Make it a beautiful one, man,' Geoffrey nodded to him as we left. 'Peace.'

Rachel arrived in a group of four – what looked like a random car-load – but stayed alone by the door, arms folded adultly. She talked to no one, although she kept waving and shouting hellos. I stood with some other girlless duds along the adjacent wall; my pits prickled as she twice refused offers to take the floor. The second loping Greek lingered awhile to remonstrate with her. Far from stepping in and saying 'Okay, mac, you heard the lady,' I waited for him to go away.

She looked confident and self-possessed all right, as young

ladies in these circumstances generally do, but, like myself, excluded rather than merely detached from the festivities. She must have soul, I thought. In my case, though, it was simply a question of being unable to dance in front of other people. Geoffrey, who was gyrating away quite giddily not ten feet from me, postulated that it was one of the best, if not in fact *the* best, ways of pulling girls. But I dance only when I am alone, in ten-second spurts, usually before a mirror, sometimes naked, more often attired in sexter-style underpants.

She lit a cigarette. That would give me five precious minutes in which to think.

I did an instant assessment. She was fairly formidable, a bit out of my league really. She didn't belong to the aggressively sexy genre, like some of the more tear-jerking girls there, whose golden thighs and teeming breasts I found about as approachable as leprosy. However: tallish, nearly my height, shoulder-length black hair conventionally shaped around strong features, she made much of her eyes, her nose made much of itself, black boots and black cowgirl skirt met at the knee, manly white blouse, expensive handbag, few bracelets, one insignificant ring, rather stern no-crap stance, intelligent lower-middle class with a good job, something bossy like public relations, living alone, older than me, possibly half Jewish.

The ethnic detail, yes, would provide me with an opening. I am in my own appearance if anything rather oppressively Caucasian, but I could always go up and say 'This party's none too kosher, is it?' or 'I see your schul-days are over.' At that moment I glanced round and guessed that I was the proprietor of the only foreskin in the room. Perhaps I should appeal to her Aryan side then, or at any rate show my sensitivity to this two-way pull she must so often feel. 'Hi there, couldn't help noticing you looked possibly half Jewish. It must be ... ' Oh, I'm a right one I am.

In fact, I only just did it. A mental chant, *timor mortis conturbat me*, and I began on my clumsiest pull ever. My legs started off, at first spasticly shooting out in all directions, then co-ordinating into a groovy shuffle. The top half of my body

34

sloped forward fifteen degrees. My arms flapped limply from the elbow. My shoulders became ear-muffs.

I opted for thick Chelsea:

'Hhulloh,' as if someone had just informed me that this greeting had an initial *h* and I was trying it out.

'Hello.' Her tone was patronizingly neutral; her accent instantly turned mine into educated upper-middle.

'*Hello*,' I said, now with prurient emphasis, a squadron-commander introduced to a fetching Parisienne. 'I notice you haven't got a drink.' This was an excellent line because there usually followed: 'Are you giving this party?'

'Are you giving this party?' she said. But here there was no gate-crasher cringing to be put grandly at its ease. Rather, a dull incredulity.

Nerve going, I elected to be literary. 'Certainly not. Parties of this kind are not given, they are received.'

There was a silence.

'Man comes and drinks the wine and lies beneath,' I said. — It was completely spur-of-the-moment, I promise you (*Tithonus*, line three.) But she wouldn't get the reference and would simply think I was being hearty. My rescue operation?

'And after many a summer dies the swan,' I added consumptively, then 'Tennyson said that,' with a little more of the old satirical edge. I laughed, as if at a private joke. She looked at me, unblinking.

'Sorry. I tend to talk crap when I'm nervous.'

'How come you're nervous?'

'The same reason you're not.'

'Which is?'

I had no desire whatever to enlarge on this cryptic reply. 'Christ, how should I know?' *Christ?* Was that wise, what with her being half Jewish and all? I held up a hand, to silence her, to call a halt. 'Why don't we talk about something that interests you? Make-up ... clothes ... babies ... ? Anything you like. Let me get you a drink.'

'How do you know they interest me?'

'You're a girl.'

35

'So?'

'They interest you. All girls like talking about those things, surely you must know that. It's all all girls ever talk about. Shops … *pillow*-slips … *hair*brushes.'

'You can't generalize like – '

'Why no – '

' – *because*, there are so many exceptions.'

'Oh really?'

She sighed. 'I'm an exception.'

'Then you're the exception that makes the rule.'

Bloodcurdling, I quite agree; yet the bookish teenager will often find himself behaving in this way.

The Costa Brava was filling up now. Wild-eyed birdlike persons cruised to and fro; the coat-stand had become cluttered with crutches and white sticks; suspiciously a nearby mutant checked me over for deformities. Why didn't I mind it here?

To my right, dentures clicking like castanets, an old man chopped through a hot-dog at insect speed. Straight ahead, a middle-aged rocker snivelled and yawned. To my left … Mad Millie herself, whose home was a wheelless 1943 Bedford van parked on the brow of Kensington's Rackham Hill. She was at present menacing the window-pane in a tired mutter. I accidentally caught her eye. She coughed me a transient rainbow of germs, and chased it with the toneless observation: 'You're the foulest little creature I've seen on the moon.' My expression replied, 'You may well have something there.' A chartreuse caterpillar of glinting phlegm crept easily down her chin. She staunched it with a wad of left-over hamburger roll and placed it primly between her lips.

In Smith's over the road I thought intently about my exams. The Tutors was plainly nothing more than a rapacious farce: loopy directress, no facilities, and apparently low on teachers, since I would have to contact the English master myself. It didn't bother me, though. A year earlier I would have wanted a real school and would have felt silly and vulnerable in anything else. Now it seemed only a detail of life, not its whole structure. Interesting. I must be getting on.

Ran into Jenny on the front doorstep. She was on her way out to have lunch with a friend. I didn't think girls did that sort of thing nowadays, and said so. Jenny laughed vivaciously, but looked not at ease. Norman was in and there was a scotch egg in the fridge we could share. I told her to be sure and have a good time.

In my room I looked out my *Rachel* note-pad in preparation for the telephone call. I flicked through it making notes, underlining the odd pertinent phrase, sketching personas. But my mind was wandering. Outside the window, Bina, only one of Jenny's democratic two tabby cats, her body tensed in dumb caution, snaked down the steps to the dustbins. I came across the only extant autograph MS of my first date with Rachel. I felt mournful, squelchy.

After a while she allowed me to go and get her a drink. When I returned from the kitchen she was gone. She wasn't gone. She was smooching with someone very tall in a white suit. I stood holding the glasses like a Negro waiter in Rhodesia House, Nashville, Tennessee. The ballad churned into its first middle-eight. About two minutes to go. What would she do then? I wanted to ask my host if there were perhaps any broom-cupboards or disused lavatories he wouldn't mind me locking myself into until the party was over.

One of the glasses of wine disappeared. I looked up to see Geoffrey.

'What happened to yours?' he asked.

'Cooled me. What happened to yours?'

'Having a crap or something.' He shrugged. 'But she's coming back. Is yours coming back?'

'You never know. What's yours like?'

'Fantastic. Bi-ig tits.'

'So I saw. But what's she like?'

'*I* don't know. Just likes dancing and drinking. We haven't talked that much.'

And he asked me: 'What's with all this "what's she like"?'

'Yeah, sorry. Is she going to fuck you, do you think?'

He nodded, eyes closed.

The record ended. I didn't dare turn round.

'Hey,' said Geoffrey, 'yours is kissing that guy.'

'Really?'

'Yeah but ... they're saying goodbye. He's pulling out.'

I looked. The white suit was backing away; Rachel swivelled on her heel and walked towards us.

'She's coming,' I whispered. 'Be flash. Say we're a group or something.'

Geoffrey was brilliant. He looked good and talked with confidence. Allusively he lowered names. He plugged me with stooge feed lines, pretended he had never heard two of (some say) my funniest anecdotes. He stole a full bottle of wine from the kitchen. And, it transpired, Rachel vaguely knew Geoffrey's sister. The dialogue was bringing regular smiles to Rachel's full brown lips – to reveal credibly flawed teeth; the top two front ones overlapped slightly, giving a sharp prow to the otherwise semicircular line of white; a felicitous touch, I always think. Everything went beautifully until the return of Geoffrey's. Geoffrey's was called Anna, and was therefore Swedish, which seemed rather to come as a bolt out of the blue as far as Geoffrey was concerned.

The general *tone* of the gathering was lowered at this point. Not that Anna wasn't perfectly charming, only that from Rachel's point of view it was so obviously me and my pull and Geoffrey and his pull getting together to plan a spotty removal to someone's house or flat or room to drink quarts of weak instant coffee and listen to records and be made inefficient passes at – precisely what Geoffrey and I had in mind. For the party was disintegrating quickly now. There remained only one or two drunken couples, some po-faced wankers, and the odd unattached (and so presumably pretty seriously deformed) girl.

'Look, I ought to help clear up,' said Rachel.

'Nonsense,' I said. 'Don't do that. Leave it to whoever was frivolous and conceited enough to give the party.'

Geoffrey joined in with some vehemence. 'No, fuck all this,' he argued. 'Why not come back to our place instead?' He stroked Anna's shoulder. Anna smiled.

'No, I really will clear up.'

'What the devil for?' I asked.

'Because it's my party. I live here. All right? I hope you had a good time.'

We watched her go.

'How fucking funny,' said Geoffrey. 'Charles, you're well away there.'

Suddenly Norman bellowed down the stairs.

'Hey, Charles, are you in?'

'Yeah,' I shouted, standing.

'Oh,' he roared back, but didn't say anything.

'I'll come up.'

Norman was in the kitchen fighting a cardboard box.

'What's in it?'

'Cider,' Norman gasped.

Eventually he wrestled all the string and paper into an arm-ful-sized bundle and forced it down the Aga, stirring the coals with a broom-handle so that the box burned up with a deep and satisfying roar.

'Where'd you get it?'

'Fell off a lorry.'

'Christ,' I said. 'Surprised it didn't smash open. Did you –'

'No, cunt,' said Norman, now crouching in front of the keg and filling two pub-style pint-glasses. '*Stolen.* Got it off a mate. Two quid. Retails at four thirty-five.'

I coughed and took off my spectacles. 'Does it make you extra pissed?'

Norman handed me my glass, drank his in one, and crouched again to refill it.

'Where's Jenny gone?' I asked.

'Up west, shopping, with some foreign tart from Bristol.'

'When'll she be back? Any idea?'

'Don't ask me.'

I watched my brother-in-law, his fat nose inches from the tap, his eyes eager, expectant. Norman was wearing what he always wore: dowdy blue business suit, boyish shirt open at the neck (the tip of a spangled red tie hung out of his side pocket); his trousers, python-tight from the knee down, came to an end a good two or three inches from some really utterly preposterous black fur shoes. Amazing. I wouldn't get ten yards dressed like that. Norman straightened up, looked with hostility at my glass, and went through the sliding doorway into the adjoining room. 'Yeah, it does make you quite pissed.' He lobbed himself on to the chesterfield by the window. 'Friend of mine', he continued monotonously, 'had three pints of this, fell out a bedroom window and smashed his head open on the railings.'

I sat down too. 'Christ.' There was a pause. I said, 'I've got to ring this girl up in a minute so I'd better be quite pissed.'

'Woy?' asked Norman in a challenging tone.

'I don't know, really. I find her sort of scaring.'

'Fucked her yet?'

'No. Nowhere near.'

'Well, no wonder.'

No wonder I feel scared, not having fucked her, or no wonder I haven't fucked her if I'm weedy enough to feel scared?

'Does she fuck? How old is she?' Norman asked, frowning.

'Nineteen, I think, same age as me. I don't know. You know Geoffrey? – mate of mine – well, his sister knows her. She's supposed to have fucked some American guy, but apparently he was her first.'

'Yeah, and what happened to him? Still around?'

'Don't know. She came out to a film with me last month so she must be more or less available.'

Norman burped. 'Did you try her then?'

'No.'

He contemplated me unhappily. Embarrassed, I finished my drink and got up to get a refill. But Norman beat me to it.

Walking over he drained his own glass and coughed disgustedly.

'It's bloody diabolical this stuff,' he said, fondling the plastic tap.

The hedonistic schoolboy just liked playing with it. He filled his own glass and began to empty it so fast that he would get to fill it again after mine. His eyes bulged; cider ran down his chin. Did he ever go to work or anything, I wondered. Did he still have other girls? Either it never occurred to him, or it never occurred to him not to.

I thought about his set-up here with my sister. Mother, who corresponded regularly with Jenny, always used to portray him as prince of the pigs – filthy, ignorant, drunken, vicious – but that was nothing more than female solidarity. Both my parents habitually and unworriedly referred to Norman as a 'bastard', but, again, in such contexts this generally means someone who has stopped idolizing his wife. Norman wasn't, however, what's known as a 'right', or a 'real' bastard, for the simple reason that he made money; real bastards are penniless bastards. This was the first time I had seen them together, except for the wedding. They had seemed okay last night.

Did it matter, for instance, that Jenny had had over five years of higher education and that Norman would probably be all thumbs with the *Daily Mail*? And there was no point in forgetting the class difference – or at least there was no point in forgetting it where married couples were concerned. Jenny couldn't really see much of her own friends; she must bitch about it. And, as in any class battle, the social inferior tends to feel a bit of a crusading visionary and thinks he can therefore be as shitty as he likes.

'Look, I'll tell you,' began Norman, handing me my second pint and sipping on his fourth. 'Say she's you, right? And you're her. Say this tart was ringing you up. You'd got a lot of tarts on so you're not worried, so you play it *easy*. What would she say that would get you interested, make you drop all the others and pull her? Now if she wanted to get you going, she wouldn't say "Oh Charles, fuck me," she'd say "Oh

Charles, fuck *you*, fuck *off*," wouldn't she? Wouldn't she, to get you going?'

I thought for a moment. 'What, I ring Rachel up and tell her to fuck off?' I asked, genuinely wanting to know.

Norman looked at me askance, as who should say 'Do you want your head kicked in?' What he actually said was, '*No*. Just be flash. I see you –' he made up-and-down motions with his hand – 'wankers, tripping on your cocks, falling over backwards, makes me sick. They don't like it either. Be flash – act like you couldn't give a fuck and she'll ... be ... begging for it.'

He finished his yawn, then leapt up, stretched, and, mouth sleepily ajar, consulted his saucer-sized, many-dialled watch (of the kind favoured by scuba divers, pot-holers, etc.).

'I'm going up Chalk Farm.'

'Shall I tell Jen?'

'If you want.'

'See you later. When'll you be back?'

'Search me.'

I had intended to ring Rachel the minute Norman was out of the way, but it didn't seem so easy now. I sighed. Could I be bothered to make some notes? Perhaps some coffee to get me thinking straight. My eyes went slowly round the room. Like the rest of the house it was filled mostly with Norman's old furniture: monstrous gauzy sofa, selection of geriatric armchairs. I could see that Jenny was sifting these out in favour of more upper-class items, with the folky bare-wood sideboards, velvet dwarf thrones, with its something-I-picked-up here and its got-it-for-thirty-bob there: tastefully timeless. In the corner, to the right of the sliding door, the grandfather clock – which, naturally, had once belonged to my grandfather – struck one. (I say 'naturally' because this is how it always is with me. In my world, reserved Italians, heterosexual hairdressers, clouds without silver linings, ignoble savages, hardhearted whores, advantageous ill-winds, sober Irishmen, and so on, are not permitted to exist. Nothing I can do about it.)

*

The other time I saw Norman was at the wedding – my first, by the way. The celebration took the form of a champagne party at a hotel followed by an intimate dinner at Norm's house (in which Jenny had long been established); caterers laid on by my father handled it all. I got extremely drunk extremely early on, so I remember the evening none too well; but apparently the thing was that my father and elder brother had gone and 'insulted' Norman. According to his bride, what happened was this. Norman was approached by Gordon and Mark Highway. My father hailed him :

'Ah, Norman, wonder if you'd mind settling something, wonder if you'd mind telling Mark here and myself your mother's *maiden* name.'

'Levi,' he truthfully replied.

My father had then said to my brother as they walked away, 'Looks like I owe you a fiver.'

However it happened, Norman took it very deeply and studiedly. As the champagne party was breaking up, under pressure from Jenny I took Norman to the hotel bar before following on to Holland Park. I suppose the idea was to get him to calm down, but I had never seen Norman as collected as he was that evening. I remember he told me that he had the previous afternoon been gobbled by the Scottish assistant manageress of his Tufnell Park second-hand refrigerator showrooms *in* his Tufnell Park second-hand refrigerator showrooms. It was clear to me, though, that he mentioned the incident merely by way of polite small-talk; this was no weary vaunt, no another-good-man-gone lament. He added conversationally that he hadn't dared actually poke her in case she still had the clap. She had had it so long and so often that antibiotics didn't mean shit to her any more.

Norman, or, temporarily, Bill Sikes, went into action as soon as we got back to the house. My parents' sub-celebrity friends all tried to behave as if they thought he was drunk; the fact that he so obviously wasn't drunk was the key to the whole performance. He asked a more-or-less dead failed philosopher how his sex-life was shaping up these days; he biffed a pancake-bosomed minor poetess on the back, whispered evilly among her jangling earrings. At dinner he abstained from the carefully chosen table-wines, fetching himself a pint beer glass which he filled with neat Benedictine. His voice went Bow Bells barrow-boy. He tucked his serviette (*'serviette*, it's called a *serviette'*) into his shirt-collar. He took soup by dipping his face in the bowl and sucking through pouted lips; he frayed the veal with his bare hands. He up-ended whole plates of gherkins and cashews into his mouth. He drank boiling coffee straight from the percolator, without blinking.

The post-prandial stage of the evening was little more than a swirling blank as far as I was concerned. And yet, as I lay on the floor of the upstairs bathroom, cradling the lavatory bowl tenderly in my arms, I could hear the horrible sound of Norman's voice, a skirling whine from below. One would have expected something bawdy, wouldn't one? However, it went like this; I couldn't catch the words until what seemed to be the last verse:

> This owd yowe was whetting her pegs,
> She run at the butcher and broke both his legs ...

slowing down

> *This* owd yowe went to fight for the prince ...

to a funereal decrescendo:

> And no living man has ... heard ... of ... her ... *since*.

The sound of hesitant applause could be heard. But Norman was off again, with a

> oooooooooooooHHHHH*HHHHH*, there *was* an
>   owd yowe wi' only one horn,
> Fifty naw me nonny.
> And she *picked* up her living among the green corn,
> So turn the wheel so bonny.

The nine-stanza cycle was repeated five times. Then there were some shuffling noises and banging of doors. When I came out half an hour later Norman was on the landing, patiently waiting to use the bathroom. He came forward and put his hands on my shoulders, as if in order to steady me.

'Your father's gone so I've made up a bed for you on the couch.'

He stared at my face and suddenly threw his head back in a roar of black, anarchical laughter. I groaned halitotically at him.

'773 4417.'

'Hello, good morning, I mean afternoon. May I speak to Rachel Noyes, please?'

Silence.

'Hello, Rachel? Ah. My name is Charles Highway. You may remember we met at a party you gave last month. Then, some days later, we –'

'Yes, I remember.'

I gave her time to whoop with delight and say, 'And I don't mind telling you it's fucking *great* to hear your voice.'

'Well!' I said. 'And what are you up to these days?'

As if to an elderly relation, she said, 'I'm cramming for A Levels.'

'What a fantastic coincidence. I'm cramming for Oxford! Where's yours?'

'Bayswater Road.'

'NO! So's mine! Whereabouts?'

'The Holland Park side.'

'Oh, huh, the *right* side of the Bayswater Road.'

'No it's not. It's on the left.'

'No, no.' I chortled uncomfortably. 'I meant right side as opposed to wrong side. The "correct" side.'

'What?'

Hang up?

No. Get flash.

'Er, listen, forget it, forget it. Say, are you going to be there tomorrow afternoon? Fine, then why don't I pick you up when they close, which is what? four-thirty? ... Four? So okay. I'll come pick you up and we could maybe have some tea together.'

There was a pause. My armpits hummed. 'What do you say?'

Normally I would have given an easy-refusal clause, such as 'unless of course you're working', or have fixed on a day further ahead which she could plausibly be evasive about. But I wanted another chance. All the homework I had done on her. Then she spoke.

'All right ... Why not.'

Why *not*. She would probably insist on paying for her own tea. 'I haven't a clue why not. You'll be there at four, right?'

'Yes, and –'

'*Right*. See you then.' I slammed down the telephone and stood there tensed, almost crouching. How had my final abruptness gone down? Applying Norman's Law, what would I feel if someone had just said that to me? Stand the rude little oaf up, obviously. But you never knew.

Noon, Tuesday. I lay immobile in the bath, like a dirty old alligator – not washing, just steaming and planning.

What clothes would I wear? Blue madras shirt, black boots, and the old black cord suit with those touching leather elbow-patches. What persona would I wear? On the two occasions I had seen her last August I underwent several complete identity-reorganizations, settling finally somewhere between the pained, laconic, inscrutable type and the knowing, garrulous, cynical, laugh a minute, yet something demonic about him, something nihilistic, muted death-wish type. Revamp those, or start again?

Why couldn't Rachel be a little more specific about the type of person *she* was? Goodness knew; if she were a hippie I'd talk to her about her drug experiences, the zodiac, tarot cards. If she were left-wing I'd look miserable, hate Greece, and eat baked beans straight from the tin. If she were the sporty type I'd play her at ... chess and backgammon and things. No, don't tell me she's the very girl to show me what egotistical folly it is to compartmentalize people in this sad way; don't tell me she's going to sort me out, take me on, supply the *cognitio* and comic resolution. I couldn't bear it.

Now I began to wash, laundering my orifices; they went all to hell if not scrupulously maintained. The works: from undergrowth nose to foamy navel – the works. Of course, I thought jovially, I know very well that my worries about this body conking out on me are pure anxiety (again, just something to take an interest in) – yes, *quite* – but knowing it was anxiety didn't make me feel less anxious.

With comb and fingertips I styled my pubic hairs. It was a good idea to spruce myself up for Rachel, the reason being that one honestly did never know. One night last July: at 10.5, in Belsize Park tube station, a girl was telling me to go away before she called the police; at 10.17 I was lying on the floor – between untouched cups of still quite hot tea – helping her off with her greasy panties. Admittedly the girl was quite hideous, had smelled unclothed of open wounds and graveyards, etc., but you still never knew. It was a theory of Geoffrey's that pretty girls liked sex more than rough ones. Take Gloria, whom I had seen only yesterday. What an excellent time I was having in London. Oxford seemed years away, like childhood.

I bundled myself up in some towels and ran on tiptoe to my room and crouched, shivering, in front of the fire: all things Dr Miller had told me to avoid doing. There was a bathroom next door that was at present too filthy to use. I could lick it out, I supposed, over the next week, which would be a good way also of paying back Jen and Norm.

I dried myself, showered in talc, and slipped into my most daring underpants. I looked down over concave chest, neat little stomach, prominent hip-bones, completely hairless legs – not half bad, I don't mind telling you. As I dressed I thought about the setting up of the room. I couldn't be as slapdash as I had been with Gloria. It was a hundred to one that I wouldn't get her even into the house, but all the same everything had to be ... just so. I assembled the relevant pads and folders, stroked my chin.

Not knowing her views on music I decided to play it safe; I stacked the records upright in two parallel rows; at the head of the first I put *2001: A Space Odyssey* (can't be wrong); at the head of the second I put, after some thought, a selection of Dylan Thomas's verse, read by the poet. Kleenex well away from the bed: having them actually on the bedside chair was tantamount to a poster reading 'The big thing about me is that I wank a devil of a lot.' The coffee-table featured a couple of Shakespeare texts and a copy of *Time Out* – an intriguing dichotomy, perhaps, but I was afraid that, no, it wouldn't quite do. The texts were grimy and twisted after a year of A-Level doodling. I replaced them with the Thames and Hudson *Blake* (again, can't be wrong) and *The Poetry of Meditation*, in fact a scholarly American work on the Metaphysicals, although from the cover it could have been a collection of beatnik verse: Rachel could interpret it as she wished. Unfortunately the *Time Out* had a rangy, black-nippled girl on the cover. What instead? Had I got time to run off and get a *New Statesman*? Not really. I looked round the room. Something incongruous, arresting. After a quarter of an hour I decided on a Jane Austen, the mellow *Persuasion*, face down, open towards the end, by my pillow. The little touch/That means so much.

At three thirty I was standing dressed in front of the mirror. Eyes narrowed, I scouted for spots. All clear. I'm not troubled by straight acne so much as by occasional sub-surface hugies, the ones that spend two days coming up and two weeks going down. An old favourite was the Cyclopean egg which put in regular appearances between my eyes, giving me a mono-browed mass-murderer's expression. But no big boys in town at the moment.

I put on, then took off, then put on again a red white-dotted scarf. Eventually I left it off: a bit obvious. Now, gazing dreamily at myself in the mirror ... Rachel would have to be out of her mind to throw up a chance like this: the medium-length, silky, thin brown hair, the ingenuous brown eyes, the narrow but wide mouth, and that jawline, really – its evenness and squareness, its cool Keatsian symmetry. I pressed my back teeth painfully together to accentuate it ... Hi there. Great, lover, and you?

On my way upstairs for some tea the telephone rang. It was Geoffrey.

'Hello,' I said, pleased. 'I was going to ring you tonight.'

'Mm ... ' There was a five-second pause. 'I wouldn't have been in.'

'Are you okay?' Another pause.

'I want to come round. I'm Mandied. I can't make it back to the Park.'

A drugged distress-call?

'Where are you now, Geoffrey?'

'Er, hang on, I'll look around. Yeah ... South Ken tube. But look I don't want to come round just yet. I've got a ... scene I'm trying ... to get together but I can't get it ... on cos there's all this ... scene ... '

'What the fuck are you talking about?' I inquired. 'Look, you can come round now and wait here while I go out to tea. Or what? Do you think it would be slightly more underground to turn up later? Say around seven?'

'Cooler,' he said, still rather guardedly.

'Or later still. About eight. Or nine?'

'Cooler.'

'Look, why don't you come round when you like?'

Silence, then a mumbled 'yeah', then more silence, then a lethargic click.

He rang back five minutes later to say that he had a couple of girls with him.

I thought for a moment. 'Fine. Bring them round and I'll try and screw the one that's not yours. Have you got any incredible drugs with you?'

'Yeah, some.'

'Bring them round too. I've got to rush. I'll probably be in from about seven or someone else'll be here. But listen: if my bedroom door's locked, don't try and get in, okay?'

'Creaming?'

'Could be.'

I allowed only eight minutes to get there. Holding my hair in place with my hands, I ran out of the house and down the steep square to the main road. Geoffrey was bringing more girls. It hardly seemed to matter what happened now.

Rachel was alone in the kitchen, emptying ashtrays into a postbox-shaped rubbish bin the colour of baby's crap. I said in a robotic voice:

'Christ I'm sorry about that I had no idea it was your party and I wondered whether you might possibly let me make it up to you and will you come to a film with me next Wednesday. God, I'm so sorry about that, I really am.'

'Don't worry about it.'

I waited, but she said nothing more. 'Shall I at least ring you,' I said, 'or what? ... Not ring you.'

Rachel smiled. 'One of the two anyway. Yes, all right. It's 773 4417. Will you be able to remember that?'

'Do you want a hand,' I gushed, 'there's quite a lot of – '

'No, honestly, I'll manage.'

Rachel came over to the table on which I was vulnerably half sitting and started to pack unused wine glasses into a cardboard box. I got that make-or-break, do-or-die feeling, the feeling not only that I must stake my claim but also that claims must be staked, the feeling not only that I must act but that actions must be put through – or some flushed confusion of these that made me stand up, and reach out, trance-like, towards her.

'Oh, come *on*,' she said.

I backed into the passage. '373 1417! Great party! See you soon!'

A quarter of an hour with directory inquiries and I rang her the next Tuesday. I had beside me: a typed-out shooting script, a photograph of Audrey Hepburn, an empty quarter of gin, and Geoffrey. Geoffrey, electrified on cut-price death-pills, nodded his head at me throughout.

Two nights later we saw a film about the ups and downs of some Icelandic subsistence farmers. Of course, I had visited the cinema the previous afternoon and had rehearsed an amusing commentary to be whispered at Rachel in the dark. But the atmosphere was wrong and I stayed quiet.

Having cashed my penultimate traveller's cheque I was big with taxis and cinema seats. Dropped her off and didn't try to kiss her goodnight, almost laughing out loud when she asked if I'd like to come in for coffee. 'Not tonight,' I said haughtily. (Moreover, her parents were there.) The evening cost six pounds. By the weekend I was back in Oxford, anyway.

Rachel's tutorial establishment was one of those dreary pastel Regency houses so popular in this part of London. With my back to the two papier-mâché pillars guarding the double-doored entrance, I practised smiles and hellos. I didn't feel dramatic enough, ought really to have lodged a milk-bottle down my trousers before coming out. Although I had crawled the last 150 yards, as if I were an expert on pavements and were studying this one, there was still three minutes to go.

To the right of the doorway was a dimly lit, curtainless classroom with male students in it. They stared broodingly at the road. I knew the kind of punks that went to this kind of place. Cuntish public-school drop-outs, dropped out for being too thick, having long hair or dirty boaters, unseaming new boys in multiple buggery, getting caught too many times with an impermissible number of hockey sticks up their bums. Would they all run out now and debag me, shouting 'Let's teach the little squit some manners'? Hobo-like I wandered back and forth. One of the boys was asleep, his head on the desk, pillowed by a twisted copy of the *Financial Times*. As I watched, there was a stir in the classroom; a cruel-faced bearded man in a pinstripe suit strode into camera. He approached his student from behind, loomed above him for a few seconds, then lustily rapped his crown with what looked like a spectacles-case. This set off a chain-reaction of twitches and snorts; the puffy young gentleman awoke blinking to the world. Loud reproaches could be heard from the pinstripe man; excuses were mouthed by the other. Teach the little turd for being so rich and lazy and for eating and drinking himself sick at lunch. Teach the fat, mindless –

The doors opened. A tall ginger-haired boy in green tweed moved gracefully down the steps. He looked at me as if I were a gang of skinheads: not with fear (because the fellows are quite tractable really) but with disapproval. Behind him at a trot came two lantern-jawed girls, calling 'Jamie ... *Jamie.*' Jamie swivelled elegantly.

'Angelica, I'm not *going* to the Imbenkment. Gregory shall have to take you.'

'But Gregory's in *Scotland,*' one said.

'I can't help thet.' The ginger boy disappeared into an old-fashioned sports-car.

The students were pouring out steadily now. Each and every one of them was shouting. 'Casper, yah, Ormonde Gate, not possibly, super, Freddie, five o'clock, *rather*, tea?, Bubble, later, race you there, beast, at Oswald's.' Double-parked Alfa Romeos, Morgans and MGs jostled and revved; those on foot moved up the slope towards Notting Hill. Where was Rachel? Ashamed to join me in front of all these bright young people? Had I got the place wrong? Apart from the catnapper, who I was pleased to see had been detained, there seemed to be no one left inside.

Rachel, again, was in a party of four, two boys and another girl. Make a run for it, I thought, as they came down the steps chatting contrapuntally. One of the boys and the other girl broke off in a pair. Rachel and the other boy approached me. I recognized him. Although now in sports-jacket and twills, the white-suited nance at the party. Rachel was smiling. She said:

'DeForest, this is Charles ... Byway?' She laughed. 'I'm sorry ... '

'*High*way, *please.*' I laughed, too.

'Highway. Charles, this is DeForest Hoeniger.'

'Great to meet you, Charles,' said DeForest, breathing heavily through his nose. He was American. You could tell that at once, because, in common with every American over eight and under twenty-five, he looked like a middle-aged American sports-writer: freckled pinhead, cropped salt-and-pepper hair.

The American? Obviously.

'How do you do,' I said, hands shaking, shaking hands.

'We thought we'd have tea at the Tea Centre,' said Rachel.

I nodded lively assent to this imaginative plan. We stepped into file: tall DeForest in the middle, Rachel on the inside, me short-arsing around on the curb, one foot in the gutter, dodging trees.

The other couple had come to a halt a few yards ahead in order to go through the motions of mutual arousal. The boy, who had diagonal hair and a long pocked face, had wrested from the girl some article – a book, a letter – which she would fain recover. He stood facing her, holding whatever it was behind him with both hands; she pawed infatuatedly at his elbows.

'Come on, you two,' said DeForest, 'tea-time.' He stepped into the road and turned to face the four of us grouped uncertainly on the pavement. Then, DeForest opened and got into a huge red Jaguar. Doors were unlocked for our benefit.

'Jesus,' I whispered.

Rachel turned to me as she stepped forward. I smiled in schoolboy wonder and closed the door after her. The others piled into the back and I wanted to close the door after, or on, them too. I got in, causing them both to shove up as if I were a suitcase.

'All aboard?' said DeForest, pulling away *down* the hill and round, going way too many places way too fast to do a three-point turn and go *up* it like everyone else.

How had I let myself get into this situation? Rachel sat erectly in front of me, her hair bright and aromatic to my peeled senses.

'No, I just love these English cars,' DeForest was telling Rachel, who nodded. She clearly loved them too.

Had Rachel planned the whole thing? Perhaps I should have given her more time on the telephone. Was DeForest in on it? Christ. 'DeForest, darling, there's this tiresome little shit who *keeps* on ringing me up and has finally bullied me into having tea with him; I thought the only half-way civilized thing to do was to jolly well *take* the hopeless little bugger –'

The Tea Centre was a sort of genteel workman's caff, done up in 'thirties, U.S. coffee-shop style; there were several circular tables surrounded by knee-high mushroom chairs and some booths at the back. With me in the rear we headed for the far corner. The girls got in first, followed by their beaux. The booth sat four. I looked round: the queer pixie's poofs were tacked to the ground; there were no movable chairs.

And there wasn't any room for me. Rachel and DeForest were talking scones, the other couple were writhing about still, now seemingly poised for a session of fully robed soixanteneuf. My head was like an electric blanket. I couldn't see Rachel because fucking DeForest's spiky insect head was between us. In a voice that didn't carry I said, 'Going out now, to make a call.'

No one reacted. They had the wide world spinning round within their heads. They hadn't heard.

Outside, I walked reflexively across the road to the line of telephone boxes opposite the tube entrance. I stopped to look in a shop window. Why hadn't I just flashed in, told them to move up? It was my hesitation that had done it. They had all wanted me to stay. No, there wasn't any room, nothing I could have done but get out. Get out. I started home.

'*Charles.* Hang on.'

I turned. Rachel had come to a halt on the island half-way across the road. She waited, still looking at me, while a stream of traffic passed between us.

How hackneyed of her, I thought emptily.

The lights changed. She paused; she walked towards me, hands in pockets, head tilted slightly. She reached the pavement and stopped a few feet away.

'Charles, come back.'

'I'm not coming back.'

She came forward two steps and stood with her feet to-gether.

'I'm sorry. Are you all right?'

'I'm fine.'

'I've got to go back.'

'Suppose so.'

'Are you cold?' she asked.

I was. I had been feeling far too vain to wear an overcoat. I was shivering.

'A little.'

She bit her lip. She came closer and held my hand for a few seconds.

'Will you ring me?'

'You bet.'

'Goodbye then.'

'Goodbye.'

At Campden Hill Square another tea-party was in progress. It consisted of Geoffrey, two strangely dressed girls – a small one, swathed in a floral curtain, and a big one, got up as a cowboy, complete with holsters – and Jenny. No Norm. A scene of almost pastoral spontaneity followed. I felt rather light-headed and, steamy though the kitchen was, I didn't ap-pear to be getting any warmer. Furthermore, I was still vib-rant from an intense Consciousness-of-Being attack, having had a highly soulful walk from the Gate.

When the tea was made I popped upstairs for a hawk. On the way back Geoffrey intercepted me; we stole into the sit-ting-room.

'Which one d'you fancy?' he breathed.

'I hardly know. Haven't taken them in yet.'

'Do you like Anastasia?'

'*Anastasia?*' This could not be. 'What's her real name?' I implored.

'Jean.'

'Oh. The short-arse? Yeah, she's all right. Boring dress.'

'Mm. Good body, though.'

'Have you fucked her?'

'Sort of. She's not as good as Sue.'

'Have you fucked Sue?'

'Sort of. She's got better tits.'

'What do you mean, "sort of"?'

'We had this vague Troy.'

'No. *Christ* how sexy. What was it like?'

'Yeah, they're dikes, too. It was okay, except I couldn't get a proper rise. Too Mandied.'

'Why doesn't that sort of thing ever happen to me?'

Geoffrey swayed on his pegs. 'Because you're a country bumpkin and I'm a city slicker.'

We talked drugs. Geoffrey had dropped two Mandrax; there was also some hash, but this was of only minor interest to the bronchitic narrator. I got a Mandrax off him to take later. My chest was telling me not to get any ideas about sleeping tonight.

That evening Mr and Mrs Entwistle laid on their very first row. It opened modestly enough. Geoffrey and I were back in the kitchen, helping to clear up. Door slams full force, missing-link footsteps, Norman's head bulges hugely into the room; seeing no one else, its albino eyes fix on Jenny. We froze, as in a television advertisement. Then he was gone, and Jenny, scooping up cigarettes and lighter, had gone after him.

'Heavy,' murmured Geoffrey.

My stage designs for Rachel were not entirely wasted. In my room, Anastasia made for the *Blake*, saying 'wow' in a reverent whisper, and Sue adjusted her six-guns, knelt on the floor and opened *The Poetry of Meditation*. I looked over her shoulder; she was reading an essay on Herbert, rather a good one despite the fact that it was called 'The Plateau of Assurance'; 'Herbert Who?' she must have wanted to ask. Geoffrey, licking at cigarette papers, instructed me to put on a record. The girls being hippies, I selected the most violent and tuneless of all my American LPs, *Heroin* by the Velvet Underground. The immediate results? Anastasia swayed in her chair and tapped a sandalled foot; Sue went glazed, craning her neck in figure-eight patterns. There you go.

Geoffrey lit up. 'Are we going to have some amazing orgy, or what?' No one reacted. He shrugged, gave the joint to Sue and tottered backwards on to the bed.

A peaceful quiescence followed.

The joint came my way; I drew on it, swallowing rather than inhaling the smoke, and in the high hippie manner, as if it were a normal cigarette. (Ostentatious and/or noisy intake is considered vulgar.) I repeated this several times, and waited. Golden Rain cinders showering my knuckles, yes, and I felt I could have puked my ribcage on to the carpet: apart from that, nothing. And it could not be said that I didn't respond to drugs; early last summer Geoffrey gave me my first purple heart: I got the screaming hab-jabs for two days, sweated liquid frying-pans throughout the third, awoke from a gentle coma on the fourth. Indeed, my metabolism is in many ways as much of a gullible weathercock as my mind. Geoffrey's hash didn't work; he must have been sold a wad of gumboot mud, or, if it was supposed to be grass, a matchboxful of crumbled tobacco, rosemary and aspirins.

I offered it to Geoffrey but he held up his hand with a hollow smile, all of a sudden not having a good time. I couldn't resist taking a certain fascinated pleasure in his remorse-stricken face; the usual triumvirate: pearly complexion, ruby lips, emerald tongue. His cheeks ballooned as if to contain a mouthful of prancing vomit.

'Is there anything I can get you?'

'Water.'

'They dehydrate you,' Anastasia explained.

As I left the room Susan quickened my stride by saying, in an indignant monotone, 'It bugs me when these guys start trying to hang on 'The Temple' this kind of *structuralized* didactic trip when it's all the hang-ups and anxieties that make it so ... integrated.'

*

Phase two of Jenny and Norman's row. It came through the walls with high fidelity.

In the kitchen I became gradually aware of screams and shouts from above. I tiptoed up to the intermediate landing outside the bathroom. The sitting-room door was open and the light off. It was from the bedroom, then, that I could hear Jenny shriek:

'You're a *murderer*. Do you hear what I'm saying to you? You-are-a-*MURDERER*!'

A very very loud scream came next.

This didn't alarm me. It was clear from the tone that Jenny's accusation was an emotional, not a circumstantial, one, probably the crest of an imprecatory tidal wave. And that sort of scream wasn't the result of fear or anger but of drawing one's breath deep into one's lungs and thinking: I'm going to scream as loud as I can now and see what effect that has on the situation.

'You're a *bastard*,' Jenny resumed, 'and you don't care, because you're a *murderer*.'

Then Norman: 'Jennifer. You're getting yourself into a state, now BLOODY GET OUT OF IT. You know you've got to do it, don't you? Get it through your fucking head –'

I switched off my ears.

In the bathroom I tweaked the light string and sat on the closed lavatory seat. How exciting. What a splendidly emotional day this was for everyone. 'You're a murderer' ... Perhaps, in the course of his work, Norman *was* called on to do the odd homicide. Perhaps he really did pull capers in his lunch-hour. Had he mown down a file of schoolboys in his Cortina, lured a blinkie into the Bayswater Road, stolen the heirlooms of a dying Jew? Had he poked a switchblade into an enlightened student (for Norman was passionately right-wing)? Had he jumped up and down on a squealing Pakistani (for Norman was passionately xenophobic: wogs began, not at Calais, but at Barnet or Wandsworth Common, depending on what direction you took from Marble Arch)? Perhaps –

yawn – she just meant that he was '"'murdering'"' her love for him.

The sound of what could have been a forearm slam came from above, then a muffled crash, as of a body making speedy contact with the floor.

I blew my nose on some lavatory paper and thought hard about Rachel. I wished Geoffrey would get a move on and puke in my bed; then Sue and Anastasia could carry him off, and I would be alone. Nip up to the sitting-room for a glass of Norman's cherry brandy? No: he might revive Jenny in order to beat her unconscious again. Instead, I hawked confidently into the basin, and returned with Geoffrey's water. Upstairs, all was quiet now.

Geoffrey had indeed been sick, not in my bed, but, rather, over the floor, walls, sink, towel-rail and lavatory of the next-door bathroom. Anastasia was there, an arm round his waist. Geoffrey turned to me diffidently when I joined big Sue in the doorway.

'Sorry glug,' he said, throwing his head back to accommodate a fresh mouthful which he then channelled into the bathtub.

'That's all right. But, Geoffrey?'

'Yeah?'

'Remember: I'm a country slicker, you're a city bumpkin. Okay?'

'Right.'

Between the three of us we cleaned Geoffrey up and gave him, in succession, an apple, some water and a cigarette. When asked, he said he felt cool. I mentioned something about a taxi but it turned out – amazingly, I thought, for one of her youth – that Sue had a car. We put Geoffrey in it and they drove off, with me asking for the telephone number of and trying to kiss neither of the two girls.

I watched them go, shaking my head a couple of times in the normal way, and walked back to the house. In the darkening kitchen, with a few glasses of water I worked the shirt-button-sized Mandrax down my throat. It was already brightly moonlit and for a while I gazed out at the navy-blue sky. Unasked, I could feel, gradually playing on my features, a look of queasy hope. And why not? I had someone to think about, no matter how fretfully; I had a face looking over my shoulder, no matter how snottily equivocal its expression. At least it wasn't my face.

There was little to admire outside, apart from the sky : just a smooth high wall, on which glittered a thousand chips of broken glass, placed there to deter the burglars over twelve foot tall who couldn't be bothered to use the back-garden door. They looked neutral enough now, though.

As I turned I saw Jenny on the chesterfield in the adjoining room, curled up on her knees, haggardly smoking a cigarette. I stepped towards her, but as I did so she made a movement, hardly perceptible, a shrug or a wave of the hand, which told me that she was content to be alone. I closed the door behind me, and went to bed.

Thirty-five minutes past eight: The Rachel Papers, volume one

Over by the window now, I effortfully uncork the second bottle of Château Dysentery. Red spots fly over my twentieth-birthday present from Rachel, the new Longman's Blake. It's very dark outside, so it seems appropriate to ask out loud:

> Can delight
> Chained in night
> The virgins of youth and morning bear?

On my desk, a sea of pads, folders, envelopes, napkins, notes, the complete Rachel Papers stand displayed. Four-eyed, I indent subject-headings, co-ordinate footnotes, mark cross-references in red and blue biros.

We have to begin with a tolerably even development, characterized though it is by chance meetings, botched preparations, half-successes. Referring to *Conquests and Techniques: a Synthesis*, I write on the inside cover of the Rachel folder itself:

> Initial 2B
> Compensatory A3 tendencies
> Emily gambit
> Marilyn variation deferred.

I erase 'deferred' and put in 'declined'. This doesn't tell me much.

The first day at school was intensely embarrassing, not for me (I felt) so much as for the directress and her staff, unhelpful as these distinctions generally turn out to be.

On my way there, walking up attractive Addison Avenue, I took out the two letters I had received that morning. It was a clear day, and so, being morbidly early for school, I slipped between the bird-pats on a pavement bench to take a proper look at them.

The fact that my mother had in her life made any written contact whatever with the outside world was in itself a moving tribute to the British GPO. My name mis-spelt, an address which even I could make little of, four 1p stamps upside down in the top left-hand corner. I put on my glasses and began worrying a few key phrases: pity missed you Sunday ... clearing up? got sick ... Your father in London two weeks but ... giving rather grand house-party ... the ? of one college is coming ... you come? ... Love to Jenny ... Norman is behaving ... Mrs Wick found vests you forgot ... My face burned. What was the point? There always was a point. Ah, sinisterly clear ending ... take care. Find out from him *how many* are coming. He can be reached at 01-937 2814.

9-3-7, W-E-S, Western: Kensington area; must be his slag's place. Why didn't she ring him at the office? Or was this some wily show of uninterest? The whole thing would have depressed me, but I happened to be having tea with Rachel that afternoon – *à deux*. And the telephone number might come in useful.

The second letter was airmail, garishly stamped. It was from Coco.

'Coco' was the *sixteen*-year-old daughter of a Lebanese economics professor (cultivated by my father when he was visiting lecturer at Cambridge the year before last). Towards the end of the summer the family had come out for three weekends. Coco was tanned, minx-like, exotic; she was, furthermore, a girl, and I was just old enough and rude enough to seem quite unimprovable to her. The first weekend I kissed Coco on the landing. The second I smoothed her shy breasts in the greenhouse. The third I persuaded her to come to my room at 12 p.m. – a perfect night, though intercourse did not take place. She was barely fifteen then and I didn't want to come out of jail when she was barely twenty-one. Besides, she wouldn't let me. I kept up our correspondence because it made me feel sexually active and in demand, and because I like showing off (doubtless to myself only) in letters. I read:

Dear Charles,
Thank you for your letter – at last! Shame on you for not writing to me sooner! I am very pleased that you did so well in your exams. My o levels were not so good!?

I skimmed for the bits about how handsome I was. The final paragraph went:

I always hope I might come to England soon. Mummy says may-be (?) next year. I think often about meeting you again and that you will not like me any more. If I come next year you will be at University and I at Drama-school!? But this belongs to Maybe Land. Well! I must go to bed now, I am so tired out! Write to me soon.
Love Coco   XXX

This required immediate attention. Taking out a memo-pad I began to draft my reply:

My Sweet,
Thank you for your long-awaited letter. I was par-ticularly intrigued to hear of 'Maybe Land'. Could you tell me more about this strange clime? What, for ex-ample, is its capital, its geographical situation, its type of government? What, say, are its climatic features, its ter-ritorial boundaries, its chief industries? Moreover, you neglected for the second time to tell me whether on your next visit you are going to let me go to bed...

I stood up, stretching like a starfish. It was nearly nine thirty. I gathered my papers and trotted off.

The school looked more like a Victorian police station than I had really bargained for. Flanked by spindly terraced houses, cordoned off with mauve railings, the building crouched inset from the road, its sooty bricks having nothing to do with the available sunshine. I sidled down the path to the rear basement entrance. The door was open.

No one seemed to be about, apart from the directress. Mrs Tauber was in her office drinking cups of coffee and smoking cigarettes, about three of each. She was surprised but on the whole delighted to see me.

We said good morning, and, after an eery silence, I asked whether I might perhaps be 'a bit early', a real misgiving since the place was empty and it was possible I had got the times wrong.

'Certainly not,' she said, gesturing to the electric clock behind her. It was nine thirty-five. 'Can't you see the time?' She seemed genuinely to want an answer.

This dislocated me. The one strictly logical reply was: 'I'm awfully sorry – I do beg your pardon – but ... this *is* the Tauber Lunatic Asylum, isn't it?' Instead I asked where everyone else was.

She said, exasperatedly, '*They're* late.'

I slapped my thigh and shook my head.

'*Ah*. Um, is there anywhere I can go until "things get started"?'

At this point her previous geniality returned, and I was led with paraded bustle to the 'library', a dirty boxroom furnished by three chairs, a split blackboard, and at least a dozen raddled textbooks forming a knee-high stack in the far corner. It was into this arena of liberal scholarship that my colleagues wandered over the next hour and a half; there were four of them, two girls, one not bad, though twice my height.

By the middle of the week Tauber Tutors held no surprises for me. The school turned out to have a second floor, the upper one consisting of a large hall/gym/cafeteria/classroom plus two small offices. The school turned out also to be a nursery school, or mostly that. There were just the five of us in the O-Level-and-after age group, and getting on for ten times that many in the Eleven-Plus-and-Common-Entrance-and-before age group. Not that age was a helpful grouping criterion, the elder lot ranging as they did from fifteen (a delinquent ghoul studying for RSAs) to nineteen (myself), and the younger lot ranging from sphincter-free toddlers to the occasional pillow-faced, taller-than-me mongol, who could have been anything from eight to thirty-eight. A high proportion of the children were obviously insane.

My time was (theoretically) to be split up between brief morning sessions in the offices with the two on-campus teachers (Maths and Latin), evening sessions with an English master in St John's Wood, and 'general study' in the spacious hall.

In practice?

Arrive ten to ten thirty. Twenty-minute Maths lesson with Mr Greenchurch. Vacuum-chamber office redolent of dead man's feet; hairless, cysty-eared octogenarian sucking noisily and ceaselessly on his greying false teeth (I thought at first he had a mouthful of boiled sweets; on the Wednesday he allows the coltish dentures to spew out half-way down his chin before drinking them back into place); mind like a broken cuckoo-clock, often forgets you're there. Ten minutes in the hall, talking to Sarah, the less ugly girl. Eleven thirty to noon with Mrs Marigold Tregear, the enormous though well-proportioned Latin widow, up whose stockingless adamantine legs it was my constant endeavour to peer; expedients included: rolling pencils off the end of the table at which we sit side by side and going round to pick them up; crouching opposite her on entry to the room and double-bowing my shoelaces; loitering beneath the iron staircase, on the off-chance: Mrs Tregear was over thirty, and I suppose very unattractive, yet she wore quite short skirts.

Another five minutes with Sarah. Brisk walk home. Light lunch and an attempted chat with whoever was there – Jenny, or Norman, sometimes neither, never both. Perhaps half an hour in the hall, cooling my three contemporaries (Sarah was mornings only). Here I attempted a few minutes' work, not easy because the fifty bawling sprogs had classes there in the afternoon, normally acting classes, or singing classes, or self-expression classes.

This, then, was the humdrum background to the fecundities of my nocturnal reading. For I had begun to explore the literary grotesque, in particular the writings of Charles Dickens and Franz Kafka, to find a world full of the bizarre surfaces and sneaky tensions with which I was always trying to invest my own life. I did my real study at home, of course, mostly on Rachel, and on English Literature and Language, which, or so it seemed to me, I was really fucking good at.

Since the night of the punch-up things were quieter between Jenny and Norman. But on the rare occasions they were to-gether the room was muggy. It wasn't day-to-day aggro, nor the drooped, guilty, somehow sexless disgruntlement I had seen overtake many relationships, where the tension never tries to become articulate. No, there was definitely something at stake, some *issue*, and I felt I ought to be able to see what it was.

Predictably, Norman's behaviour was more illustrative than that of his wife. Now, in the early evenings, he would moon over the kitchen table, toying with his car keys or staring, glaucous-eyed, at the wall. At some point he'd slope off head-long towards the door – but he was going out just to get out; he had lost that air of breezy purpose.

After my first morning at school, I was in the kitchen, en-joying – rather sweetly, I thought – a sandwich and a glass of milk for lunch. I hardly noticed Norman's entrance. He came in – again, not to the traditional manic flurry of crashes and shouts, but with hesitation, uncertainty, as if only on reaching the kitchen would he be sure he was in the right house. 'Oh, hello,' he said. 'Jennifer around?' ('Jennifer', in Norman's par-lance, tended to mean 'that bitch Jenny'.) I said I supposed she was out. We both shrugged. Nodding to himself, as if in thought, he opened the door of the fridge. 'Any food?' he asked, his eyes quartering the room. Norman's eyes saw: a sinkful of crockery, a soiled cat-tray, a basket of fetid sheets, knitting kit splayed on the table, a cooker like a tinker's stall.

The odd thing about what followed was that I had never seen Norman take any interest whatever in domestic affairs, behaving usually as if he were living in a tent or semi-permanent pre-fab – chucking newspapers on the floor, undressing on the stairs, pasting his beetle-crushers over clean upholstery.

He took a step forward and booted the rubbish bin beneath the sink; he sent a pot slithering up the draining-board with the flat of his hand.

'These fucking slags,' he yelled, head thrown back. 'All they can bloody *do* is gorge down great fucking fry-ups and squirt ponce all over themselves.' He flicked on a tap and rolled up his sleeves, tone getting jerky with righteous sarcasm. '*You* work all bloody day and they're wiggling their bums in fucking *dress*-shops and spending pounds in Sleazy fucking Wheezy's or whatever the fucker's name is. You're up the shop while they're on their arses doing their eyes.' His voice rose half an octave. 'Juskers they wear the tits doesn't mean –' He cut out on a long, shuddering growl of rage and frustration.

Norman finished the washing-up (with Boy-Scout meticulousness), put on his jacket and left the house.

But that wasn't it. If it had been it, then nothing on earth would have made him do what he had done.

My next encounter with Rachel was on the Friday, three days after the Tea Centre Incident.

It couldn't have been more spontaneous if I had planned it. All the more startling, because I had resigned myself to dumping the entire Rachel opus. Shaving on Wednesday morning I cringed and winced as I recalled the mawkishness of my thoughts the night before. At best she had felt merely sorry for me; at worst it was phase two of her and DeForest's plan. I was too scared and ashamed to ring her that evening. Perhaps tomorrow. Nothing ventured, nothing lost.

But, as I say, when I did see her it couldn't have been more spontaneous. I was quite unprepared, caught completely on the hop. Semi-shaven, dishcloth hair, *duffle*-coat, baggy brown Farmer-Giles corduroys. Didn't have a single note-pad on me. So I ad-libbed.

I was in the Notting Hill Gate Smith's at the time, standing with my back to the front entrance and scratching my scalp – not in puzzlement, but because it itched. Badly shaken by my fell-off-a-lorry slip the other day, I had just put down a book on Cockney slang ('Cheers, Norm, where's the trouble and strife? Up the apples and pears having a pony and trap?'), and was just picking one up on 'Criticism and Linguistics'.

She came on me from behind and poked me too hard in the ribs.

'Hello then. Wotcher reading?'

'Oh, hello,' I said, surprise borne out by the falsetto croak in my voice. But then I was off. 'Oh, you know, some tired old hack reproducing boiled-up earlier articles and pretending they form a unity.' I paused and made (three) impatient gestures with my hand. 'He says they're all about "the problem of words".' I pointed to the subtitle on the cover, rich in adrenalin as a phrase from a novel took shape at the back of my mind. 'But what they're really about is him – his taste, his poise, and how much he likes money. Just look at the price.' Rachel just looked at the price, and then back up at my face, which smiled brilliantly.

Posturing, wordy, inept, if you like – but not bad for a viva.

Again quite impetuously, we began a tour of the shop. This allowed me a wide variety of tableaux: the boyish fascination I still took in children's toys; my mischievous quizzing of a saleswoman in Stationery; how refreshing it was that I liked vulgar greetings-cards (kittens with balls of wool, dogs resembling old men). Rachel seemed to be enjoying herself, rather than the reverse, but it was hardly the response I had been banking on. For instance, she hadn't grabbed my cock once.

We ended up in the record department. There we watched a small middle-aged man (with unusually big brown ears, like tea-dunked ginger-biscuits) denouncing an equally small but much younger salesgirl. She was yawning at him a lot. He couldn't get the record he wanted in mono.

'You mean to tell me that it's only *made* in stereo?' he asked in a reedy voice. I couldn't believe his ears.

'Yes. but it –'

'That's all very well for the people who own stereo record-players.'

'The rec–'

'What about the people who *don't* own stereo record-players?'

'It says on the –'

'It makes you sick.' He said this with all the verve of discovery, as if having long been of the opinion that it didn't make you sick, or even that it made you well. He turned to address the whole store. 'It makes you sick,' he repeated, walking along the counter in an attempt to individualize his audience. 'Aren't we a lot of sheep, eh?' he said; he looked from one face to another in a you-you-and-yes-*you*-sir style. He approached me.

'Have *you* got a stereo?' he asked.

' – Sir?'

'Do you own a stereo record-player?'

'Absolutely not.'

This satisfied him in some way. He strode off.

I had intended to buy a new LP, but didn't, being as yet ignorant of Rachel's musical tastes. Instead, I suggested coffee. Rachel agreed, after consulting her watch, and with the proviso that she had to be back at the Tutors in a quarter of an hour. This caused my smile, originally welcoming, to become derisive, shitty – eloquent, I should have thought, of great sexual menace.

On our way to the door I had a brainwave.

I halted suddenly as we stepped on to the pavement. I was frightfully sorry – it had almost slipped my mind – but I'd promised Cecilia Nottingham that I would ride with her in Hyde Park that afternoon. Did she mind?

'But Rachel,' I said. 'How about Monday? Do you think we could have tea together?'

She thought about this. 'All right,' she said.

'Really? Four fifteen, then.' I hailed a cab. 'At the Tea Centre?'

'All right.'

'Marvellous. The Dorchester, please. See you then.'

A smarmy ploy, this: and its shrewdest reproach was Rachel herself. She seemed less posh, less assured, altogether less formidable. She seemed physically smaller, too, and emphasized this by pouting a lot, playing dumb, deliberately mispronouncing long words – the whole routine. I didn't mind, even when she crinkled her nose in girly indecision, or popped her eyes in cute astonishment. If she's stupid, boring, ugly and affected, I thought, it's all right by me.

Anyway, I had had to show some independence, counterpointing my abjectness of the Tuesday. And I needed a breather, time for more research. And my face was in no condition to take the Centre's somewhat unkind neon. And the ludicrous business about going riding at least explained my wrecky clothes. And there was nothing I could do about it; my conceit is an unmanned canoe, leaping imaginary rapids.

I *think* it was that afternoon I began work on the Letter to My Father, a project which was to take up many a spare moment over the following weeks.

Now, I thought, assembling fountain-pen, inkpot and notes, I'm really going to hit the bastard with everything. Forty minutes later I had written:

Dear Father,
    This has not been an easy letter to write.

When I went upstairs for some tea, Jenny was in the kitchen bathing the half-faded shiner Norman had given her on Tuesday night.

'How is it?' I asked.

'Not too bad now. That flipping doorknob.'

Jenny, these days, was silent, but her silence had plenty to say. In the days immediately after the punch-up she went on As Normal: Don't worry about me I'm perfectly ... all right, patrolling the house at two miles per hour in search of extra-gruelling chores, every time she bent over or began to climb the stairs letting slip – for all her courage – a groan of exhaustion or a pained sigh.

Towards the end of the week, certainly by Smith's Friday, she had taken to her bed, becoming a spectral, ever-dressing-gowned figure, occasionally to be glimpsed on the staircase or preparing starchy snacks in the kitchen. Sometimes you could hear her cruising round the top floor and making descents to the bathroom. Sometimes, in the early evenings, when Norman was out, she would come down and have a cup of something with me. On these occasions I always tried to look tranquil, approachable, full of dear-Marje wisdom; with no results.

Saturday week, nearly a fortnight after my arrival, six days after Norman's great pots-and-pans speech, I was off to the Tate Gallery, and had gone upstairs for a quick tup in the sitting-room (just to keep the cold out). I stood looking down the square, shivering as the mouthfuls of warm gin began their priestlike task. Jenny's voice, both languid and anxious, came from the bedroom next door: 'Noorman ... ?' So I popped my head brightly into the room and said that it wasn't in fact Norman, but me, and asked if I could get her anything.

Five minutes later I was trying to slot a tea-mug in among the rubble on her bedside tray. The room smelled of make-up and breasts: half-full coffee-cups, overflowing ashtrays, dank eiderdown; a collapsed pile of magazines on the floor; beneath the dressing-table Bina and Tiki batted empty lipstick tubes. However, Jenny, in red cotton nightie, bloomed – warm-cheeked, nice greasy skin, lustrous hair, bringing to my notice once again the fact that I would not be averse to seeing her in the nude.

I sat down on the edge of the bed and tried asking her how she was. Jenny drew her knees up into a supine crouch.

'Fine,' she mouthed, as a mascara tear welled up out of her puffy right eye. She sniffed, and reached for her mug with an apologetic smile.

I felt a lump in my throat – of grief, I was pretty sure, not phlegm. I opened my mouth to speak, but there was nothing there.

'Just tired,' said Jenny.

We had both wanted to talk, I think; I don't know why we didn't.

Spent a whole day getting ready for my Monday tea date with Rachel. I shouldn't think I'm being very representative here. Indeed, such deadpan contingency-meeting must largely be the preserve of the over-thirties. Yet, given the frail, heapy, anxious teenager ...

Press-ups, knee-bends, and further sexual callisthenics. Complete body-service (sorry about all this): pits clipped, toes manicured, pubic hair permed and styled, each tooth brushed, tongue scraped, nose pruned. (The next day I would have time only to run back after school and scorch my rig under the hot tap.) I read two early Edna O'Briens and annotated my sex-technique handbooks. Horlicks at nine o'clock.

Nor did Rachel stand me up.

That afternoon, over boiling pink tea, ruddered by perceptive questions, encouraging smiles and apt generalizations from myself, Rachel Noyes told the story of her life.

It read like dingily enlightened 'sixties fiction. She wasn't Jewish at all (thereby cutting out any You-marry-white-boy? gambits). Born in Paris nineteen years earlier (one month older than me). Of course, her father had dutifully 'gone off' when Rachel was ten ('He just couldn't be bothered any more, I suppose'), and her mother (who 'had some money of her own', let's be thankful for small mercies) moved to London almost straightway.

For what it's worth:

'I spent most of the time with Nanny Rees when I wasn't away at school. She was lovely. I still go and see her in Fulham. Mummy had to let her go when I was sixteen. Huh, I cried for a week. Then Mummy married Harry, which was probably a good thing because he's sweet and she was getting terribly lonely by herself. She knew him for *ages* before, and I suppose they were lovers for quite a long time. He's so sweet – you'd love him, everyone does. He's a very steady ... *sane* sort of person, and Mummy needs that because she's a bit neurotic about some things. She can get herself into awful states. I don't think she ever quite got over Daddy. He was such a bastard to her. Then they [her mum and sponger Harry] got the house in Hampstead and I left Lawnglades and here I am.'

I asked about her real father.

'I see him every now and then. He's an artist, still lives in Paris, in *le seizième* [full accent] with his "mistress". They haven't married. I stayed with him for two weeks this summer. She was there. I liked her. She's a sculptress, much younger than him. I can't see why he still insists on seeing me, he's only beastly to me whenever I do see him. He keeps on ringing up home when he's drunk and shouts at me.'

I asked what sort of thing he shouted.

'Oh – why haven't I written, when am I coming over again, am I getting my A Levels out of the way. And he says nasty things about Mummy, that she's a liar and things. But that's only natural, isn't it? – for divorced parents to be at each other's throats over the children. There's bound to be rivalry ... don't you think?'

I did.

'He rang last week, actually. Wanted to know whether I was on the pill or not, can you believe. I said, "Look, mate, if I get pregnant I won't come running to you!" That shut him up.'

I betted that it had. The *pill*. How sexy.

'We never mention him at home. No point. That's one of the sweetest things about Harry. Never mentions him. We're all very lucky to have him [Harry], stops us all from going crazy. His wife left him, too, so they're rather a good pair. She left him with Arnold, when he [Arnold] was fourteen, which is a terribly difficult age to leave a boy. Have you met Archie?'

'No, I haven't.' I didn't say that I had seen 'Archie' at the party and already nourished much hatred for him.

She looked at me as if in reappraisal, almost certainly the result of being allowed to talk about herself for so long.

'You must come up and meet them.'

I fluttered my eyelashes.

'Shall we go?' she asked.

I thought for a second that this was a gentle, rather Whitmanesque invitation to come and meet them right away. But it wasn't. I picked up the tab. Meanwhile Rachel blew her nose into a ragged tissue and put on some camp round sunglasses: both actions made her nose look big and red.

As we left the café and idled over the road to the bus-stop I felt a listless bewilderment come over me. Rachel's character was about as high-powered as her syntax. Where *had* I got the idea she was clever? Geoffrey? No. Geoffrey's sister? No. Me? Yes. What sort of mumbo-jumbo world, I asked myself, do you think you're living in, bub?

Seemingly, in one afternoon, the entire Rachel Papers rendered defunct. All that scholarship ... wasted, utterly wasted.

'Don't you even like Blake?' I complained.

'What?'

'I was wondering if you liked Blake, because if you do I thought we might go and look at his paintings at the Tate next Sunday, if you haven't already seen them.'

I had, of course, planned to say this. But it sounded very flat now. I wasn't stroking her shoulder, nor was I staring at her in the compelling way outlined in my hip-pocket note-pad. I wasn't even looking at her. I said,

'I just thought you might like to ... I'm not ... '

Her bus appeared round the corner. I stayed where I was while Rachel edged forward with the queue. I wasn't going to get anywhere. My disappointment and fatigue seemed to prompt a loud groan, and I would have uttered it too, if Rachel hadn't suddenly been saying:

'Oh Charles, I'd love to, *really*, but ... things are so complicated.'

She glanced accusingly at the bus. She looked fretful, importunate, almost bouncing up and down, like a little girl wanting to pee. It seemed totally spontaneous. I moved closer, intending to seize her hand with involuntary earnestness. But they were both in her pockets.

'It's DeForest. He's coming to lunch. He might stay.'

'Oh well.'

'But *ring* me. No *do*. Will you?'

A stocky old woman with what looked like a triangular polythene bag on her head shouldered me brutally out of the way at this point and joined Rachel on the crowded platform.

'You never know,' I shouted. Irony and blood returned to my features.

Don't I ever do anything else but take soulful walks down the Bayswater Road, I thought, as I walked soulfully down the Bayswater Road.

Very well: demonically mechanical cars; potent solid living trees; unreal distant-seeming buildings; blotchy extraterrestrial wayfarers; Intense Consciousness of Being; pathetic fallacy plus omnipresent *déjà vu*, cosmic angst, metaphysical fear, a feeling both claustrophobic and agoraphobic, the teenager's religion. The Rev. Northrop Frye fetchingly terms it 'queasy apocalyptic foreboding'. An Angus Wilson character terms it 'adolescent egotism', thereby driving me almost to suicide last Christmas. Is *that* all it fucking is, I thought. For the question that interested me about this feeling was not 'What is it?' so much as 'Does it matter? Is it worth anything?' Because if there isn't a grain of genuine humility there, it's the electrodes for me. Does it simply get weaker and weaker, like one's sense of uniqueness? Or do some of us hang on to it? Then, I suppose, I'd have to throw in my lot with all those twitchy twenty-five-year-olds I had noticed about the place, the characters who find egocentricity numinous in itself. Intermittently articulate, something held back, a third eye hovering above their heads, intrigued and forever gripped by the contrast between them and everything else. Look round: everything, except you, is (wait for it) quite unlike what you are, altogether dissimilar, a totally different kettle of fish. Yet this is what interests them most about the observable world. Well, I'll have to make up my mind at midnight, twenty and all, one way or the other. How about you?

I telephoned Rachel the next evening. We chatted like friends.

When I brought up Blake she spoke of that engraver with enthusiasm and surprising familiarity. Obviously, if we did go, I would have to mug up on him.

'Yes, but there's at least as much blank fear in the Milton paintings as there is spiritual afflatus.' I paused, counted down from three. 'And the point is, will you be able to come?'

'Charles, I feel –'

'Hang on, you'll have to speak up. I've got some people here.' I slammed the door, so that the sounds of the radio-play on the kitchen wireless were reduced to an underground rumble. 'That's better. Yes?'

Her tone was no less firm. 'Charles, I feel rather uneasy about the whole thing. DeForest is coming on Sunday and I can't just … you know.'

'You do want to come, don't you? Well then, don't worry about that. I'll think up some amazing lie for you to tell him.'

'That's just it. I won't … tell him a lie.'

Oh, for Christ's sake. 'Oh, I see. Couldn't you just sort of say you were going to the Blake and not with who?'

'Well, we went together not long ago. And it would be unlikely that I'd get it into my head to go again.'

Surely there was no telling what could get into that battered hold-all. I went hang-dog.

'I suppose I could say I wanted to see the Gray Illustrations,' she said.

'Which are the grey illustrations?'

'The illustrations to Gray's poems.'

'Oh, of course. Say that, then. But he'd still want to come along, wouldn't he?'

'Not if I said I was going to see Nanny Rees afterwards.'

I waited. 'Would we really have to go and see Nanny Rees afterwards?'

'Do you mind?'

I thought fast. 'Not at all. But you said she lives in Farnham, and, well, that's quite a – '

'No, *Ful*ham.'

'*Ful*ham? Oh, great, well let's do that then. She sounds marvellous, I'd love to meet her. Is she Welsh, or what?'

I went along to the Tate, I need hardly say, on the Saturday before, decked out like a walking stationery department, also with a pocket edition of the poet's work and the well-thumbed Thames and Hudson.

Half an hour of wandering round: I sneered at the militarist paintings on the ground floor and laughed at one or two of the Hogarths. Then it was down to work. I mapped out an approximate route and noted points of general interest. In the hope that he would acknowledge me on the day, I approached (practically on all fours) a winded attendant and talked to him about how much he hated Americans and children of all nationalities. I had a thorough look at the Blakes, marking them up in the Thames and Hudson, and generally got the feel of the place. I was a bit ashamed, actually, having not been along before then. Because I really quite liked Blake – and not just for the fucks he had got me, either.

Two hours later, over barley wines in a pub off the King's Road, I swotted up some quotes and drafted a few speeches. One on *God Creating Adam*, to be delivered as we were leaving, by the large windows at the southern end of the gallery; unless I missed my guess, albescent reflections of the sun playing on the river would flit eerily over my face as, voice hushed and brow creased, I spoke these words. I wrote:

There's so much sexual energy in the horizontal ... *movement* of the painting. The faces of God and Adam [pause] – pained, yet distant. [Ask what she thinks and agree] Yes, it's almost as if Blake imagined the Creation as an inherently ... tragic act. [Laugh here, getting out of your depth] Quite sexy, though. Obviously quite an experience.

Then, in note form, I sketched out a short polemical piece on why I hadn't been to see (and apparently hadn't heard of) the Gray Illustrations.

suspicions justified – hopeless insipidity of the material – prim humour – no apocalypse

My face darkened.

over-demure – reactionary platitudes – fuck all that

The pub started to fill up with blue-and-white-scarved soccer hooligans, who looked disconsolate, and uniformed senior citizens, who seemed giddy with precarious cheer. Finishing my barley, I read through what I had written. I looked round, coughed, and read it again. *Nobody talked like that.* Still, Rachel knew a fair amount about Blake, and it was a sort of last fling anyway. After this, I thought, I'll have to go Lawrence.

I patted my pockets for loose change. Enough for a taxi, or a double whisky plus the tube. Perhaps I should do neither, force down a pie or something. It was a funny thing. I had never been much of an eater, and was relieved now that Jenny had become too preoccupied or whatever she was to cook those marshy dinners for Norman and me (which I had always gobbled up in case Norm thought I was queer). But instead of being merely bland, food had begun to seem irrelevant, superfluous, wholly alien. Must be Rachel. I remembered a Dickens character, Guppy in *Bleak House*, telling Esther, for whom he had the hots, that 'the soul recoils from food at such a moment'. 'Such a moment' : it bothered Guppy only when he was in a flap. It stayed in my body like a dull allergy. It occurred to me that I might be in love.

I chose the whisky, but that liquor pleasantly numbed my fear as I walked down on to the King's Road and along it to Sloane Square. Illuminated by bright shop windows, packs of Continental youths stood talking in loud voices, either among themselves or to heartbreakingly beautiful girls. They didn't mind me. Things got slightly sweatier when I changed trains at Notting Hill, a small riot being in progress on the eastbound Central Line platform. But I stuck close to a pair of fat old women, actually nipping into the seat between them on the train itself.

When I returned I got drunker with Norman. We talked for an hour and a half about girls. He didn't mention Jenny and I didn't mention Rachel.

Later, instead of going to sleep, I stared at the ceiling all night and got a lot of coughing done.

'If ever you think your prick smells bad,' mused Geoffrey, weighing a tube of glue in his hand, 'just get a load of this.' He held it up to my nose. 'And you needn't worry.'

I sniffed. A swimming-pool of cock-camembert. I wondered.

'When you say "bad" – '

'I mean bad,' he said, nodding.

Geoffrey was trying to stick a poster of a naked girl on to the south wall of his Belsize Park sitting-room. He continued :

'No, man, don't get too wanky with her. And cut out all this intellectual shit. Chicks don't want to be over-*awed* ... Thanks,' he said to his (new) witch-like girlfriend as she handed him a joint so ill-made that it resembled a baby's winkle. 'Just be yourself. If you make it, cool, if you don't, then no sweat because it wouldn't of worked anyway. Be yourself ... what's ... wrong with that?' He strained to adhere the top of the poster to the wall, and stood back, hands on hips.

'Crap,' I said (deducing that if he didn't care what he said in front of Sheila, I needn't). 'Who ever acts naturally with a girl? Do you think you do? How much of the time isn't it lovable vague Mandied Geoffrey, or big-cock groover Geoffrey, or just plain old honest-to-goodness *Geoffrey*, who doesn't put on any acts or play any games?'

He yawned. 'I don't know what you're talking about,' he said, and collapsed on to a pile of cushions, returning the joint to Sheila. As she puffed on it he kissed her neck and ears.

'Relax,' he murmured, to me rather than to Sheila. 'Flow with it, never try to change ... the course ... You can't alter ... '

'Geoffrey,' I said. 'Have you been reading all that Chink crap again, that I-Shaing or – '

Geoffrey stuck out an amphetamine-verdured tongue and made covert gestures with his free hand. Sheila stood up, brushed herself down, and brought the joint over to me. I gently refused it.

'How're you feeling?' she asked. 'Bit better?'

'Yes, a bit better.'

'Like some more coffee?'

'Love some.'

Sunday, one o'clock. Two hours before I was to meet Rachel.

That morning, I awoke, bolt upright, at nine fifteen, with a bit of a hangover. I woke because Norman was 'doing the dustbins', a thing he did two mornings a week. This duty was, I imagined, also a pleasure; at the end of it Norman got to throw the two empty bins down the ten-foot drop outside my room. It made quite a lot of noise.

I waited for the second crash. It came, even louder than the first. Out of bed, across the room, I toppled into the armchair by the fire, which, naked, I lit, fourth match. With quivering fingertips I kneaded my forehead and scalp. When I had got them working again, I moved to the window and gingerly parted the curtains. Norman was standing above me, the two dustbin lids in outstretched arms. Cymbal-like, he clapped them together, and released them. I veered back into the room.

*

'... change the way you feel, but you can change the way you think.'

There was enough of a pause for me to say: 'Well, I'd better pull out.'

'Here,' Sheila said. She handed me a paperback. *The Well-Tempered Spiral: An Ascent*, by Professor Hamilton Macreadie. 'Read it,' she said. 'It's a very beautiful book.'

I flipped through. Four hundred pages of hippie sententiousness. 'I will. Thank you.'

'Be sure you do.'

Geoffrey said that he would see me out. In the small vestibule, he took the book from my hand.

'Don't bother about that – I'll hide it.' He made a space between the telephone books on the floor. 'She's really into it seriously ... so –'

'Is that why you were trying to shut me up earlier?'

'Yeah, save hustles.'

'See? You do it too. You go along with all that. What's the difference?'

Geoffrey opened the front door. 'I only do what I have to do, like everybody else. But I don't say anything I don't mean. With me, it's not all part of some great ... scene.'

'Scene?'

'You know – strategy, angle. You go out of your way to do it. I never even really think about it. Never thought about it till today.'

'Yes, but you've *got* Sheila. I haven't got Rachel, so I've got to work on it.'

'Yeah. Anyway, fuck it.'

'Yeah, fuck it. She's nice, that Sheila, though, despite all the –'

'Yeah. Ring me. See you.'

'Yeah. Bye.'

'G'luck.'

To stabilize myself I had trekked slowly through the morning routine. Duffle-coat and gyms; up the stairs; gruff hellos, make some coffee, jokes and nudes in the morning papers.

Then I took the coffee to my bathroom (which a few not very arduous days had made usable) and sat on the lavatory seat, leaning over every now and then in order to hawk into the basin. The point of the coffee was to camouflage any darker substances I might chance to cough up; similarly, I used red-tinted toothpaste to abolish signs of what might or might not be bleeding gums. But I didn't dare look at all that morning, flushing the whole lot down with an imperious blast of the hot tap. I caught my eye in the mirror. My face looked, at once, dreary and vicious. My hair hung on my head as if it were a cut-price toupée. My mouth was crinkled like a frozen potato-chip. Moreover, my chin seemed curiously mis-shapen, or off-centre. Suddenly my hand flew to my face. A Big Boy.

For five minutes I savaged it with filthy fingernails.

Then I rang Geoffrey.

'Lovely. Then I suppose it was ewe decided to go to The University?'

Rachel spoke for me. 'Yes. He could have gone to *a* university but he decided to wait another year and try for Oxford.'

'Just in case,' I put in, not the silk-hatted layabout I seemed.

'Very good,' said Nanny. 'And have ewe been studying hard, my lovely?' She leant forward and slapped Rachel on the thigh.

She, Nanny, wasn't too bad: a red-faced, fat but strong-looking woman of about sixty-five or seventy. A Taff all right.

I sat with Rachel on the sofa, facing the two-bar electric fire. Nanny was on the moist armchair to Rachel's right, her shiny old knees drinking up the heat. As she poured tea and turned animatedly from one of us to the other, Rachel's leg would brush mine. I had, therefore, a painful, half-buckled erection which, in the teenage manner, wouldn't go away. A cup of tea turned stone-cold on the throbbing saucer above my groin without me once daring to raise it to my lips. I wore a smile, one of decent approval of all before me.

The day was going well, particularly in view of the fact that Rachel's first words were:

'Hi. You've got an enormous spot on your chin.'

I laughed with her, in a way relieved that we weren't going to spend every second of the afternoon not mentioning it.

'I know all about it, thank you,' I said. And I did, too. That morning, man and spot had become one, indivisible. Now, it felt like a surgically implanted walnut. But Rachel didn't seem to mind, or was good at seeming not to. I would have minded.

I had read my notes so often that they had long lost any meaning they might once have had. So I tried some extempore stuff. Rachel did a good deal of the talking – by no means all of it nonsense. To save face, therefore, I ran through an edited version of the *God Creating Adam* speech, adapting it to the ghostly lighting effects of the lower gallery, rather than to the pallid flickers of the afternoon sun: with widened eyes and more oracular remoteness of voice. When I finished, Rachel looked up at me and spoke these words:

'See that little boy over by the stairs? He's got his pyjamas on underneath his trousers.'

We stayed for two hours. On the way out I heart-rendingly bought Rachel a 3p postcard of Blake's *Ghost of a Flea*, offering it to her with boyish diffidence. She (quite rightly) kissed me on the cheek, just missing my spot.

'Then she lost her thumb in the grinder at the factory,' Nanny was saying. 'She've got compensation of course, one hundred and forty-five pound. "Unsafe", they said it was. Pity, mind, because they can't employ her now. Lucky to've got the money, but ... *pity*.' She beamed at us.

'That's *terrible*,' said Rachel. 'She should've got hundreds –'

'No no,' said Nanny, shaking her head with pedantic calm. 'She got good money. I read in the *Post* only Friday, boy lost his right leg in the printing works down the Broadway. They said –'

I looked round the room. There was only the one door off it, and we had come in by that, so it was safe to assume that these four walls (or six: the bedsitter was L-shaped) bounded

Nanny's existence – apart from sorties to some rancid bathroom, which would anyway have crap and catatonic Irishmen all over its floor. What happened when they got too aged and fucked-up to climb three flights of stairs every time their awful old bowels gave (surely most unreliable) signs of moving? In the far corner was a sort of kitchenette unit: a sink, a one-ring electric plate, a tiny Fablon-decked table. There Dora Rees breakfasted on tap-moistened All-Bran, lunched on devilled tea-bags, dined on a mug of hot water into which she had cautiously dipped an Oxo cube. And the spread she had laid on for us. Two kinds of sandwiches, raisin cake, sliced ham, unlimited tea. I noticed that Nan wasn't eating, so, after a couple of sandwiches for politeness' sake, I laid off the food, claiming a heavy lunch whenever she pressed more on me: 'Have some more of next Wednesday's breakfast. Do try tomorrow's dinner.' The garrulous Rachel, however, ate as fast as she talked.

I began listening again. With Rachel in the lead, they were taking a roundabout stroll down memory lane, I supposed for my benefit. Rachel talked with volume and great freedom of association; Nanny Rees just stared at her besottedly, directing the odd appreciative glance at my big boy: every now and then she would say something like 'Yes, my beauty,' or 'And don't forget so-and-so, angel, he was –' before Rachel hectically resumed.

'That Sunday on the Heath when those boys from Camden Town wouldn't give me my hoop back and you chased them all the way down to the Vale of Health and one of them shouted –'

That sort of thing. I had to do a hell of a lot of laughing, and had also to maintain a stream of unbelieving *Nos* and *You're kiddings*, but I didn't mind. Rachel was looking so good; what *did* she think she was doing here with me?

'... I think we must be going, Nanny,' said Rachel, this announcement forming the coda of some oily tale about a pet frog Rachel used to have. It had crawled beneath one of the three wheels of a prowling cripple's car, apparently a hit-and-run cripple, too. I stood.

'Give my regards to your mother,' said Nanny, 'and to Mr Seth-Smith.'

'I will. And Mummy says she's going to try to come and see you soon.'

'Tell her not to put herself out. Goodbye, Charles, lovely to've met ewe.'

'No, please don't get up,' I said. 'Goodbye, Miss Rees, thank you very much for the delicious tea. It was very nice meeting you, and I hope I see you again soon.'

I turned away, letting them complete a short but intense session of hugs, kisses and promises. Rachel joined me by the door and preceded me out. As I followed I looked back to give Nan a final wave, conceitedly indicating that I, in a mere two hours' acquaintance, had perhaps learned more about this sad indictment of our society than Rachel probably ever would. Nan didn't see me. She had brought her swollen red face back towards the fire, seeming to smile in a strange ripple-featured way. Rachel had her back to me, head bowed over open hand-bag in an attempt to light a cigarette, having not smoked while she was there. She was oddly stiff, or intent, or something. I took another glance inside. Nanny was still. Nanny rested her head on her left hand and brought her right hand up to her forehead so that the hands nearly touched, face very shiny in the glow from the fire. Perhaps it was sweat, or grease, or sebum – but, you never know, it might have been tears. I liked to think it was.

As I closed the door, Rachel turned in the semi-darkness, cigarette alight in her mouth, and led the way down the gaunt staircase to the hall. The hall smelled of boiling cabbage – or, let's be accurate, it smelled as if someone had eaten six bushels of asparagus, washed them down with as many quarts of Guinness, and pissed over the walls, ceiling and floor.

My tentative plans. A walk along the Embankment, melodious insights on Nanny Rees. Or a showing of *Bicycle Thieves* at a local Classic, after which I would discourse tellingly on the theme of its all being very well for us. Or an

85

unsmiling taxi-ride back to my place, where we'd churn the sheets in locomotive lust.

I didn't feel up to any of these. As we left the house, I said, 'Can we go and have a drink somewhere?'

'Fine. Where? I can't stay too long. Got to be back at nine.'

'The Queen's Elm. It's the other end of the Fulham Road. It'll be open by the time we get there.'

The sky was greying now, and the light shower earlier had brought no warmth to the air. Rachel fastened her coat tightly and did a Walt Disney shiver. I was informed by my viscera that now was the time to put an arm round her shoulders. I ignored them.

'God, it's freezing,' she said, as we walked up to the main road. 'Can we get a taxi? I'll go halves.'

I felt reluctant to do this. Taxis now seemed vulgar, in bad taste. Puritan guilt after parting the soiled net curtains to Nanny's world? Although I couldn't refuse without seeming mean, I hated my blithe talk on the way about what a marvellous old girl old Nanny was, such resilience and warmth and, well, *good*ness. Mind you, I realized even at that moment how shaky were my claims to any social concern. Like most people, I feel ambiguous guilt for my inferiors, ambiguous envy for my superiors, and mandatory low-spirits about the system itself. Was this better than Rachel's obliviousness? She didn't use the misery of others to cultivate her own smugness, true, but at least I didn't go about eating all their food.

'Shouldn't we have helped clear up?'

'Not on your life. She wouldn't of let us.'

Naturally, I paid for the taxi, even though Rachel made a few token rummages in her bag.

'Don't worry,' I needn't have bothered to say.

'Uh, Rachel,' I said, putting the drinks down on the table (a tomato-juice for her, *ergo* a shandy for me). I paused worriedly, gearing her for a heavyweight interlude. 'I'm not trying to be sweaty or anything, but, um – just out of interest – how long have you known DeForest?'

86

'About a year. Are we going to talk about him now?' She was smiling, so I said:

'Yes. It's DeForest time. It's DeForest hour. Where'd you meet him?'

Rachel lit a cigarette. 'In New York, actually, the end of last summer.' We fell silent as two persons dressed up as milkmen complained about the meanness/crookedness of the saloon bar fruit-machine. 'I was on holiday, staying with a friend of Mummy's. She's a dress designer. On the West Side. DeForest was staying there too. He was her nephew.'

'Does he live in America?' I asked, pleased to hear her refer to DeForest in the imperfect tense.

'Well, yes. He's over here studying. He'll probably be over here for at least four years. He wants to go to Oxford. He's –'

'Which college?'

She said. It wasn't mine.

'What if he doesn't make Oxford?'

'He will. Anyway London have offered him a place.'

Why did she have so much confidence in him, and why had she planned out everything with him, and why was she so unruffled discussing him with this strange, oddly compelling young man, this Charles Highway?

I strove for intimacy. 'Was he coming to England in the first place,' I whispered, 'or did that sort of change –'

'No. He was coming anyway.' She puffed on her cigarette, giving nothing away.

This wasn't going well. Her reticence about DeForest could be connected with her refusal to lie to him, part of some in-sane principle completely unconnected with how she really felt. Or perhaps she loved him and hated me.

But I tried to step back from the situation, to look at it sensibly, structurally, and for once it didn't seem quite the hilarious, whirligig adventure that my self-consciousness would have me believe. This was the fifth occasion on which we had met. Did that mean anything, or did people do it all the time? I wondered what Rachel thought of me and could come up with no answer, not even an opinion. I shrugged.

'What will you do when he goes to Oxford?'

'God, that's so far ahead. We haven't really – '

'I mean what do you think you'll do?'

'I don't know.'

'How do you feel about him? Are you going to tell me?'

Now, to growled obscenities, after much sparring and feint-ing, one of the milkmen began actually to fight the fruit-machine, rocking it on its base with flat-palmed jabs. Rachel glanced towards the bar, and back again.

We were sitting at right-angles. She was looking at me, I faced straight ahead. It was no accident that my spot was on her blind side. Rachel's eyes dropped to her lap, where she was fondling a ball of stained tissue. Big boy beating like a young man's heart, I hung my head, exhaled a chestful of air, and spoke.

'I feel vaguely ridiculous saying this, it may be quite out of line – I can't tell any more where I stand with people – but listen. I ... well, I just think about you all the time, that's all, and I thought I'd better find out how you feel so that we can see what's best to do.' I waited. 'And because I'd really like to know. I'm getting tired – '

The fruit-machine burped, gave a deep, guttural judder, and, while the milkmen whooped, started to cough out a string of clamorous tokens.

'It's difficult – ' Rachel began.

'What? I can't hear.'

She bit her lip, again, and shook her head.

The machine hawked. The milkmen shrieked.

I patted the hand on her lap. 'Well. Never mind,' I said, relaxing, sinking, drained and battered into my seat. I felt com-pletely hollow, as if I were a child. She could have sneaked away then without me lifting a finger, without me noticing.

'Let's get out of here.'

Rachel said that.

Outside: in the middle of the pavement; my hands on Rachel's upper arms, her hands playing with my jacket button. I could see the line of her centre-parting, and she smelled agreeably of hairdressing salons. I cupped her chin, lifting her face to mine.

'Are you crying?'

She dropped her head again. 'Not for you.'

I held her reasonably tight and gazed across the road at a dimly lit antique-shop. There was some reflection. I looked better fun than she did.

'Listen,' I said. 'Are you listening?' She sniffed and nodded. 'I don't care what happens now. Honestly. I can wait as long as it takes. But remember I'm thinking about you non-stop. And don't worry.' I stroked her hair. 'How're you getting back?'

'Taxi, I suppose.'

'*Taxi!*'

I wasn't shouting it back at her, but hailing a cab that had pulled up at the lights. I opened the door and Rachel gave instructions to the driver. She turned, and would doubtless have said goodbye had I not silenced her with a potent, vale-dictory stare. Rachel might have looked out of the tinted win-dow to catch a last glimpse of me so I stood on the pavement and waved, with sinister beckoning motions, until the taxi was out of sight.

I regained the saloon bar, finished my shandy, killed a further two barley wines, and (tousling my hair and accent) managed to get a game of darts with three very serious car mechanics. Then I walked down the Fulham Road to South Kensington Underground, pausing several times to look at myself in shop windows, or just to think.

Nine: the bathroom

Flipping through my *Odds and Sods* file just now I came across two rather curious items, stapled together, which is in itself unusual because I'm always trying to keep things fluid.

The first is dated the eve of my eighteenth birthday. It says:

> As regards toilet training. Remember when I was 8 (?) asked mother how turds should behave. She said that, ideally, turds should be brown and should float. Looked next time – black as night and sank like a stone – never looked since. Hence, possibly, my anal sense of humour?

... I don't see why. I've always thought that an anal sense of humour was very common among my age group, though I may be mistaken. Surely, nice things are dull, and nasty things are funny. The nastier a thing is, the funnier it gets.

Anyway, here's the second item. It's dated August 1st, no year given, so it must have been penned during my summer holiday in London.

> Told Geof how much I wanted to fuck an Older Woman. He said it beat him why, since I was always going on about how horrible they looked. He asked how the fuck I knew, anyway, having never poked one or seen one naked. I had no reply.

... I wonder. Transferred disgust of my own body? No; too boring. Dislike of women? Hardly, because I think male oldsters look just as dreadful, if less divertingly so. Sound distrust of personal vanity plus literary relish of physical grotesqueries. Could be ... Sheer rhetoric? Yes.

I go over to the chair and sit down carefully, my legs on one arm and my head against the other, as if it were cradling me: teenagewise. I free the staple with my fingernails and marry the two items with a paperclip, instead. I don't think they can be *that* closely connected.

Telephone pips.

'Hello, is Charles Highway there please?'

'It's me. Hello Gloria,' I said, my voice adapting to Cockney cadences. 'How're you?'

'Charles.'

'What?'

'I know you're going to murder me if I tell you.'

'What?'

'If I tell you.'

'Tell me what?'

'I can't.'

'Go on. I won't mind, I promise.'

'It's so awful ... I got this pink slip this morning.'

Oh. Was that all. 'What do you look like in it?' I asked sexily.

'No, in the *post*, Charles. It says I've got an infection, and that I've got to tell everybody, you know, I've –'

I steadied myself against the banisters. 'What sort of infection?'

'Try chum ...'

'What? Spell it.'

'Pardon?'

'*Spell* it *out*.'

'T,r,i,c,h,o,m,o,n,a,s. – But it's not serious. I went to the clinic and the doctor gave me these pills you take for five days and that's all. Then you're all right. Charles?'

'I'm still here.'

'Are you really furious with me?'

There was no one in so I spoke quite loudly.

'I see, I see. Trichomonas. So what do I do? what do I do? what do I do? Just go to the doc's, slam it on the table, tell him I've got a tricky dicky and he gives me the pills and I take them and that's that?'

'You are furious with me, aren't you.'

I sighed. 'No. Not with you. Wasn't your fault.'

'Oh, Charles.'

'Who was it, by the way? Any leads? Any ideas?'

'Yeah. Terry. Haven't been with anyone else, and the man said it couldn't be you, because of the ... '

'Incubation period. Oh well. How long before you can start going to bed with people again?'

'I didn't ask. Not long.'

'Why haven't I got any symptoms?'

'Men don't with this. Only girls do.'

'What sort of thing?'

'You know. Itching, hurts when I go to the toilet.'

'Mm, I know.'

'I'm sorry, Charles.'

'Oh, don't worry. Perhaps I'll see you, when it's all over.'

This be Nature's way of recommending monogamy.

From the gyppo in Belsize Park, of the grimy stomach: crabs – ant-hill groin. The cure: five nights running with nova balls. You apply milky ointment, and wait, biting a penny, cigarette up either nostril. Five nights running I was back in the bathroom, trying, with no effect, to wash it off again. The unearthly anguish goes on taking you by surprise. Then, once more, ten days later, for luck.

From Pepita Manehian: clap. That was nine months ago. Pepita was an inmate of one of Oxford's many A-Level/secretarial colleges, establishments which supply the town with a large proportion of its eligible womenfolk. She wasn't very good-looking, of course; if she had been she could have taken her pick of the undergraduates and wouldn't need blackheaded sixth-formers. Made the girl mine in a lavatory at some week-end party. (All the bedrooms were occupied; but it was quite a spacious closet, with a rug, some towels, and tissues a-plenty.) We did well, even though, in the dying moments, Pepi

93

smashed her head three times against the lavatory bowl, this giving the cramped cleaning-up operations a still more incongruous air.

However, on the following Friday or thereabouts I woke up to find that someone had squeezed a family-size tube of pus all over my pyjama bottoms. A toxic wet dream? On visiting the bathroom I found also that I was peeing lava. Palpably, something was up. To deal with the first symptom I fixed up a sort of nozzle over my helmet with a wad of Kleenex and an elastic band. To ameliorate the second, I took care always to use the narrow downstairs lavatory, where, with palms pressed flat against the walls, like Samson between the pillars of the Philistine temple, I would part company with angry half-pints of piss, pus, blood – you name it.

Then I wondered what to do.

Obviously, I could never sleep with anybody again, but (God knew) that would be no deprivation. I thought I might as well get cured. Yet Pepita was of foreign extraction and this meant that I would have to go to Madagascar or somewhere to get it treated. 'Ah. Congo Clap,' the doctor would say through his teeth. 'Witch Doctor Umbutu Kabuki's your man – the *only* man, as a matter of fact. You turn left off the Zambesi, second tributary, third hut on your right. Offer him these brightly coloured beads ... '

All weekend I cried, beat my head against the bathroom door, thought of ways of committing suicide, ran off into the woods and screamed as loud as I could, considered lopping off my rig with a razor-blade, slept in a nettle-bed of nerves. I half wanted to tell my father; I knew he wouldn't mind, but it would have disgusted me to have his efficient sympathy.

On the Monday, after six hours of incognito leprosy at school, I had a coffee in George's with Geoffrey. Via girls, Durex, promiscuity, I brought the subject up – quite hypothetically, of course. Geoffrey thinks he knows all about this sort of thing because his father's a doctor. When I asked about the cure his reply was therefore vehement:

'It's hell, apparently. They stuff stuff up your arse to sort of

... bring it on. Then they bung this needle-thin umbrella down your cock and press a button that fans it out. Then, *then*, they yank it out, really hard.' He made a tugging gesture with his spoon.

'What, they give you an anaesthetic first?'

'No. No point. It's too sensitive. Don't be silly, man. Anyway, you've got to be able to get a rise first before they can get it in. Obviously. Then they *wrench* it out, and all the scabs and crap come out with it.' He sipped his coffee. 'You usually faint.'

'Jesus Christ. How long before you can screw again?'

'Not sure. Six months, a year. At least six months. With regular treatment.'

Nothing of the kind, needless to say: just two jabs of penicillin up the bum and much humiliation at the local clinic.

Then I wrote to Pepita. Did I write to Pepita. I still have the reply somewhere. My letter was savaged by the caretaker's corgi; the addressee's name was unintelligible so the headmistress opened it and was most put out by the contents. (The letter was one of my polemical best, strong on imagery.) Pepita was chucked out on her ear, a letter sent to the parents, etc.; this all struck me as perfectly right and proper at the time. Pepi told the story in her answer – a forgivable attempt to square the moral blame – ending with the claim that she 'had never mean't so as to give it to' me. (Love that 'mean't'.) I later discovered that she had given it to half Oxford, too; her personal hygiene was evidently so flexible that the symptoms had slipped by unnoticed for an entire term.

What now, though? What now? I went down to my room, locking the door for some reason, and lay on the bed in the dark.

There was nothing to worry about. Geoffrey knew a queer doctor in Chelsea who was always keen to deal with such maladies. He had fixed Geoffrey up only last month. Geoffrey had caught some rather complicated NSU off that Swede. The Swede – significantly, it seemed to me – had had a scar like a giant's fly-zip right down the middle of her stomach. Geoffrey said that he had gone through with it out of pure altruism, and I believe him. (Erections, as we all know, come to the teenager on a plate.) He had done it because he did not wish to hurt her feelings. There was a moral there. The doc had charged him five guineas; I could borrow that from Norm. It might postpone Rachel, it might mean a couple of weeks off the booze, it certainly would mean a hellish afternoon, but otherwise *there was absolutely nothing to worry about.*

Try telling me that. It was curious. All Saturday I had been strung up about Rachel: would she stand me up? what would I do when she cooled me? All Sunday – too busy being with Rachel to worry much in a general way – I had been strung up about my spot: would it turn cancerous? would it permanently alter the shape of my face? would it erupt over Rachel's white shirt? All Monday, yesterday, after a bad night and, this morning, an unusually productive bronchorrhoea session, I had spent the day with the growing conviction that my lungs were on the way out, that soon I would be coughing up not just gilbert but stomach-lining, key sections of my vitals, that surely I could not live beyond a Keatsian twenty-six.

Now all these problems seemed laughable. I couldn't imagine why I had given them even a passing thought.

And there was something that frightened me much more. If I went to the doctor's tomorrow, and was cured by, say, the weekend, there'd be no relief from anxiety, just different anxiety. Even as the antibiotics hosed down my genitals, the mind's bacteria would be forming new armies. I'd come up with something to get me down.

I went over to my desk, put on the lamp, and got out the note-pad entitled *Certainties and Absurdities.* I wrote:

ANXIETY TOP TEN. Week ending September 26th
(Last week's positions in brackets)
(–) 1 Clap
(1) 2 Rachel

(2)	3	Big Boy
(7)	4	Loose Molar
(10)	5	Owing Norm Money
(3)	6	Bronco
(6)	7	Being Friendless
(9)	8	Insanity
(–)	9	Rotting Feet
(4)	10	Pimple in Left Nostril

Ones to watch: Having a smaller cock than DeForest; incipient boil on shoulder-blade.

Clap has taken the charts by storm, ousting Rachel after her confident two-week run. Spot in Nose is definitely following Disintegrating Toenails on its way out of the Ten – but watch out for Boil on Back!

So see you next week. Right? Right! Goodnight.

Was this the case with everyone – everyone, that is, who wasn't already a thalidomide baked-bean, or a gangrenous imbecile, or degradingly poor, or irretrievably ugly, and would therefore have pretty obvious targets for their worries? If so, the notion of 'having problems' – or 'having a harder life than most people', or 'having a harder life than you usually had' – was spurious. You don't have problems, only a capacity for feeling anxious about them, which shifts and jostles but doesn't change.

It struck me, not for the first time, that I owed it to the world to write some kind of dissertation before my untimely death. The trouble was that I never got further than the title and dedication before I started thinking how it would be received, its reviews and my trenchant answers to them. The long-awaited open letter to *The Times*:

From Professor Sir Charles Highway
Sir, I should like to point out, for the last time, to Messrs Waugh, Connolly, Steiner, Leavis, Empson, Trilling, *et al*, that the argument of my *The Meaning of Life* was in-

tended to be anti-comic in shape. The recent television publicity has done a good deal to becloud the issue ...

And so on.

Beneath my bed was an unopened quarter of whisky, my liquid sleeping-pill. Were you allowed to booze before you started on the antibiotics? I wondered, as I drank it all anyway.

When drunkenness arrived I made for the bathroom. I spent a lot of time, especially at night, moving from bedroom to bathroom, from underground bathroom to underground bedroom, the hidden worlds of sleep, dreams, weariness, shame. Now where had I got all that from? Ah yes, I remembered some essay which claimed that the bedroom and the bathroom, the secret, private area of human life, was the world of 'death ... from which all human imagination comes'. (Geoffrey, by the way, didn't have one. He said he had once crapped while a girl of his had a wash. There you go.)

I ran a bath and stripped. Lowering my jockey-pants, a razor-blade on the basin shelf caught my eye. I looked down and looked up again. There was my rig and there was the razor-blade. 'Come on, don't be wet, have it off,' my mind coaxed. 'Just lop it off, lop the bugger off. Go on. Go *aarn*.'

Tucking it between my legs, like a dog in disgrace, I got into the bath and lay back. The ceiling was slightly cracked in the corner. A house-proud spider worked on its translucent web. Eat a fly or something, I told it; be symbolic.

For goodness' sake, I had had only one real infection. The rest was temporary scares and growing neurosis about my private parts – parts (it bore pointing out) that had come to enjoy greater privacy over recent months. Now I looked at them only when I had to, and even then covertly, as if I were a queen and they were someone else's. Any spot or abrasion, even when I knew perfectly well it was a zip-scar or the remains of some tortured blackhead, meant going through the routine. It meant working it over. It meant waiting for the one-by-one elimination of my senses. It meant another trip to the local library, another afternoon browsing pinkly through medical dictionaries, ship's doctor's manuals.

Let it just try anything when I had a pee and Christ would I show it who was boss. I washed, got out, slipped a towel over my shoulder – had a pee. I couldn't tell whether it hurt or not. So I worked it over anyway, and good.

Normal procedure: I flicked it; slapped it; I garrotted it with both hands; a final searing chinese-burn – a last attempt to tempt out a drop of that most dreaded commodity, discharge. None was forthcoming. It looked at me as if bullied, picked-on. Cautiously at first, I applied a nailbrush to the helmet. I combed, with the rigour of an orphan matron, my pubic hairs. I swabbed my balls with after-shave. Perhaps a pipe-cleaner, steeped in Dettol?

I experienced thrilling self-pity. 'What will that mind of yours get up to next?' I said, recognizing the self-congratulation behind this thought and the self-congratulation behind that recognition and the self-congratulation behind recognizing that recognition.

Steady on. What's so great about going mad?

But even that was pretty arresting. Even that, come on now, was a pretty arresting thing for a nineteen-year-old boy to have thought.

'Yes. Very. One somehow gathers these responsibilities – or they seem to somehow gather on you. Because affection is a cumulative thing. People go on as if it were purely chemical. But it's not. How could it be? You just *do* feel fond of people you've known for a long time.'

'They get dependent on you and you start taking them for granted. And then maybe you think it's the safest thing. And you start worrying about how they're going to get on without you, and about you getting along without them.'

'But that's the trap. Worrying about being without them is a cop-out. And you mustn't let yourself get hustled into a false position.' My use of the split-infinitive and the hippie colouring of my speech were attributable in part to Rachel's hippie satchel – one of those tasselled, ropey-looking nosebags – which, or so she claimed, was made entirely from natural fibres and dyes (i.e. snot, hair, ear-muck). I had remarked on how nice it looked.

'Yes. That's the trouble.'

I felt the pre-pass flush come over me. After all, here she was, sitting on my bed and talking to me without any real sign of dislike. Over lunch at the Tea Centre, my sympathy vis-à-vis DeForest had been so discreet, my manner so genial, so ... right, my invitation to 'forget school', to 'live a little', so re-laxed, so unpushy, that – here she was, sitting on my bed.

Fortunately, my room was in a state of red alert nowadays and Rachel's telephone call hadn't caught me with my pants down.

She had said matter-of-factly that she was fine and that DeForest wasn't going to be at school that day and that per-haps it would be 'a good thing' if we met for lunch and 'had a chat'. Her blandness had frightened me at first. I didn't like that 'chat'. There was something honestly all for the best about it. But I, as cool as you like, had not contacted her since Nanny Sunday; so the initiative was mine.

'Can I put the other side on?'

She was referring to the Beatles record (late-middle period – between pretty-boy rock and bleared occult) which had just come to an end. This had seemed a safe choice, since to be against the Beatles (late-middle period) is to be against life.

All I had had to do, really, was make the bed more thoroughly (sprinkling talc between the sheets), readjust the record stacks, and, as a last-minute thought, place two unfin-ished poems on the coffee-table, to be shyly gathered up when and if I got her in there.

I watched Rachel crouch in front of the gramophone. She was wearing a fawn crew-neck jersey, a tight (and quite short) pinstripe skirt, and brown knee-high boots. As she knelt her arse formed a ... whatever you like – an arse-shaped semi-circle above the heels of her boots.

Rachel settled herself again on the bed and, with modest

sways of the head and in a small but pleasing voice, began to sing along with the gnomic George Harrison: about the space between us all, about those persons who wilfully conceal themselves behind a wall of illusion, and so on.

I was still soggy with retrospective alarm about the miraculous escape I had had eighty minutes earlier. When I followed Rachel into the room the first thing I saw was a huge notice on the mantelpiece. The notice had this to say:

FOR THE LOVE OF GOD DON'T LET HIM TOUCH YOU
HE HAS GOT AN UNUSUALLY REVOLTING DISEASE

The notice was written on a small bottle of pills (pressed into my shaking hand twenty-four hours before). The notice was in code form; it said:

Flagyll. One to be taken four times daily.

I pocketed the pills while Rachel was looking at the copy of *Encounter* on my bed. Later I put them on the shelf in the bathroom, out of the reach of children.

Seconded by the boyish Paul McCartney Rachel now urged me to send her a postcard, drop her a line, stating my point of view and indicating precisely what I meant to say. Instead, I tried to read an *Encounter* article on the relationship between art and life. Rachel was leaning back on the bed. She fell silent. She looked out of the window. And she lit a cigarette, her first since we had got back, her first for an hour. I peered over the rim of my spectacles. Even supine Rachel seemed erect, reminiscent of early Jennifer. Her knees were hunched up so that I could see the opaque darker-brown tops of her tights and the elusive shadow above.

It was natural that I should pick up the improvised saucer-ashtray from the coffee-table and only polite to glide over and put it on the backless bedside chair. It seemed fair enough to stand by the window for a while, to be expected that I should drop the *Encounter* to the floor, totally credible to sit on the lower third of the bed, and quite on the cards when my left foot brushed against her boots. This was how it seemed to

Rachel. To me, as always, the pass was a new and unexpected turn: dreamy and inevitable enough, but alien, altogether different from what had gone before.

Lovely Rita meter maid
Lovely Rita meter maid

sang Rachel. Then she stopped singing.

Do I speak?

There was a warm, musty silence. The diagonal curls of smoke from her cigarette were spangled by a thousand grains of dust highlit by the shaft of autumn sun. The shaft of autumn sun struck through the recently dismembered tree in the front garden, squeezed between the railings, quartered itself against the window-frame, wormed its way into the room.

Rachel stubbed out her cigarette.

I squeezed her leathery ankle.

She turned towards me, exhaling smoke, smiling.

Her lips were smudged with some pasty brown substance, almost the colour of her skin. I stared at them, leaning over. Those diamond-hard, slightly crooked teeth. Those lurid gums. Did I dare offer up my grim stripe to that pristine orifice?

The orifice was still smiling when I kissed it.

It yielded, but by no means voraciously, so mine kept its distance, varying the angle every few seconds. Rachel was still on her side. The manœuvre had involved leaning over her legs and lower torso. I supported myself, with some effort, on a single quivering arm, positioned near the small of her back, with enough purchase to keep some distance between our bodies. With my free hand I did things like describing the outline of her hair against her face, stroked her jawline, let a finger hover above her right ear. But I could keep this up for only so long.

After a first kiss there are normally two things you can do. Either extricate your mouth, grin with it, and say something (necessarily) cinematic; or move on to the neck, throat and ears. My posture suggested the first, since I couldn't get at the rest of her face without falling backwards on to the floor or collapsing wheezily on top of her. But I preferred the second method, having, indeed, never tried the other. The kiss had been underway for better than thirty seconds now. I made it more positive, introducing tongue a quarter of an inch. Rachel's mouth widened the same distance. Right.

Great strength was called for to lower my body down to just above hers, so that I could bring in the support of my right elbow (crooked for this purpose) to take the pressure off my left arm. In one movement I shifted my nine stone on to said elbow, slid my legs over Rachel's to the other side of the bed thereby settling in beside her, withdrew my mouth, and lay my head on her chest.

I listened to the fizz of cashmere and the crumpling of (more or less) empty brassière. My knees came up to rest against Rachel's, keeping a good six inches between her skirt and my groin. I lay there still.

As hoped, Rachel's left hand came up and stroked my hair. Smirking at the wallpaper, I stayed in position for a quarter of a minute and laid an arm across her waist. Then I looked meekly up at her. She was gazing at the ceiling, deep in some maternal fantasy perhaps? I doubted it.

Tactically, this was less than ideal. Too wistful, and this gives time for regret. I brought my face to within an inch of hers, having crunched my back teeth together. I kissed her again, far more emphatically this time, paying special attention to the corners of her mouth and to the points at which her teeth and gums met – both very sensitive areas. Meanwhile, I 'did' her left ear with the index finger of my right hand. If 'done' skilfully this can cause the subject to become ga-ga with arousal. The thing is *hardly to touch* the ear, to touch it as lightly as possible consistent with touching it at all. The nearer you get to not touching it the better. (I knew because I had had it 'done' to me, in the St Giles bus shelter, by a wonderful waitress. I had almost fainted, but I was seventeen then.)

Rachel responded tolerably well. Her tongue, as yet, was held in abeyance. However, she was jostling her lips a fair amount and made some of the right noises. When I pressed a corduroy kneecap against the point where hers met, though, her legs could not be said to have leapt apart. Nor, to be honest, did she have so much as one finger up my bum.

Just as well.

With my left hand I was making swirling motions on Rachel's stomach, outside her jersey, not touching her breasts but coming mischievously near them sometimes. Thus I maintained a tripartite sexual application in contrapuntal patterns. This sort of thing: insert tongue, remove finger from ear; withdraw tongue, stroke neck, trail pinkie of left hand along narrow gash between her jersey and skirt (tastefully avoiding navel); kiss and semi-lick throat and neck, 'do' ear, and place hand unemphatically on knee; stop 'doing' ear and stroke hairline, bring mouth towards hers and hand up her leg at similar speeds; with mouth almost there, hold her gaze for long second while hand takes off at aeroplane trajectory from the runway of her thigh and lands ... on her stomach again just as mouths meet. That sort of thing.

While doing this I thought how lucky I was to be out of action. In Dr Thorpe's queer words: 'Don't go sticking it up any pretty ladies for a bit, now will you? Come back next Monday, all right? and we'll take another peep at it.' Lucky because there was no chance of me getting 'worked up', of getting *carried away*, I believed was the phrase??? There was no danger of me thinking about anyone's pleasure but Rachel's. I made polite groans, naturally, but with the professional sincerity of the wine-taster as opposed to the candid slavering of the alcoholic.

My rig, of course, wouldn't know. And yet, to give it its due, that organ had behaved immaculately the day before. As I stood beside Thorpe's white-sheeted chaise-longue, about as relaxed as a drainpipe, trousers frilling my shins, baggy but spotless Y-fronts midway down trembling thighs: as Thorpe cruised towards me, as he reached out his manicured hand, head down, saying 'Well let's just take a look at the old codger then, shall we?' I was *convinced* he'd set off some awful glandular button, that my prick would spring to life joyfully in his fingers, that he would lift up his face to mine in eager recognition. But it couldn't have been better. I had wanted to buy it a bag of sweets or something afterwards.

Now. I completed a really very complicated set of man-œuvres. It featured, among other things, the worrying of her hip-bone with my elbow, stroking her eyelashes, and kissing her ears with dry-tongued care. I did some talking, too – shameless flattery most of it, but circumstantial and disinterested, which, I find, makes it far less embarrassing, since during their delivery compliments are borne and only in retrospect are they enjoyed.

'You know, you're looking straight at me and I can still see the whites of your eyes all round your pupils. Look at mine. The brown always joins the edge at some point. But yours are amazing. I suppose that's why they're so striking – the first thing I noticed about you. Why do you ever wear sunglasses?'

And again:

'What's this stuff on your lips? It doesn't taste like make-up. It's difficult to tell where your lips stop and your face starts. Your skin's such an absurd colour, like damp sand; very nice.'

Rachel, for her part, said at one point: 'You've got such sweet breath. Not sickly.' She laughed. 'Just sweet.'

Although utterly inexplicable, this was true enough, often pointed out to me by girls ('cucumber and peppermint' is the best description I've ever screwed out of them). That tasty liquefying gook in my lungs? Rachel's remark impressed me deeply all the same. I wished I could, so to speak, come off duty, surrender to this experience as something related not to the past nor to DeForest nor to trichomonas nor to the future. But I had to get her first, then there would be time.

To signal this promise, I abandoned the tactile skirmishes. I lifted both hands to her face, held it with my palms resting flat against her cheeks, and kissed her lightly on the lips. Some-times, in this sort of situation, in a sexual context, girls look sad when they are not sad. This was how Rachel looked: frowning, beautiful, clear-eyed, pained.

We had been at it for thirteen minutes. I knew because the record had come to an end (I timed it later, for the books: four tracks' worth). But the record didn't go on to automatic reject like any normal record; those cheeky Beatles had indented the final groove, so that it went

> Cussy Anny hople – wan
> Cussy Anny hople – wan

ad infinitum, until you could be bothered to go and lift up the needle. (Geoffrey said it was 'I'll fuck you like a superman' backwards. I had never checked.)

Pretended not to notice for half a minute or so. Then: 'Oh, Christ.' I let my body go limp and swivelled over. I sat facing away from Rachel. The record had been hardly more than a murmur, intended to drown the muffled snorting and wincing of the pass. Without it, the room seemed hollow.

'Your jacket's awfully creased,' said Rachel, as if from a great distance.

I bunched a fistful of the material in my hand. It was creased. I stared at the rug. 'Where is DeForest, anyhow?' I thought this would sound more powerful with my back to her.

'Oxford. Getting interviewed.'

'Oh really?' I said in a tight voice. Why wasn't I getting interviewed? 'When's he coming back?'

'Tomorrow. But then he's going shooting in Northamptonshire.'

'Shooting? What do you mean?'

'Hunting. You know, with guns.'

'Oh. He does all that, does he?' Elitism *and* butchery. Ought to be some milage there.

'Not really.' I heard her stifle a yawn. 'A friend invited him for the weekend.'

She stressed 'weekend' on the first syllable. DeForest's influence. I turned, smiling.

'That means you can come to a film tonight. *La Rupture* is on at the Classic.'

She closed her eyes and nodded, seemingly in regret. I stole a worried kiss.

Suddenly there was clamour from the direction of the stairs, as if a victorious Cup Final team were running down them. Rachel and I had only just enough time to sit up and look startled and guilty before the door swung open. Norman's beachball head loomed over us. It ignored Rachel.

'Come on. Upstairs. Your dad's here.'

'What? *Here?*'

'Yeah, come on.' He turned to leave.

'Look, Norman, slow down,' I said. 'Can't you tell him I'm ill or something, or out? What the hell's he doing here, any-way?' I was making little allowance for Rachel's presence, having explained to her that my sister had gone and married, quite unaccountably, this mad cockney – perfectly harmless, something of a character, totally off his head of course, don't be alarmed by *anything* he says or does, and so on.

'No, you've got to come up. Jenny said. She thinks I'll nut him or something unless you're there. This Rachel?' He looked her up and down in insolent appraisal.

'Yes. Rachel, this is Norman.'

'Hi,' said Rachel chirpily. She had sat up, arms wrapped round her knees.

'Tsuh.' Norman threw his eyebrows and head back with disgust or envy – I couldn't tell which. Nor could I tell how anyone could be so offensive and give so little offence.

'Come on, then,' he said, 'both of you.' He frowned and gestured towards the door encouragingly. 'His tart's here, too,' he added, as if they had arrived independently.

'You mean his *mistress?*'

Half after: right Charlie

A moment ago mother came in and asked me if I wanted any supper. I said no, of course, and added that I would appreciate not being disturbed again. That sort of thing can put you right off your stride. Now I have to lie on the bed for a few minutes and let the solitude gather round me once more.

I assumed that for all her social varnish Rachel must have been feeling rather overwhelmed, so I was relieved when we were hailed outside the kitchen door by an unkempt, hurriedly made-up Jenny. She was making a big tea. I introduced them, and Rachel immediately started to help, assembling trays, grilling toast, transferring milk and sugar into genteel containers.

'What *does* he think he's doing here?' I asked.

'Gosh,' said Jenny. 'Norman must be up there. Oh Charles, do go up.'

I wanted to know how long they'd be. Jenny said not long. I disappeared.

My father, arms folded and needly legs crossed, was at the far end of the room. To my right: a small blonde in white shirt and black velvet trouser-suit. To my left: Norman, back to the window, in brick-jawed relish of the uncomfortable silence.

Gordon Highway was startled but, all in all, quite pleased to see me. He stood up and held out an arm towards his tart. She was called Vanessa Arnold. I leaned down and shook her jewelled hand. Vanessa was a midget, and had a drawn, over-tanned face, but she wasn't unattractive.

'No, I don't believe we *have* met.' I sat down beside her.

'Yes, I was just telling Norman here,' said my father in a declamatory voice, 'Vanessa has just flown in from New York.

It's topping ninety there! It's hot, dirty, expensive, bad-tempered – the blacks are going crazy, everyone's striking, the students are restless again ... ' He laughed. 'What a God-awful country!'

He continued, exchanging the odd political or ecological platitude with Vanessa, until the deliverance of 'Ah, here we are.' The girls placed both trays on the drinks-table between the windows. I introduced Rachel, with some pride.

My father told Jenny and Rachel what he had just been telling Norman and Charles here. Rachel said she had been there the year before ... oh really? lot worse now what's going to happen mugging Nixon riots Central Park pollution even in the day-time.

Norm and I grimaced at each other. He hadn't spoken yet, I only once. The tea got round, then the toast, which my father refused. He wanted neither milk nor sugar. Was there a lemon? Jenny would run down, occupied as she was. No, Rachel would. Where were they kept? She left the room.

'They aren't going to put up with it much longer,' Vanessa was saying. 'Nixon is up to here' (neck-high) 'in bullshit.' She blew on her tea. For someone who hated America so much she had a very mid-Atlantic accent. 'Soon the students and the Panthers are going to get together, and then ... ' She shook her head.

There was a pause.

'And what do you think of this frightful situation,' said Norman in a pontifical voice. 'Charles, I mean what's it all coming to?'

Rachel broke the stillness. She bore a saucer on which lay a single slice of lemon.

'Ah, thank you so much.' My father held out his cup, a smile fossilized on his face.

'I'll tell you, Norman,' I said. 'I think it's got very little to do with the government. It's the people.'

'Ah, now what do you mean by "the people"?' my father queried. 'Aren't "the people" and the government, in effect, the same – '

'I'll tell you, Norman. Americans will always be hell no matter who's governing them. They're –'

'Okay, so you don't like Americans,' said Vanessa.

'No, I don't like Americans.'

Rachel sat down in a straight-backed chair to Norman's left.

'Ah, but why? Has that got anything to do with the matter at hand?' My father lifted his cup, watching his weight and watching me.

Stop saying 'ah' like that every time you open your fucking mouth. I felt hot. I didn't think much. I said: 'Because they're violent. Because they only like extremes. Even the rural people, the old reactionaries in the farms, go out blowing nig-gers' heads off, roast a Jew or two, disembowel a Puerto Rican. Even the hippies are all eating and mass-murdering each other. The generations of T-bone steak and bully-beef, as if they're doing a genetics experiment on themselves. No wonder they're so violent, with bodies like theirs. It's like being permanently armed.' The room sighed. 'And I hate them because they're so big and sweaty. I hate their biceps and their tans and their perfect teeth and their clear eyes. I hate their –'

I was interrupted by Vanessa (abusively), her boyfriend (magisterially) and Rachel (with amused dismissiveness). I let them ride over me without protest. The tirade hadn't been contrived wholly for Rachel's benefit. I had, in fact, before even meeting DeForest, written a sonnet on this theme – of whose sestet the speech was, in part, a prose paraphrase. It had not seemed such limelit nonsense in verse form.

Jen finally took time out from serving tea and toast. She sat on the floor at her husband's feet. Norman, staring at me with curiosity and some affection, laid a palm the size of a violin on her head. Jenny frowned when she felt Norman's hand, but looked grateful. It was the first time I had seen them touch since the night of my arrival. Two and a half weeks.

The argument continued. I was unable to see how the three of them could have disagreed with me so fervently and yet go on disagreeing among themselves. Vanessa had decided that it would be more swinging partially to come round to my view (she blamed the system, and 'genocide-guilt'). Rachel was taking a conventional stand against 'this kind of generalization'. My father umpired. I listened for a few minutes, then went downstairs.

After some words with Valentine ('Fuck off and get Mum') and a new au pair ('Yes, I'm terribly sorry, *would* you mind waking her up, it is rather important – I do hope I'll see you next time I'm there'), I got mother. I let her scale the lurching rope-ladder first to consciousness, then to recognition, and, at last, to intelligibility.

'Er, no dear, yes. I wanted … I wanted just to know how many people your father was bringing. There's Pat and Willie French, I know, but I wondered if they were bringing … someone else. Because I shall then have to move Gita out of the green room and put Sebastian's things…'

I looked for a connection. 'Who are Willie and – Pat, is it?'

'Willie French, the journalist, and his … Patty Reynolds. She's a very old friend of mine. She…'

Reynolds. I put my hand over the receiver and shouted, 'Father?' The conversation above ceased, and then, more quietly, resumed. I listened. Mother was still lost in monologue when my father's head appeared over the banisters. I held up the telephone for him to see.

'I've got mother here. I think she wants to know whether you're bringing' – I waved my head – 'her, up for the weekend.'

He descended to the bathroom landing. 'Yes. You see … ' He began down the stairs towards me, 'Vanessa's sister is –'

'You are? Right. Yes, mother, Pat will be bringing her sister.'

' … oh. Well, I'll … there'll probably –'

'I'm sorry, mother, I can't talk just now … Yes, I might come. No one will be using my room, will they? I'll ring if I am. Bye now.'

My father stood half-way down the stairs. 'You will come,

Charles, won't you. Old Sir Herbert is coming along and I think you should be there. He can –'

'Next time,' I said, 'next time, let her know, okay? There's enough room to sleep an army in that fucking house. Let her know. So she won't have to go through this pathetic charade to see if she can find a bed for your girl. Okay?'

'Oh, come on, Charles, pull yourself together. Your mother and myself have already discussed the matter. And nothing whatever is going to happen with my "girl" in "that fucking house". Do you understand me. Do you understand me?'

I turned away and then back again. He was managing to look quite elegant and plausible, there on the stairs. I nodded.

'Charles, you're such a ... ' he laughed, 'you're such a prude.'

I felt ashamed. All worked up and nowhere to go. I looked down at the telephone, breathing deeply.

'Come back upstairs.'

I went.

'Gordon,' said Vanessa, in an outraged voice, 'Rachel is Eliza Noyes's girl – Harry Seth-Smith's *step*-daughter.'

I followed my father into the room.

'Really,' he said, steering past Jenny's legs to the tea-tray where, with rock-like hands, he filled his cup. 'Well, in that case you must come this weekend also. Charles, why don't you bring Rachel? I'm sure there'll be plenty of room.'

Rachel looked at me blankly.

'I saw Harry only the other week. He does regular work for us, very old friend of mine. Do come.'

Rachel shrugged in my direction.

I had had no intention of going. 'Can you?' I asked.

'Well, Mummy might –'

'Nonsense,' said my father. 'I shall ring her myself this evening. Charles, have you started at the Tutors yet?'

'Yes. Beginning of last week.'

'Good man.'

I took Rachel to a French film, *La Rupture*, as an oblique way of indicating to her how good in bed I was going to turn out to be.

I realized that there were plenty of sound, indeed urgent, reasons for hating French films: the impression the directors gave that the shoddier and less co-ordinated their products were, the more like life, and therefore the better, they were; that habit of *lapsing* into statement whenever suggestion got too difficult or ambiguous. And my critical sense told me that the English–American tradition of exploratory narrative had obvious strengths. Yet I preferred the more rickety and personal conventions of French – and, occasionally, Eyetie – cinema: the more radical attitude to experience, the scrutiny of the small detail and the single moment.

I said as much to Rachel, I told Rachel so, as we walked up to Notting Hill Gate. She agreed.

At one point Rachel took my hand. (Relax, I told myself; you don't have to do all this. She just fancies you.) She said, 'What happened when you called your father out of the room?'

'Nothing much.'

'Do you get on with him? You seemed, I don't know, frightfully tense.'

Rather flattering. I said: 'It's funny. I hate him all right, but it doesn't feel like hatred. Even at home. If I was sitting in the kitchen reading, and he came through the room, I'd look up and think, Oh, there he goes, I hate *him*, and return quite happily to my book. I'm not sure what it is.'

Rachel said that – hold your hats – she had 'given up' hating *her* father long ago. I didn't explain.

Owing to the mendacity of the girl who answered the telephone there, we arrived at the cinema just in time to catch the last hour and a quarter of the B feature. The B feature was called *Nudist Eden*.

It was grisly. The film presented itself as a documentary, just taking a look round a real nudist camp. The narrator gave facts and figures, interviewed satisfied customers. The camera patrolled the grounds, examined the facilities. Grubby colour, low-budget incompetence; it had a nightmare quality: you can't tell whether you're going mad or whether everyone else is going mad; you stare round the cinema to check your bearings; you expect the audience to make some gesture of spontaneous protest. What was more, the producers could afford only middle-aged actors and actresses.

I shifted in my seat as the camera inexpertly focused on a parade of oldster genitals. The men had pricks like hand-rolled cigarettes, balls like prunes. The women did not differ significantly in this area, as far as I could see. Caved-in bums, deflated breasts – these were to be seen everywhere: by the pool, round the camp-fire (a scene scored by an ill-synchronized Deep River Boys number to which the nudists attempted helplessly to mime), in the chalets, at the canteen, and so on.

I began to feel distinct alarm, what with Rachel being so posh, when the camera lingered for a full half-minute on the naked body of a seven-year-old girl. High-spiritedly she was arching herself backwards, to reveal (i) that little girls in nudist camps are healthy and can do the crab, and (ii) her cunt, in order to sate the more recondite predilections of certain cineastes – one of whom, a mackintoshed compost-heap, was sitting immobile, like a toadstool, not even wanking, in a wide circle of unoccupied seats.

The time came to say something. After a most cunning scene, in which, for three minutes, a dangerously overweight couple were to be viewed jumping up and down on a trampoline, I turned to Rachel and said – unanxious, empirical, resigned – 'That's motion pictures.'

Rachel started laughing, quite loudly, shoulders hunched, right hand cupped over her nose. 'I love this sort of thing,' she whispered. 'How much of it will there be? Have we missed much?'

'Not much,' I said. I grabbed a kiss. 'There'll be plenty more.'

I gazed at Rachel's profile. Goodness me, I really did like her. A novel turn in our relationship. What had it been up until then? It didn't seem like affection, far less desire: rather a kind of gruelling, nine-to-five inevitability.

As it turned out, the nude film was a delight and *La Rupture* left us cold.

Later; at the bus-stop, I quizzed Rachel about the weekend. She was evasive, pointing out that even if my father did ring it might still be difficult.

'Mummy's really neurotic about things like this. Maybe because of Daddy. She was so young then, and I think she thinks the same will, you know, happen to me.'

I sighed.

Rachel's hand writhed in mine. 'But if you came up and met them to sort of reassure her ... ?' She pinched the loose skin on my knuckles.

'Okay,' I said. 'Yeah, I'll do that. Tomorrow? What, just come up for dinner, or a drink or something. Yes, I'll do that. I'm quite good at all that.'

' ... although Eden, then, is the "goal" of all human life, it remains strictly an imaginative goal, not a social construct, even as a possibility. The argument applies also to the literary utopias, which are not the dreary fascist states popularizers try to extrapolate from them, but, rather, analogies of the well-tempered mind: rigidly disciplined, highly selective as regards art, and so on. Thus, Blake, like Milton, [hesitate] saw the hidden world, the animal world in which we are condemned to live, as the inevitable complement to man's imagination. Man was never meant to escape death, jealousy, pain, libido – what Wordsworth calls 'the human heart by which we live'. [perplexed three-second silence] Perhaps this is why Blake paints the created Adam with a serpent already coiled round his thigh.'

So ended my short, derivative, *Roget*-roughaged essay, complete with stage-directions.

'Ye-es,' said Mr Bellamy. 'Which utopias did you have in mind?'

'Mm. Plato. More. Butler.'

He thought about this. 'And Bacon, of course. Sherry? ... or *gin*.'

'Gin, please.'

'Pink one?'

'Probably,' seemed a safe answer.

The church clock across the road struck six. Mr Bellamy chuckled as he made the drinks. 'Beng on time,' he said. 'Yes, "utopia" in fect means "nowhere", and *Erewhon* is an ene-grem of the same word. Yes, I liked thet. One of the more stylish essays I've heard for some time. Better, I should say, than most undergraduate essays.'

I found this unsurprising.

'You do seem to have read a great deal, I must say.'

'One of the advantages of being a delicate child.'

His brow puckered in genial inquiry.

'No.' I shrugged. 'I spent a lot of time in bed with illness. I read a lot then. Even dictionaries.'

Mr Bellamy rocked on his heels before the marble chimney-piece. He had so many hairs sticking out of his nose that I was unconvinced, after nearly an hour in his company, that they weren't a moustache. He sounded about fifty – he went on as if he were fifty – but he couldn't have been more than thirty-five. I assumed he had a private income. How else could he sit about drinking gin, girdled by bound books, in a Hamilton Terrace drawing-room, pretending to teach English and wish-ing he were an Oxford don with real live queer undergradu-ates to bore?

'Most imprissive. I think they'll snep you up. More gin.'

He was a short-arsed little bastard – about five-five. Hirsute brown jacket, knobbled face, rusty Brillo-pad hair. Being posh and rich and unhurried, he managed to get away with it, though what he did with it then was open to doubt. He had virtually no sexual presence, didn't look as if he could be bothered even to masturbate.

Bellamy returned with my glass. He reached out to his left and put a book in my hand.

'*Perry-dice Lost*, second edish'n. It's … virry lovely, isn't it,' he said tremulously. 'Yes, I believe a distant encestor of mine wrote a utopia novel. *Looking Beckwards*, it was called. I've never rid it.'

'Really. It's a lovely edition,' I said, handing back the Milton.

'No. I should like you to hev it.'

I began shaking my head and saying things.

'Uh-uh-uh.' He held up his hand. 'I insist.

'Read it,' he said, 'It's rather good.'

It was light enough to risk the walk to Kilburn. Thirty-ones were capricious buses; even so, I wasn't due at Rachel's until seven forty-five. There might be some time to kill. Underneath a still bright sky, Maida Vale was reassuringly well-lit against the incipient dusk.

I had been to Kilburn once before, when Geoffrey made me come with him to investigate a second-hand guitar shop. Again, it looked like a small town in wartime : beleaguered, shuttered-up, people on the streets, camaraderie after a blackout. I went into a ramshackle Victorian pub, and came out of it, very quickly. Chock-a-block with teds, micks, skinnies, and other violent minority groups. Any other day, to consolidate Bellamy's gins, I would have chanced it. But I was wearing a three-piece charcoal suit – from school, admittedly, yet quite flash all the same. A lemonade, instead, then, with the students and au pair girls in a shadowy coffee-bar next to the cinema. There, and on the bus twenty minutes later, I leafed through my present from Bellamy, and thought about the weekend.

What, for a start, was my father's game? When I got back from the cinema on Wednesday, Jenny and Norman were watching television in the breakfast-room. Simultaneously, Jenny asked me if I'd like some coffee and Norman asked me if I'd like some whisky, so I had had to say that I didn't want anything.

'Why', I wondered, 'did old shitface come round? What was he after?'

'Old shitface's tart', said Norman, 'has got a ten-year-old daughter with nowhere to go this weekend because her mother's going off with old shitface.'

'And he wants you to baby-sit?'

Norman nodded.

'Are you going to?'

'Of course,' said Jenny.

'What for?'

'The poor little thing's got nowhere else to stay.'

'So?'

The television crackled. Jenny let out a short, sharp scream.

'What's the matter with you?' asked Norman.

'Oh, nothing. I was just wondering what the dickens was going on.'

'Thass funny. I was wondering what the fuck was going on, myself.'

I sat at my desk for an hour, shaking my head, working on the Letter to My Father. At midnight I crossed out 'Letter' and put in, above, 'Speech'.

I alighted at Swiss Cottage and turned left up the hill into Arch Hampstead itself. In a nearby side-turning, two streets from Rachel's, I tried to lose in advance the evening's phlegm, expectorating two puddles of assorted greenery. I rested against a brick wall and watched a man clean his car.

Richardson Crescent – and the house Geoffrey and I had broken and entered eight weeks before. This time, I stalked up to the door and rapped, with an upper-crust rap, on the knocker.

A young princess disguised as a maid opens the door, stows my coat, leads me upstairs. I am shown, unannounced, into a room full of people. Rachel, in white, a monochrome blur, appears, takes my arm. I am urged to come and meet Mummy. Together we weave through elongated finery to reach hunched-up finery. Probably three women among all that jewellery and hair-do. Two dinner-jackets? A big silver lady receives my hand. 'Highway Mummy this.' Mummy, however, looks over my shoulder as I bow towards her. She replies: 'Minnie, you *came*. Whatever happened?' With a tomato-juice smile I relinquish her pud and back off to let Minnie close in. Make a run for it. Two minutes later, somehow alone in the middle of the room, hiding, there is a glass in my hand and a hand on my shoulder. 'Haaay there ... great to see you again, Charles,' said DeForest Hoeniger, through his nose.

Only at dinner did it first strike me that I might not be going to faint. By then I was drunk and very left-wing. DeForest couldn't have been nicer, or more welcome, in some ways. And since Americans can't help being good cinema, he wasn't even all that boring. Finally, every time I emptied my glass, he took it, put more whisky in it, and gave it back to me, saying 'No problem', again through his nose.

In the dining-room I was shown by another incognito princess to the 'dud-seat', or, alternatively, 'the inferior guest's seat'.

'Thank you, thank you,' I said, sitting down between Rachel's aunt and Rachel's step-brother, Archie. There were fourteen people at the table. I was at the quiet end, Harry's end. Rachel was up the noisy end with her mother, and DeForest.

Harry, I now saw, was a very tall, Anglo-Jewish-looking man, with a forehead the size of a buttock and fat, glistening lips. He wore a trendily cut grey suit, and matching shirt and tie. To look at him, you'd think he was posh and stupid. In actuality, he was common and stupid, having obviously trained his loud, pompous voice to affect an upper-class accent while in his twenties (a fixture probably contemporaneous with 'Seth – '). Thirty years on, he had just as obviously forgotten it. Luckily he was too smug to notice his twanging 'eows' and 'ois'. Old Harry had a strange figure, but quite symmetrical really. From ankle to knee he was thin. From knee to thigh he was fat. From thigh to waist he was very fat. From waist to ribs he was very very fat. From ribs to shoulder he was very fat. He had a fat neck. His face, apart from his water-melon lips, was thin.

Harry sat down and began to swap reactionary pedantries with the handsome undertaker on his right. Between them quailed an equine young woman. The aunt, Rachel's aunt rather than Archie's I later gathered, sat to my right, Harry's left. She fingered her napkin and listened to Harry. Harry peered at me from time to time. He seemed to think I was a friend of Archie's.

The room was dark – thatched walls and a low ceiling – lit only by a few intimate candles. I looked up the other end of the table. Rachel was next to DeForest. DeForest was next to Rachel's mother, whom he was arousing with freckled whispers. Why hadn't she told me he'd be here? He was looking very places-to-go, people-to-see. Perhaps he'd fuck off after dinner.

But it was high time someone asked me what *I* thought I was doing here, and 'Search *me*' was the only possible answer. It clearly wasn't enough to go on sitting here eating bread and seeming nice. Archie sipped wine, elbows on table. I studied him with distaste. Prosperous cowboy's fringed suede jacket, chocolate velvet trousers swaying as he tapped a snakeskin boot. Archie had a car, a Mini-Moke.

This won't be difficult.

'Hi,' I said, with a stoned, heavy-eyed smile and a noble-hippie accent. 'Jesus, do *you* know all these curious people? How long will it go on for, would you say?' I took an ironic slug of wine. 'At least there's plenty of lush.'

Archie regarded me with frank consternation, like an attentive but slow-minded schoolboy. He raised his eyebrows, then turned to speak to his other neighbour, who, I now saw, was a fabulously beautiful girl. Cooled. As I bowed my head to the floor, an elegant hand appeared high up on Archie's leg and trailed its fingertips between his thighs.

Arnold Seth-Smith was seventeen years of age.

Rachel's aunt, then, as the only comparably unattractive person in the room, became the object of my attentions. Once the food arrived Harry and his friend were too busy sweating and eating to talk much, so our conversation could be heard by anyone bored enough to listen. We covered a good range of topics, in this order: avocado pears, oil-tankers, Mauritius, tailoring terms, the size of the room, the price of London property, candles, tablecloths, forks, coffee-spoons. Surely we must have something in common. At one point I wanted to ask: 'How do you *spell* "homo sapiens"?'

'What about the weekend, then?' I asked my young hostess, downstairs in the kitchen, feet from the baby's-crap-coloured rubbish bin, where I had tried to kiss her the night we met. I was kissing her now. 'Did I do all right?'

This wasn't as preposterous a question as it might sound. Half the guests, including DeForest (after a minute of sweet-nuthins with Rachel), had wisely got the hell out as soon as dinner was over. I had then had a brief audience with Rachel's guardians. I merely sat there while they talked to each other about where they might or might not be going that winter. I didn't hawk or fart once.

'I think it'll be okay. Harry's worked for your father, and he thinks very highly of him.'

(Nothing would thrill me more, by the way, than to be able to say that my father was an ad-man or a PRO. But, among other things, he was the editor of a business-law fortnightly magazine. This sounds promising, I know, but the paper has an excellent arts section, with the best cinema critic, and the book page had recently won outspoken praise from a forum of distinguished academics.)

' ... so there's not much she can say.'

'Incredible. Does DeForest know yet?' Rachel shook her head. 'Hang on,' I said, before she could get rueful, 'I've got a present for you.'

I went out to the passage and back again. 'Here. I should like you to have it. No, I insist.'

'But it must of –'

'Read it,' I said. 'It's rather good.'

Outside, I looked up at the drawing-room windows. Harry,

drinking brandy from a glass like a coffee-percolator, was bearing down on the equine young woman. I felt I ought to shout out something defamatory, or lob a brick at them – make a gesture of conclusive disgust.

'Yes, you're left-wing, all right,' I said, hailing a taxi.

The next morning I ran down the square and gave twenty pence each to the legless buskers.

'Thank you, sir, thank you. Gob less.'

'I'll try,' I said.

I was keyed up all day. The feeling was so unfamiliar, and made me so light-headed, that I got my head whomped in (almost) by one of the boys at school.

My maths lesson with Dead Feet, or 'Mr Greenchurch' as some called him, had been postponed until the afternoon. (A major irritant because I had planned to get away straight after the morning session, to wash, perfume myself, etc.) What happened was this. The Feet, alighting from his Morris 1000 (what else?), flings his head against the top of the door-jamb. Happily, he is so old that he doesn't feel a thing, doesn't, in fact, *notice*. With blood trickling down the side of his face, forming a delta around his snaggled ear, and splattering his shirt and cardigan, he shuffles cheerfully into the school. Eventually alerted by the gasps of Mrs Tauber and the screams of the children, he puts a hand to his head, examines its contents, and keels over backwards on to a straight-backed chair, which keels over backwards under him. He is rushed to the casualty ward of the local hospital, there to receive three stitches on his lucent crown. I assumed that, if he didn't actually die, he'd at least be on his back for a few weeks. Not a bit of it. He made a greedy telephone call direct from the hospital, telling Mrs Tauber that he wasn't going to lose a day's tuition fees after all.

I waited for him in the (temporarily bratless) main hall, with the three others. There was Brenda, the uglier girl; Elvin, fat, cow-eyed, generally hopeless but affable enough; and Derek. Derek was true borstal-bait. At seventeen, he had already faced a variety of charges – including, it was said, GBH and petty larceny. The guile of expensive lawyers had secured his acquittal. As I sat at the table, brooding, trying not to think about the weekend, it occurred to me that there was something uniquely unpleasant about his face. Cherubic features moulded into a satanic complexion – a desert of flaked, crumbling skin relieved only by oases of dermatitic pimplery: like the scummy death-mask of Troy Donahue, Peter McEnery, or some other noted pretty-boy. Just the eyes, glinting perfect blue, emerged intact.

Anyway, there we were. It took place about two o'clock. I happened to be retching – fairly quietly, I thought – into a handkerchief. Derek looked up from an O-Level text.

'Someone shut him up, will you.' He made hawking noises. 'It's enough to make you sick. Go somewhere else, do.'

I blew my nose unhurriedly. 'What did you say?'

'U-word. You, fucking, heard. I said it's enough to make you puke.'

'Oh really?' I said. 'And what do you think people feel when they look at your face? What, would you say, was running through *their* minds?'

Brenda laughed, so I continued. 'Look at that huge … archipelago of blackheads on your conk. Christ, why don't you try washing every now and then?'

'Shut up,' said Derek, with a robotic smile.

I could tell this was excellent advice. But I looked at Elvin, who grinned, and, besides, it made me feel so young. 'Yes. Why don't you give washing a whirl one of these days? It can't be much fun walking around with all that crap, all that *greaze*, all over your face. But – got to keep the spots fed, I suppose. Tell me, Mr Sebum, tell me, Monsieur Têtes-noires, how does it go down with the girls? I bet they –'

I was wearing a double-breasted jacket with modishly wide lapels. Derek grabbed these, hoisted me to my feet, and drew his right fist back at shoulder height.

'No, *please*,' I shrieked, 'for Christ's sake!'

At that moment the double-doors at the end of the hall swung open and Mr Greenchurch strolled grandly in.

'Churls!'

He wasn't reproaching us, merely calling out my name in his senile yodel.

Derek instinctively relaxed his grip.

'Coming,' I said. I stood up, slapped Derek's hand away with my own, and followed the Feet to his pungent little room.

What extraordinary behaviour. Patently, I was in a state about something. Not so much about Rachel – for I was cock-free until the end of next week, so nothing dramatic could happen. Perhaps it was the idea of having some sort of show-down with my father. During the lesson, under the pretence of making notes, I planned the weekend – anecdotes about the village, nature speeches – and outlined a brief coda to the (by now) 2,000-word Speech to My Father.

Ten five: the spinney

Less than two hours to go and more than two months to come. But things get simpler as I get older.

Now I open the window that looks on to the woods. It's December, and very cold, so I close it again soon.

On the train to Oxford, Rachel took up the subject of her father – apparently, he had written her a 'stinking' letter that morning. She developed the real-bastard theme and filled in some early history. Her last brush with 'Jean-Paul d'Erlanger' (Rachel used her mother's maiden name; don't ask me why) had been earlier that summer, when DeForest himself had taken her to Paris for a couple of weeks. Apart from some unpleasant incidents, a 'marvellous time' was had by all. I bucked up slightly when Rachel made it clear that these unpleasant incidents had consisted of M. d'Erlanger hinting at and then articulating his immense hatred and contempt for DeForest, who had in fact got one of his ears further cauli-flowered by the passionate Frenchman. Rachel invited me to see this as a testament to her father's boorishness. DeForest, I learned, was most understanding about it all and had never mentioned the matter since.

When I asked what the letter had said Rachel stared out of the window at the Reading suburbs for a full half-minute before telling me that it was too awful to repeat. I decided to let it go at that, giving her the scene with good grace. To fill in time, and to offer her some indirect comfort, I told a few rather vague lies about parental atrocities I had suffered, featuring my father in the role of Bacchic hooligan, moody night-owl, au pair-buggerer, and so on.

We were the first to arrive.

Mother appeared to have contracted hydrophobia at some

point in the afternoon. She was in such a blind frenzy that, before hellos or introductions, Rachel and I asked immediately if there was anything we could possibly do – while there was still time, still hope. It seemed that what Rachel could do was help the (quite fetching) au pair peel potatoes. What I could do, indeed what I *simply had* to do, was drive into Oxford and fetch Valentine.

'But I can't drive,' I said.

'But you had lessons?'

'I know.' (Driving-lessons were the statutory seventeenth-birthday present in the mobile Highway family.)

'And you took the test?'

'I know. But I failed it.'

'But you took it again?'

'I know. And I failed it again.'

'Well, it's too late now. Where did I put the keys?'

I went in mother's Mini, and nearly got old woman all over the bonnet, too.

After going through an affected little toll-bridge – the toll was the twee sum of three and a half pence – I got up to forty miles per hour as the road straightened out. At this kind of speed it was advisable to place the stiletto-heeled shoe, kept in a side-pocket for this purpose, over the gear-stick to prevent it jiggering like a pump-drill. As I did so, I noticed a scrawny figure two hundred yards ahead, motionless in the right-hand half of the road. To break her reverie I parped the horn. Instantly, she flew into a spastic life-or-death dash across my path, abandoning her hat, her shopping and a single brown slipper in a galvanized frog-march to the opposite curb. I changed down, slowed, and drifted to a lazy halt beside her.

'It was all right,' I said, returning her accoutrements, 'you could have just stepped back on to the pavement. Are you okay?'

She stared unseeingly before her, thinking: I'm fucked if I'm going out again.

I parked the car in front of Valentine's school, one of the better Oxford primaries, which nevertheless resembled a cluster of Monopoly hotels greatly enlarged, dirtier red, and with windows. Valentine, or his silly name, had been 'put down' for a second-rate public school but my father had decided not to send him to a prep school also. I searched for damaging significance in this policy as I walked up the lane dividing the school from the playing-field in which Valentine was supposed to be having his game of football. I warmly looked forward to interrupting it. My pace slowed.

Had I got over my obsessions about Valentine? More or less. Those days were gone. Watching him marshal his hosts of friends, being asked to tick off the Harrods toy catalogue on December 1st, dressed up by his mother like a spruce three-foot adult (he and I had switched from short to long trousers the same year: I was thirteen, he was four); on that spring day, eighteen months before – I was there, when Val rode his drop-handle racing bike down a schoolgirl-packed street, no hands, singing 'Hey Jude'. And that mad, wonderful summer: I sabotaged his bicycle, spiked his Lucozade with steaming urine, spat in his stew – I went as far as contemplating one ruse involving, well, a portion of vanilla junket, actually, but felt that I had already made my point. (As a rule, I too would deplore such behaviour. But this was – how shall I put it? – this was family.)

In the right-hand corner of the playing-field, about twenty yards away, four boys, one of them my brother, stood in a semicircle round a fifth. The fifth was a Fatty. He cringed against a shed-like pavilion. I crept up behind the goal-posts, and watched.

The Fatty wore a crochet jersey, odd socks in Clark's sandals, and patched short trousers (everyone else, especially my brother, was in longs). Home-cut hair capped a face well used to – seemingly almost bored with – fear: non-existent bush burned off every day at school, head kneed in every night by his over-glanded father.

Having looked round for encouragement or approval, one of the boys leaned over and slapped the piggy in the middle quite hard on the face. The other three took a step forward and joined in. I watched a bit longer, on the off-chance that Valentine would do something exceptionally odious, then signalled my presence with a yell.

I walked towards them. 'Piss off,' I told the Fatty, hoping that my intervention would be taken as a breaking-up of unruly horse-play rather than a bulliable rescue. The Fatty collected satchel and cap, and wandered off, breaking into a run as he approached the gate.

'Piss off,' I said to the other three. They hesitated and backed away. As an afterthought, I shouted out: 'My brother's too posh to mix with the likes of you.' They might beat him up on Monday.

'Hello, Valentine,' I said, 'had a good day? Enjoy your game of football?' He stood his ground, chewing lemon chewing-gum, hand on tailored hip. 'Why'd you pick on him? What did he do?'

'I didn't hit him a lot,' said my brother. 'The others did, mostly.'

'Did he do anything? Why were they hitting him?' Hatred was dissipating me.

'Everyone does.'

I stared at him. I could think of nothing to say, so I caught hold of his shoulder and boxed him on the side of the head. But without much conviction.

Rachel and I lay still on my bed. It was nearly dinner-time. (The pre-twenties aren't required to socialize; apart from meals they can come and go as they please.) My room, one of the three long, low attic rooms, was okay, allowing for the fact that I hadn't had a chance to do anything to it. Faddy ephemera covered its walls: posters of Jimi Hendrix, Auden and Isherwood, Rasputin, reproductions of works by Lautrec and Cézanne. The bookcase retold my adolescence: *Carry On, Jeeves, Black Mischief, The Heart of the Matter, Afternoon Men, Women in Love, Gormenghast, Cat's Cradle, L'Étranger.* A chess set, a drawing by my little sister, postcards on the mantelpiece. It was straightforward enough – nothing much you *could* do to it. However, the one vital adjustment had been made before we arrived. That morning, before school, before I had run out to pay my graft to the legless buskers: a panicky telephone call. I got Sebastian, and bribed him with the promise of ten cigarettes to fucking go up and change the light. There had been a pink-tinted bulb in the bedside lamp, so that any village girls I lured up there would know at once how sexy I was. Seb, as instructed, had put in a normal one. A bit outré for an urbanite like Rachel.

Most of the guests were there by the time I got back with Valentine. I joined Rachel and the au pair in the kitchen, gave beefy assistance gathering chairs and shifting the dining-room table. I led Rachel to her room on the first floor, then to mine on the second. Some low-pressure necking took place, soon modulated by me to include drowsy conversation. We talked as it got dark. We talked about our fathers, pretty well agreeing that women had it harder than men:

'Women have to cope with babies and periods and things, they carry the real responsibility.' I sighed. 'If a girl sleeps around she's a slag, if a boy sleeps around he's quite a guy. Society *and* Nature seem to be loaded against –'

'Do you think so? I don't think I do,' mumbled Rachel to my armpit. 'You'll probably say this is rather ... pissy, but babies are the only things women can have that men can't. And they should be proud of that. It evens things out, too.'

I considered attacking this view as doctrinaire, brainwashed, sexist, etc., but I said, 'I don't think that's at all pissy. How do you mean, it evens things out?'

'Well, let's face it, women usually look pretty terrible by the time they're thirty-five. *Scaly* faces. Figures go, hair gets matty and dry. Men often get better. At least their faces don't get all ... ' she yawned and cuddled nearer, 'scaly, like wo-men's. So it's good that they can have families. Like your mother.'

Rachel was wearing a short red dress – no stockings. I placed the palm of my hand on the back of her thigh, where it became her bum, where the rim of her silky panties was.

131

'Maybe,' I said, moving my crotch back to make way for the erection. 'To give them something to do, you mean. But my mother's really in the shit. What'll she have when Valentine's grown up?'

'Mm. Suppose so.'

'Anyway, I'm glad you could come.'

She grunted. 'Mm,' she said.

I excused myself and slipped downstairs for a hawk and a pee. For some reason, I felt neurotically high-cheek-boned as I closed the door.

My father was in the passage to the bathroom. He was wearing a fashionable black polo-neck jersey (fashionable, that is, among the weasly middle-aged) whose sleeves he was rolling down. He not only looked quite good, he looked quite *nice*.

'Ah, Charles,' he said, in the voice he used for ballockings. 'Now I hear from your mother that you hit Valentine earlier on. On the head. Is that correct? Well you mustn't. It's extremely dangerous. Not on the head. Is that clear? All right, ticking-off over. See you at dinner.' He smiled and began to move past me.

'I wouldn't have hit him anywhere, but he and his friends were beating up another boy.'

He fiddled with his sleeves, in order not to meet my eye. 'I dare say they were, but your mother and myself –'

'Fine. Next time I catch him at it I'll just break his arm. And what do you *mean*, "your mother and myself"? When was the last –'

'Oh, for Christ's *sake*.' He allowed a few seconds to pass. He looked puzzled, amused, like the time at Norman's. 'Charles, are you seriously going to claim that you didn't behave badly when you were his age?' He took a chain-mail watch from his trouser pocket. 'Perhaps, when you're older, you'll see that the – that the wrong that's committed to make a right, the second wrong, is invariably shabbier than the first.' He finished putting on his watch. 'Perhaps when you're older you'll see that.'

'Great copy,' I said. 'And that's quite meaningless coming from you. You may be *old*, but my mother hasn't – '

'What do you care?'

My father paused, and continued in a softer voice. 'I can see there's little point in discussing this.' He put his hands in his pockets and waggled a bunch of keys. 'We only say things we regret. Charles … '

'*Nothing, sorry.*' I weaved past, erasing with my hand any further reply or question. 'Don't worry, won't say a thing. Mum's the word.'

In the bathroom I peed, hawked, steadied myself by chanting 'don't get full of yourself, don't get full of yourself,' and tried not to cry.

The room was dark when I returned; Rachel was asleep. I went over to the window and watched the woods. Gradually my chest stopped heaving. There was nothing to tell Rachel anyway. I lay down beside her, chest-first to dull my lungs, and waited until someone called upstairs for dinner, which wasn't long.

I kept an eye on the old goat all through the meal, but with little to show for it. He was too busy being worldly socialite Gordon, lavish house-party-thrower Gordon, to have much time for erring husband or wily philanderer Gordon. Nevertheless, he sat between his tart and her (twin) sister, while at the other end my mother coped with Sir Herbert and the journalist, who honestly was called Willie French. Rachel and I sat opposite each other half-way down the table. She was being self-possessed enough; all the same I found I had to intercept and remould pretty well everything she said.

However, a brilliant argument was taking place between Sir Herbert and Willie, all about youth. I couldn't for the life of me make up my mind which one I disliked more. Dismissive cameos. Sir Herbert resembled nothing so much as a pools-winning dustman. Snouty open-pored face (itself topped by a sprig of sinister golden hair) clashed with his Savile Row suit and stiff collar. Shaving-cream bubbled inside the nearer of his question-mark ears. In stockinged feet, Sir Herbert stood four foot eight inches tall. To look at Willie, on the other hand, you'd place money on the fact that he had just dismounted from a motorbike on which he had spent his entire life at high speed. His ginger hair was driven back to form a curving mane from brow to nape of neck; he had inside-out lips, as if most of them took place within his mouth; speckly red eyes. For all this, he appeared to be losing the exchange, which served him right for having – in order to show how *simpatico* he was – a machine-gun stutter. Sir Herbert only ever let him get as far as saying 'I' or 'Wha' a few times.

Herbie now propounded the toiling paradox that the ostentatious 'unconventionality' of youth was, in point of fact, nothing other than a different sort of *conventionality*. After all, was not the non-conformity of yesterday the conformity of today? Were not these young people as orthodox, in their very different way, as the orthodoxy they purported to be subverting?

How refreshingly different, how refreshingly different.

Sir Herbert's liquid eyes roamed the table with such twinkling conceit that even my father fell silent and frowned interestedly. Herb then consulted me, praising my eccentrically restrained dress, my weirdo good manners, my daring cleanliness. The reply I gave was far too nasty not to be quoted in full. (It reads well because I plagiarized a key paragraph from the Speech to My Father.) By way of apology I squeezed Rachel's ankle between mine, before saying:

'I couldn't agree more, Sir Herbert, though I confess I've never looked at it from quite that angle. It occurs to me that the analogy can be taken further – moral issues, for example. The so-called new philosophy, "permissiveness" if you like, seen from the right perspective, is only a new puritanism, whereby you're accused of being repressed or unenlightened if you happen to object to infidelity, promiscuity, and so on. You're not *allowed* to mind anything any more, and so you end up denying your instincts again – moderate possessiveness, say, or moral scrupulousness – just as the puritans would have

134

you deny the opposite instincts. Both codes are reductive, and therefore equally unrelated to how people feel: so fucking give me a scholarship,' or words to that effect.

Willie signalled his intention of taking issue with me here by saying 'Doe' a lot. After a couple of minutes, Herbert suggested, 'Don't?' Willie nodded.

'Don't you think that total puppappapermissiveness is preferable 2-2-2-2 total repressiveness, including cell-cell-self-repression?'

Sir Herbert, soon himself to be rendered unintelligible by food and drink, cruised back into the argument.

I gave my father a steely glance, and shrugged at Rachel. She was contemplating me with what seemed a mixture of emotions.

The next day, Saturday, was an epoch-maker, I now see.

Invoking the teenage prerogative, Rachel and I opted out after dinner, and went to bed, separately. I felt the hawks coming on, so I claimed tiredness.

It was one of those nights: my bed a roller-coaster, my brain a garbled switchboard of poems speeches essays plans, sheets of scrambled type the contact-lenses of my mind's eye, coughing a kaleidoscope of commas and dots.

'What's the matter with you?' someone asked.

'Christ. Sebastian? What's ... I'm falling apart here.'

'Eh?' Sebastian put the hall light on and leaned against the door. 'It's three o'clock,' he said. 'You were shouting.'

'Oh? Really? What?'

'Couldn't hear. Got my cigarettes?'

'On the table. Don't tell mother I got them.'

He disappeared again.

I read till seven, watched the dawn through the window as if it were television, bathed, shaved, and went downstairs. Cat's crap on the strip-lit kitchen floor, musty wine-shop smells from the dining-room, objects tingled to flayed senses.

Then, bath-robed, I took coffee and orange-juice into Rachel's room. She was sleeping in a foetal bundle: white cotton nightie, kneecaps for breasts, her little brown thumb planted tritely in her mouth. Quite sweet really. I parted the curtains and massaged her awake.

'What time is it?' she asked.

'Practically eight thirty.'

When she finished her coffee, Rachel stretched and smiled at me. I said something like 'Alive again,' and moved up the narrow bed towards her.

'Is that the birds singing?' she asked at one point.

'No, it's the radiator pipes. And while we're on the subject, have you slept with DeForest?'

'Mm?'

She had.

'Only him, or others too?'

'Only him.'

I said: 'Never mind.'

At mid-morning the adults tooled off in Sir Herbert's tank-like Daimler to have lunch with some small-shots on the other side of Oxford. They were to spend the afternoon admiring the colleges. When they left I asked Rachel if she'd like to take a bus in, go punting perhaps. Rachel said she was happy here.

The house had no real garden: fields began after a stretch of lawn at the back and on either side the grass drifted into shrubby wastelands. But there was a spinney only yards from the front door and we went for a walk in that. I'll never forget it. The wood was unspectacular; fat oaks every couple of hundred yards, a distant rank of chestnuts lining the road to the village. Otherwise it was mostly long whitened grass, frizzled bushes, and hundreds of ropey little trees, fifteen feet high. But at every turn in the path my childhood ganged up on me, and every twig and tuft seemed informative and familiar. Drugged and amazed by exhaustion, my mind fizzed with memories and anticipations (and Wordsworth) as we stumbled along in silence, like guests.

There was a place where a hazel had keeled over between two clapped-out rhododendrons, sheltered from the wind but not from the sun. We sat. I took Rachel's hand and lay back, thinking that there was a lot to be said for going without sleep, letting the rays boil up images on my closed eyelids, toying parenthetically with the idea of telling Rachel I loved her. The setting was good. Girls never minded so long as you pressed for no reply. Enjoy the moment a moment longer.

I opened my eyes and let them swim around, declining to focus them on the curled leaves and blades of grass.

'Come and look here. There's a sort of hollow in the bush where I used to come and smoke fags when I was young.'

I stood up, walked forward, and knelt to part the foliage and branches. Rachel looked over my shoulder. Inside the tent of leaves we saw : beer bottles, a tin can, trodden newspaper, grey tissues, shrivelled condoms like dead baby jellyfish.

Rachel groaned.

'Popular spot,' I said. I let go of her hand when I straightened up. She followed me as we started back to the house.

Early evening. On the sitting-room sofa, we lay snogging, as teenagers will. Very mild stuff, on the whole. Occasionally, of course, I would go all sinewy and urgent in her arms, or halt her in mid-sentence with a (probably absurd) demonic glare. I, for one, was beginning to find it a bit unreal – but what could a poor boy do?

So. Let me describe the way DeForest looked when he came in.

There was the noise of a car. The oldsters' return? We separated, not far. The front knocker sounded and we heard someone go to answer it. A tap on the sitting-room door preceded DeForest's entry. He gave a smile of furtive recognition and came over towards the sofa, all the time staring straight at the mantelpiece, as if tolerantly giving us time to get dressed. I remember I almost let out a shriek of terrified laughter when I noticed he was wearing plus-fours.

No one spoke.

Still staring at the mantelpiece, DeForest lowered himself on to the edge of an armchair, little feet together, hands on lap. I glanced at Rachel, as if to say, Is it all right if I hide under the sofa until he goes? Then, DeForest put his head in his hands for perhaps five seconds, took it out again, and looked up at Rachel: mischievous but ashamed, like a schoolboy caught stealing.

'What *is* it?' Rachel asked in a frightened voice.

'Are you okay?' I joined in. 'Can I get you anything?'

A brave child can bear anything but commiseration, and DeForest's tiny square head jerked backwards suddenly and his chest trembled, searching for air. He started to cry.

Rachel moved forwards and knelt in front of him, her breasts on his thighs, her arm round his knees, her free hand stroking his face and hair.

'DeForest, DeForest, shsh, shshsh, DeForest, shshsh,' she whispered.

Incredulously I suggested out loud to myself: 'I'll go into the kitchen.'

Ten minutes later Rachel followed me. I asked how DeForest was and Rachel said he was all right now. She said she thought she had better go back to London with him. I said I wished she wouldn't do that. She said she had to.

As a juke-box turntable moves along the row of upright records before picking one out, so I prowled my mind's filing cabinets. But all I said in the end was, staring into space:

'Oh no. I know what's going to happen. You're going to walk out of here in a minute and I'll never see you again.'

Who can say how I got through the weekend? My heart really goes out to me there.

Charles listened to the car drive away and walked up the stairs like a senile heavyweight. 'Seven o'clock,' his watch told him. In the master bedroom he rifled through drawers, examining bottles of pills. Back in the sitting-room, he washed down a fistful of hypnotics with a quarter of lukewarm vodka. He complained to the mirror that this only made him feel worse.

Charles went upstairs to Rachel's room. It looked exactly as it had when he showed her into it twenty-five hours before. He searched methodically but without success for the note that would read: 'How I love you – R'. Next, he kicked one of the bed's iron legs, not quite as hard as he could, but hard enough to make him squawk with pain and surprise.

In his own room he took off the shoe. The big toenail of his right foot came away cleanly in his hand. Charles thought about this for a few seconds before resourcefully sticking it back on again with a piece of festive Sellotape.

He found his Rachel note-pad (not to be confused with the Rachel folder) and wrote some things in it. He sank down on the bed, but a minute later his head reappeared; on it was a vertiginous scowl. Now sitting, now lying, he got rid of most of his clothes. He swore every few moments, or gasped in breathless grief.

Let us leave him, then, as the scene fades: upright in the armchair, comatose; naked except for watchstrap, a single sock, and a scarlet cushion nestling on his thighs.

First thing the next morning I ran round the house telling lies about Rachel. Domestic tragedy, financial ruin, multiple bereavement, jumbo blaze horror, and so on, were responsible for her disappearance. I didn't worry about the lies being exposed. I needed self-respect only for the weekend, and after that no one would be insensitive enough (or concerned enough) to raise the subject again.

My chief preoccupation was how to get sufficiently drunk to ring Rachel. Due to a whim of my father's, the Sunday papers weren't allowed in the kitchen until the afternoon – probably he thought it more amusing and civilized to loll around the sitting-room with them. But the sitting-room was where all the drink was kept, and Willie French, because of professional interest, and Sir Herbert, because of his great age, would assuredly be in there till two.

In fact, there wasn't much problem. After a heist on the pantry, I spent the later part of the morning with half a bottle of (exquisite, it seemed to me) South African sherry. I made diagrammatic plans of the Telephone Conversation. They were fairly cocky diagrammatic plans. My behaviour of the night before now struck me as overdone. Even Rachel could not have been genuinely affected by DeForest's grotesque theatrics. She had acted out of fatigued loyalty.

Sure, kid, I wrote, *it must have been tough for you too.*

But you never knew. And I had been sure last night that I would never see her again.

I went down to the sitting-room, slunk unnoticed past the dyspeptic Sir Herbert (who was grappling with the *Sunday Telegraph* as if it were a giant sting-ray), and scooped a bottle of port off the drinks shelf. There was an old television set in the attic 'nursery', where Sebastian had been billeted, and I thought it might steady me if I watched some. Sebastian had gone into Oxford to see an X film ('any X film', he said) and to moon round looking for girls with his spotty mates. Valentine was playing football in the garden – refereeing, and captaining both sides if his querulous whines were anything to go by. I locked myself in all the same, forced down the alcoholic syrup, and worked desultorily on the Reunion Speech.

Sunday television is a mixed bag in the provinces. University Challenge: the contestants seemed to be alarmingly well-informed but, on the other hand, reassuringly hideous. A panel-game in which a cross-section of dotards and queer celebrities tasted wines and, with diminishing coherence, talked about them. A comedy show that recounted the attempts of three beautiful girls and one ugly one to pay the electricity bill and not sleep with their boyfriends.

A sports programme followed – not the Saturday afternoon kind, where alert-looking old men lean on desks keeping you up to date, but a canned, filmic report on a tennis championship currently being disputed somewhere in the southern hemisphere. I was about to turn over when a pea-headed American gravely announced that what we were about to see was the women's semi-finals.

Now I greatly revered women tennis players. When they came on to the court, smiling in trim uniforms, they seemed plain, remote persons: yet, after an hour of sweat and malice

... A couple of years back, there had been a particularly simian little number: squat torso, arms like legs, and a face as contorted and spiteful as you could possibly wish. She had obsessed me all through the Wimbledon fortnight. Not an afternoon passed without me thinking how much I'd like to corner her after an eighty-game, four-hour final (which she had lost), wrench off – or aside – her porky shorts, bear down on her in the steamed-up dressing-room or, better, much better, in some nicotine-mantled puddle, and grind myself empty to her screams.

Neither of the present sportswomen was up to that standard. In my excitement I missed the initial roll-call, and had to sit through twenty minutes of elegant variation – 'the 28-year-old Australian', 'the young Wiltshire housewife' – before I caught the ladies' names, so intent were the unctuous commentators on concealing the fact that they had bugger-all to say. However, of the two I vastly preferred the enormous Aussie. The British Wightman Cup player made the mistake of trying to appear recognizably feminine, doubtless in order to show the older woman that you don't necessarily have to look like an orang-utan to play a damn good game of tennis. The wife of the Great Bedwin dentist skipped up to the net to volley and pirouetted when she served. The Darwin-born PT instructress, on the other hand, her glossy shoulder-muscles rippling in the ninety-degree heat, threw her bulk round the court in frank virility – as she bulleted passing-shots, as she leapt four feet to punch the shit out of last year's quarter-finalist's weedy lobs. That mother of two wailed like a tragic heroine whenever she lost a point; the ex-junior champene showed emotion only when she double-faulted (with strident bellows that brought the commentary to nervous ten-second silences) before pounding back into the match. – At last I got their names: Mrs Joyce Parky and Miss Lurleen Bone. Miss Bone took Joyce apart in the second set. Joyce, quaking at the net on match-point, love–six, got a mouthful of tennis ball from Miss Bone's top-spin drive. She limped off the court in tears, without shaking hands.

'Here's to you, Lurl,' I said, glass raised.

There followed twenty minutes of one-day cricket, a make-shift eleven of boozy has-beens versus some itinerant Negroes. It left me wondering why, according to the commentators, Malcolm Sprockington, or whoever, always managed to 'turn' or 'steer' the ball *between* the slips, when it was all Cyprian Uwanki, or whoever, could do to 'snick' or 'chip' it *through* them. But it was sorry stuff after that gladiatorial combat between innocence and experience.

I collected my notes, had a drop more port, and fell down the stairs to my parents' bedroom.

Rachel's mother answered. She wanted to know who it was but didn't reply when, with drunken mellifluousness, I gave my name. Now, in the fifteen seconds silence, the fear I had been hiding from all day came to find me. I saw the gormless face in the mirror. Through the window I heard the children cry. I stared down at the folder open on my lap, at my tiny, immaculate handwriting.

Rachel said hello and started telling me about the crash she and DeForest had nearly been in on the way back. I wondered what was going on, tried to interrupt, no voice. Stop all this. She stopped. But she couldn't hear me. Could I speak up? I inhaled and exhaled. Rachel wanted to know whether I was still there.

'Stop all this. What are you talking about? Tell me – '

'I can't *hear*.'

'Wait.'

I put the telephone on the bed and unthinkingly took a piece of paper from my breast-pocket. It said: 'Of course you had to leave, don't worry about me. I just feel sorry for De-Forest. How is he?' I accumulated twenty words' worth of breath and picked up the receiver.

'Listen. Please tell me what you're going to do. Don't tell me about ... fucking car accidents, tell me – '

I had time to slap my hand over the telephone, so she didn't hear me cry. When I listened again Rachel was saying,

'Charles, I'm sorry. I'm sorry, I'm sorry.'

Twenty-five of eleven: the Low

Now I weigh the Longman's Blake in my hand. On the inside cover, I notice, Rachel has written, in pencil: 'To Charles, with love from Rachel'. Between my finger and thumb I take a rubber and bounce it up and down on the desk.

Elaine, my elder brother's girlfriend, sat on the sofa with a glass of iced whisky in her hand. She really did say to me:

'Gerry, the cat I was balling before Mark, yeah?, sort of poet, free-lance lecturer, ICA, that scene, was way into this Selby–Miller–Purdy trip, like we're all children, tender sometimes and beautiful maybe, but like we kill each other and fuck each other up all the time. So Gerry gets into these doomy oppositions, God and Satan, creativity and napalm, love and thalidomide, fucking and cruelty, birth and death, youth and shit.'

'I dig,' I bluffed.

'And his pomes get doomier and doomier, and his acid experiences get more and more negative, he won't lecture any more, can't make the night-time, won't go to the bathroom alone, gets freakier and less organic, won't eat. I mean, I can dig where his head's at but ... '

'Yeah, that's nowhere. You get all upti–'

'*Right*. And it was like kind of a drag too.' She laughed. 'Sometimes he'd be really into me, digging me, telling me I was beautiful' (which she was), 'and other times I could tell I was turning him right right off. He'd get the shudders in the sack.' She laughed again. 'We'd make it maybe once a week, yeah? He could like get it *together* ... but he couldn't get it *on*.'

'I know *exactly* what you mean.'

Half an hour earlier, out of the bathroom window, I watched

my father seeing off Sir Herbert, Willie French and the ladies (to whom he gave identical kisses). As they drove away, mother, in cerise trouser-suit with green fringe and gold buttons, joined him. My father put his arm round mother, and she responded hurriedly, putting her arm round him. They said things I couldn't hear. But I could tell from the angle of my father's head that he was being nice.

They were still outside the porch when two cars appeared at the turn in the lane. Out of the first, Mark's MG, came Mark, all arse and smiles, plus the Elaine. Out of the second, a DeForest Jaguar, surfaced three handsome gangsters and a second, taller girl; up her legs, encircled by a belt-sized skirt, I caught a gout of scarlet panties. On the strength of this I had a heartless and pleasureless wank before joining them downstairs, my face still flushed, but more ambiguously so. I hawked a lot, too, because you hawk more when you cry.

My father and my brother and the rest came into the sitting-room through the frog-windows. They talked about improvements to be made to the house. Mark outlined plans for landscaping the rear plot. Then he led his friends over to the drinks shelf and gave them more gin. They laughed and bantered and seemed really to like each other, as tall, healthy people will when things are going right for them. Elaine emphasized her detachment by continuing her experiments in stream-of-consciousness narration.

'Hello, people,' said my brother, sitting creakily on the coffee-table before us. 'What's the matter with you, Charlie? You look like shit. I mean it.'

'I feel like shit, too,' I said.

Elaine sucked on an ice-cube, so Mark took her glass and refilled it.

'Elaine. I have to talk big-business with Dad. So Tracy and everyone's staying for dinner, okay? We'll drive back –'

'Look, I *told* you, I've gotta be –'

'Yeah. You told me.' He dropped a bunch of keys in her lap. As he withdrew his hand he playfully tousled my hair. 'Keep at it, little-britches.' He coasted off to join the others by the window.

'Why do you go out with that fat shit?' I wondered out loud.

'You got me,' said Elaine.

I asked if she could give me a lift back to London and she said she could.

Elaine kept her eyes on Mark, who, one leg wiggling in his trousers, exchanged tall stories with his Dad about how quickly they had been known to get from London to the house, and back again.

'That motherfucking ... ' She hesitated. 'Christ. *Sorry.*'

'Oh. Oh, that's okay.'

So begins a stage in my descent to manhood which retrospectively seems avoidable, without significance, second rate, not worth it. The following three weeks form what might be called my Low, or the conventional *nadir* period. The only claim I have to originality here is that I didn't fall behind with my work. Of course, I stopped going to school, but, without fail, I did some Maths in the morning and always an hour of Virgil in the afternoon. On top of this I conscientiously read the literature of nausea, melancholy and absurdity – Sartre, Camus, Joyce. I strolled the frosted symmetries of Graeco-Roman tragedy in Penguin translation. I unfurled myself once more to *Lear* and, not *Hamlet*, but *Timon*. I clocked up the jejune libidos of Shelley and Keats, and took Hardy's Befuddled Will into account. I did my research.

Otherwise, I was careful not to wash, encouraged insomnia, failed to clean my teeth, smoked twenty Capstan Full Strength a day. I fidgeted with matchsticks to grime up my fingernails; I consigned my feet to cheesy death; I nourished ray-gun halitosis. I went for walks, wearing too little, sat in tube stations for hours lapping the soot, went to films in the sullen afternoons, coughed into dimly lit shop windows. I sipped whisky and played three-card brag with Norman most nights. I rang no one and no one rang me. I went to bed drunk, slept in my clothes and woke up every morning, terrified; I grew old pain-fully.

To pay back Norman (prick-fees and gambling debts), I even got a job, not on the railroad, but licking plates in a Shepherd's Bush restaurant, just for a week, in the evenings, quid a night. The restaurant was such an immobile concern that all I really did was sit smoking fags in the well-equipped kitchen and listen to the grumbles of Joe, the cook. Joe, a young and ambitious cook, was fed up to the teeth with cooking steak and chips for the odd Pakki, would far rather have been cooking exotic dishes in a flash restaurant. Accordingly, when people ordered steak and chips, and *soup*, Joe tended to hawk in it, to show his contempt for such an unimaginative choice, and also because he had heard that flash cooks always hawked in the soup if given the chance. I washed up after him.

On my last night, we had only one order : steak and chips, and soup. After mature consideration, Joe offered to let me hawk in it, as a treat. I did so, with enthusiasm.

Joe looked at it and looked at me. 'We can't give them that,' he said.

The turning-point, the *cognito* or *anagnorisis*, was hardly less corny than the Low itself.

I was joy-riding on the Circle Line one Monday afternoon. At High Street Kensington a youthful but hunchbacked tramp I knew got on. (I had seen him in the Gate – so often that we were virtually on nodding terms.) Because his legs were all gone to hell he disported himself about town by means of two second-hand crutches. These exertions caused him to sweat and smell a fair amount, enough, at any rate, to earn him the nickname of Mobile Armpit.

Mobile levered his way into the carriage and nose-dived on a greasy sweet-wrapper. I helped him to the seat opposite. He seemed to be in difficulty – sniffing, snorting, rifling through his damp pockets. Then he took a newspaper from the floor and was evidently about to offer its entertainments page up to his nose. Always well stocked with handkerchiefs, it appeared the least I could do to give him one, and I did.

The everyday response to this incident would be shame-faced reappraisal; comparatively, it was all right for me, etc. But what I found disturbing about my trite and rather appalled gesture of charity was an even triter and more appalled one of kinship. We'll be underneath the Arches together, you and me, I felt I could have said, as Mobile yelped into bunched fists.

I got off at the next stop, Notting Hill, went home, had a bath, gargled with after-shave, changed my clothes, spring-cleaned my room, and rang my doctor and dentist making appointments for the next day but one. That night, Norman sat alone at the breakfast-table, shuffling the cards and glancing uncertainly at me. However, I plucked up the courage to say I was too tired, and so he went to his room and had a row with Jenny instead.

On the Tuesday I put in an appearance at school. Everyone behaved either as if I had never been away or as if I had never enrolled there in the first place. Dead Feet tied himself up in knots trying to explain why x to the power of zero always equals one. The clay-thighed Mrs Tregear told me why she thought it was Dido's own fault that Aeneas cooled her. Derek forgot to beat me up. I signed forms enabling me to take Oxford Entrance on November 21st and 22nd. This was some four weeks away now.

Later, I sat at my desk with a cup of tea. The sun found its way into the room about this time, and, drugged by its warmth on my shirt, I used often to stare at the coalshed wall and railings. Occasionally my mind would go quite blank for as long as ninety seconds or two minutes and I would close my eyes and almost sigh with gratitude.

I wondered why I felt saddest about Rachel at early evening. I couldn't muster much jealousy for DeForest and I was unconvinced that Rachel had behaved cruelly. If she had, and if DeForest were some snarling fat-cock, then I would have known what to do: there'd be some well-charted escape-route. Impartially, shrewdly, I considered suicide, though not in my worst moments. The bottle of pills. The note: 'No hard feelings, everyone, but I've thought about it and it's just not on, is it? It's *nearly* on, but not quite. No? Anyway, all the best, C.' Only it might be a bore for Jenny and Norm. And where would I find a responsible literary executor for the Notebooks?

I tried writing letters to Rachel but although elegant and conscientious they made no sense to me and I merely filed them away. I seemed incapable of using words without stylizing myself. And the telephone was out. I wanted to send her vials of my tears at dusk, Tchaikovsky's *Romeo and Juliet*, Keats's 'Bright Star', a videotape of me getting into bed and coughing and going on being here alone.

Kensington Town Hall seemed a reasonable enough place. I didn't dare go in, but when a stray Nigerian staggered out of it at five fifteen or so, having no doubt fucked up some O Level, I assumed an American accent and questioned him about supervision, seating arrangements, and so on.

I drank an orangeade, rather solemnly, in the High Street Bar-B-Q Lounge, and thought about ringing Gloria. During the first week of the Low I had gone to see the queer doctor and he had let it slip out that I was all clean and needn't come and get touched up by him again. (I probably flatter myself; my rig was too shrunken with fright to arouse much more than laughter.) Yes, Gloria. For old times' sake.

I *did* ring her, too, as soon as I got back. I had to keep it down to a sexy whisper because there were voices coming from the breakfast-room – principally Norman's. First, I waited while the urchin who usually answered Gloria's (neighbour's) telephone ran down the street to get her. Then, when she came on, I wisecracked for a bit, got her laughing, and wondered what she was doing later. Gloria switched from breathlessness to gravity. She told the foul-mouthed little oik to stop pinching her arse and bugger off. 'How about it,' I said. In a lowered voice Gloria informed me that she was sorry but

she just so happened to be 'courting' (really) – Terry Trichomonas, what's more – and therefore had no wish to endanger
her happiness at this moment in time. She was convinced I'd
understand.

Sweating with shame I crept into the kitchen and steadied
myself against the table.

'Do please come in and meet someone,' called Norman.

Blotchy head between the half-closed sliding doors: Norman was on the sofa with two girls, an arm around each of
them. The girls were Jenny and Rachel.

'Christ.'

'*Come* on, wanker, get a cup.'

'There's one here,' said Jenny.

'So there is.' Norman went on: 'Met her down the road.
Went out for a *News* – there she was. *She* told me she had to
get home' – he squeezed Rachel's shoulders – 'but *I* told her she
had to come and have some tea.'

Rachel looked at me in helpless apology, as she had when
my father asked her up for the weekend.

'Why were you coming back so late? You finish at four,
don't you?'

'I had to stay and finish an essay.'

Hence no DeForest. I found I was staring at her with goofy
delight. 'Really? What on?'

'*Daniel Deronda*. Have you read it?'

'Certainly not,' I said, untruthfully.

Norman frowned. 'I've seen that. BBC 2. It's not bad, is it?'
He glanced at his watch. 'Hey, look. Bugger all this tea. I'll get
the drink.'

'Can't we go up?' asked Jenny in a plaintive voice.

Norman dismissed the suggestion with a wave of his hand.
'Be a sec.'

Jenny picked up the tea-tray. Rachel helped. I looked out of
the window. Shortly Norman returned, rattling like a milk
float: a crowded tray that resembled a miniature Manhattan,
bottles of wine in either hip-pocket, and a further one of
Dubonnet down the front of his trousers.

Then I had time to risk taking in the chestnut orbs, the sandy complexion, the hair you could see your face in, and even the nose, quite shiny also, and the smudged brown lips. The white smock made short work of her breasts, but on the other hand it twirled airily high up her thin Bambi thighs.

Eleven ten: The Rachel Papers,
volume two

Here come the sexy bits. I'm having a hell of a job, all the time whipping from *Conquests and Techniques: A Synthesis* to the Rachel Papers and back again. My files really are in need of thorough reorganization. A good way to spend my twentieth birthday?

I'm sure Norman planned the whole thing. Firstly, he got us all drunk. He poured Rachel out a gin and tonic, insisting that girls never drank anything else, as she well knew, and kept topping it up. Next, he ordered her to ring home and say she was staying to supper. Rachel demurred, until Norman said: 'What's the number? I'll do it.'

Rachel did it.

Then, five minutes later, he said he was taking Jenny *out* to dinner and that there were some sausages in the fridge if we wanted them. He winked at me and Jenny shrugged. As she and Rachel discussed modes of preparing and serving sausages, Norman pointed his great Watney's thumb at a bottle of wine and looked at Rachel with a molten leer.

But I was beginning to feel ridiculous. She didn't want to be here. When we were alone I would apologize, offer to ring her a taxi, make excuses for Norman's intimidating high spirits. As that entrepreneur now took his leave, I winced at his smutty gnomes. 'Be good,' he said, 'and if you can't be good be careful.' Jenny followed him as if bribed to do so.

'Bye,' said Rachel.

It was about seven thirty and the room was darkening. To suspend the moment, underline our aloneness, the street-lights played on the smoke from Rachel's cigarette.

'Can you really stay?'

She nodded.

I poured out more drinks, dutched myself up on neat gin. What's it going to be? I appraised certain gambits – a waste of time; not because of any swinging intensity, but because I felt tired.

'How's DeForest?'

She didn't reply.

I gathered from the female novelists I had been reading (there was a page or two on it downstairs) that the malleable, soft-centre syndrome was no longer considered attractive and that the confident autonomy syndrome was steadily gaining ground.

'Tell me how DeForest is,' I said.

Still no reply. What did she want? Some kind of purer response? It was back to tried and trusted methods.

'There's a stanza in Blake,' I droned, '*Songs of Experience:*

> Love seeketh only self to please,
> To bind another to its delight,
> Joys in another's loss of ease,
> And builds a Hell in Heaven's despite.'

By rights, Rachel should have quoted the complementary stanza, but she probably didn't know it. 'I'm glad you're here,' I said, 'because I've missed you so much. But I still want to get at you although I know how unsatisfying it would be.' I sipped my gin. 'Here's the other stanza:

> Love seeketh *not* itself to please,
> Nor for itself hath any care,
> But for another gives its ease,
> And builds a heaven in Hell's despair.'

Rachel received this idiot outpouring with a pathic nod. (I don't care what anyone says: poetry, if you can bring yourself to recite some, never fails. Like flowers. Give them a posy, speak a verse – and there's nothing they won't do.) Thus:

'I was going to ring you.'

'Were you? But when I rang that Sunday you started going on about cars and roads and things.'

'No, I was going to ring you *yesterday*.'

There was an appreciative hoarseness in my voice when I asked: 'What for?'

She couldn't or wouldn't answer. I knew anyway. I thought of saying, 'Forgive me, I should like to be alone for a few moments,' but what I in fact said was: 'Hang on – just going to have a pee.'

Within two minutes I had sprayed my armpits, talc-ed my groin, hawked rigorously into the basin, straightened my bed-cover, put the fire on, scattered LP covers and left-wing week-lies over the floor, thrown some chalky underpants and a cache of fetid socks actually out of the window, drawn the curtains, removed The Rachel Papers from my desk, and run upstairs again, not panting much.

'Let's ... let's go downstairs for a bit.'

She stood up and looked at me demandingly. I had nothing appropriate to say, so I went over and kissed her.

'Didn't it work with DeForest, or what?'

'No good.'

My left hand slid off her right buttock and twirled round the neck of the wine bottle.

'Let's go downstairs. Chat about it there.'

But we were diverted by another kiss and soon folded on to the sofa. We talked in one another's arms.

DeForest had more or less fallen apart during the weeks roughly corresponding to the Low. Of course the scatty bitch hadn't *told* him she was coming to stay with me, and he minded her not having told him. Also, though DeForest didn't mention it, Rachel had a hunch that he thought I had banged her on the Friday night. I was flattered to learn that Rachel eventually told him she hadn't banged me – out of the blue. He appeared to believe her, but, five minutes later, burst into tears. Cracked. That was ten days ago. Since then? Smashed up his car twice; crying all the time; stopped working; once came into Rachel's classroom and dragged her out of it; the headmaster had taken Rachel aside for a talk: the lot. Rachel closed with the not unaffecting low-mimetic remark that she didn't want to make two people miserable so she'd make one person happy, if she could.

'Me?' I asked blankly.

'If you still want me.'

Right then.

As regards structure, comedy has come a long way since Shakespeare, who in his festive conclusions could pair off any old shit and any old fudge-brained slag (see Claudio and Hero in *Much Ado*) and get away with it. But the final kiss no longer symbolizes anything and well-oiled nuptials have ceased to be a plausible image of desire. That kiss is now the beginning of the comic action, not the end that promises another beginning from which the audience is prepared to exclude itself. All right? We have got into the habit of going further and further beyond the happy-ever-more promise: relationships in decay, aftermaths, but with everyone being told a thing or two about themselves, busy learning from their mistakes.

So, in the following phase, with the obstructive elements out of the way (DeForest, Gloria) and the consummation in sight, the comic action would have been due to end, happily. But who is going to believe that any more?

Ready?

Now, as an opener, I decided to try something *rather* ambitious. I rose, poured out drinks, held her eye as we sipped, took her glass away. You really need to be six foot for this, but I gave it a go anyway: knelt on the floor in front of her, reached out and cupped her cheeks, urged her face towards mine ... No good, not tall enough, she has to buckle inelegantly, breasts on thighs. Rise to a crouch, start work on ears, neck, only occasionally skimming lips across hers. Then, when leg begins to give way, I do not churlishly flatten her on to the sofa nor shoo her downstairs: I pressure her to the floor, half beside half on top of me. (It was bare boards so it must have seemed pretty spontaneous.) Reaching to steady her my hand has grasped her hip; not sober enough to be over-tactical, I let it stay there.

Hardly seemed worth bothering with her breasts. In one movement, her skirt is above her waist, my right leg is between her legs, and my hand floats on her downy stomach. 'Doing' one of her ears I bulged my eyes at the floor. Phase two.

Move my hand over her bronze tights, tracing her hip-bone, circling beneath the overhang of her buttock, shimmer flat-palmed down the back of her legs, U-turning over the knee, meander up her thighs, now dipping between them for a breathless moment, now skirting cheekily round the side. It hovers for a full quarter of a minute, then lands, soft but firm, on her cunt.

Rachel gasped accordingly – but the master's hand was gone, without waiting for a decisive response, to scout the periphery of her tights. And her stomach was so flat and her hip-bones so prominent that I had no problem working my hand down the slack. By way of a diversionary measure (as if she wouldn't notice) I stepped up the tempo of my kisses, harrying the corners of her mouth with reptile tongue. It must be so sexy. How can she bear it?

Meanwhile the hand is creeping on all fours. At the edge of her panties it has a rest, thinks about it, then takes the low road. The whole of me is along with those fingers, spread wide to salute each pore and to absorb the full sweep of her stomach. Mouth toils away absently, on automatic. I nudge her with my right knee and give a startled wheeze as she parts her legs wide. Still, the hand moves down, a hair's breadth, a hair's breadth.

On arrival, it paused to make an interim policy decision. Was now the time for the menace? Had the time to come to orchestrate the Lawrentiana? What I really wanted more than anything – yes, what I really wanted more than anything else in the world was a cup of tea and a think. Covertly I looked at

Rachel's face: it included clenched eyelids, parted lips, smallish forehead wistfully contoured; but there was no abandonment to be read there.

Nor to be read here. I begin to find all this rather alarming. It makes me feel confused, frightened, sad. Because we have come to the heart of the matter, haven't we? This is the outside looking in, the mind moving away from the body, the fear of madness, the squirrel cage. How nice to be able to say: 'We made love, and slept.' Only it wasn't like that; it didn't happen that way. The evidence is before me. (If any respectable doctor got hold of these papers he would have no choice but to cut my head off and send it to a forensic laboratory – and I wouldn't blame him.) I know what it's supposed to be like, I've read my Lawrence. I know also what I felt and thought; I know what that evening was: an aggregate of pleasureless detail, nothing more; an insane, gruelling, blow-by-blow obstacle course. And yet that's what I'm here for tonight. I must be true to myself. Oh God, I thought this was going to be fun. It isn't. I'm sweating here. I'm afraid.

Back on the breakfast-room floor, my fingertips awaited instructions. They had me know that I was dealing with mons hair of the equilateral-triangle variety, the pubic G-string variety, the best, not that of the grizzled scalplock, the tapered sideburn, the balding fist of stubble, fuzz and curls. So, impelled – who knows – by a twinge of genuine curiosity, a mere presence now, the hand went *over* the mound, straining against the pull of her tights and pants, and, once in position, began its slow descent.

This is what I thought. Since Henry Miller's *Tropic* books, of course, it has become difficult to talk sensibly on the question of girls' cunts. (An analogy: young poets like myself are forever taunted by subjects which it is no longer possible to write about in this ironic age: evening skies, good looks, dew, anything at all to do with love, the difference between cosmic reality and how you sometimes feel when you wake up.) I remember I overheard in an Oxford pub one undergraduate – a German, I believe – telling another undergraduate that Swedish girls were okay, he supposed, but 'their conts are too big.' In the same place on a different occasion I talked sex with a pin-cocked Geordie who dedicated himself to the proposition that Oxford girls weren't nearly as good as Geordie girls, the reason being that their cunts were too small. Narcissistic rubbish. Size doesn't matter – unless, that is, you have troubles unknown to the present reviewer.

Which isn't to say that cunts are homogeneous. Now Rachel's was the most pleasing I had ever come across. Not, for her, the wet Brillo-pad, nor the paper-bagful of kedgeree, nor the greasy waistcoat pocket, the gashed vole's stomach, the clump of veins, glands, tubes. No. It was infinitely moist but not wet, exquisitely shaped and yet quite amorphous, all black ink and velvet recessed into pubic hair that resembled my own as a Persian carpet resembles a mat rug. And it was warmer than me; it was, actually, *hot*.

Meanwhile my fingers paddled there, enclosing it with the flat of my hand, entering with one, two fingers, one, two inches, flicking the clitoris. Rachel was quaking and warbling away: however, it seemed right out of context when I pressed my mouth against her ear and (well I never) my sharp erection against her thigh, and said, with a nicely gauged crack in my voice:

'How do you undo this dress?'

Her movements ceased at once. Her eyes opened. 'I'm not on the pill.'

'No, really?' I said.

But then, you see, we did the sort of lyrically zany thing that the under-twenties do fairly often. On Rachel's suggestion, after some tweedy humming and ha-ing from me, we decided that we'd jolly well go up – fuck them all – and *buy* some contraceptives at the late-night chemist in Marble Arch. Nonplussed at first, I soon fell in with the requisite mood. We drank wine, put on coats, and made our whacky way down the square.

Even if we tenderly pooled our money we couldn't afford a taxi – Rachel had to have enough to get back – and besides I thought it more in keeping to take a bus. There was still enough summer about for it not to be really dark, and also you never got beaten up when you were with girls.

It seems improbable now, but on the way there we talked about DeForest's infrequent and ham-cocked performances in bed. (We laughed, too, wholly without malice: an example of prelapsarian high spirits which as of tonight will be another experience unavailable to me.) DeForest's chief, though by no means his only, problem was that he tended to come before either he or Rachel could say – 'Jack Robinson'. He would slap on the contraceptive and surge into her with the look of someone who had just remembered that he ought to be doing a terribly important thing elsewhere, like attending his mother's funeral. (I merely annotate Rachel's imitation.) Then he would screw up his freckly face and sink down on top of her, while his prick slithered out as fast as it had slithered in, not to reappear until he had completed a fortnight of stalling, apologizing, rationalizing. I soft-pedalled my amusement through most of this, partly out of real admiration for Rachel's tolerance and lack of embarrassment. But I nearly burst out crying with laughter when she recounted one of DeForest's wheezes to prolong their delight. He took a *history textbook* to bed, which, so the idea was, he would pore over as Rachel shinnied away beneath him; when they were level-pegging, Rachel was to attract her lover's attention in some way. DeForest would hurl *Tudor England* aside, and be granted four or five seconds of impetuous transport before melting into her dream. It didn't work, I need hardly add, though DeForest clocked up a minute on one occasion.

Whether by design or not, this had the effect of making me feel rather cocky. I had come on impact once or twice myself, but only when I couldn't be bothered not to. I would have readjusted my anxiety chart, only I was unable for the moment to think of anything to fill the DeForest's-prick-size slot.

'Have you ever had an orgasm?' I asked, as we got off the bus.

'Never,' said Rachel.

'Just you wait.'

But I soon came up with something. Of course: I had never used a sheath before. With those girls who weren't self-contracepting I had practised coitus interruptus, practising it all over their stomachs or in between the sheet and their bums, depending on locale and whether or not I liked them. (There was no definite rule here, yet you were always prompted to go one way or the other.) I was conversant with Durex lore, however, having naturally peed and wanked into them a good deal as a youngster, and Geoffrey once took me along to score a pack. Further, I had read widely in prophylactic literature. The great things were to squeeze the air out of the tip, lest they burst, and not to put them on inside-out, because then they catapulted off and you opened yourself up to ridicule scrabbling about after them in the dark.

The chemist's was like a chunk of America, a neon labyrinth of bristle and cellophane, ranks and display pyramids of things to minimize your smells, things to soften your hair, bully your spots, reclaim your feet, flush out your ears. We stood in the doorway, shy latecomers to a formal party. The activity and splendour made me feel drunk and empty-stomached. Store detectives, housewives and dotards cruised the aisles. At the far end a quartet of junkies awaited the return of their forged prescriptions.

'Whereabouts?' I said from the corner of my mouth. Rachel put her hands in her pockets, looping my arm. We moved forward. Only nail-polish remover and badminton rackets seemed to be on sale. Feeling our merriment ebb, I pointed out a not all that unlikely-looking counter. A liberal middle-aged man was in charge of it. What would it really sell? Scabies ointment. Baby powder. Cock-enlarger cream. Dildoes.

'Do you want to come or do you want to wait?'

'I'll come,' she said.

A kooky smile seemed in order.

As a matter of routine, the moment I committed myself to approaching the counter the enlightened-looking man disappeared beneath it, in favour of a woman with silver hair and a glacial uniform. Oh, come *come*, I wanted to say, you must of course see that this is *too* much like low-brow American fiction.

'Can I help you, young man?' She smiled on cue to reveal oppressively false teeth, dull dying white, the colour of newspapers three weeks old.

'I hope so. May I have a packet of contraceptives, please?'

She glanced at Rachel. 'Certainly, sir. Lura, or Penex?'

'The Penex, please, if I may.'

'Twenty-five or thirty pence?'

'Oh, I think the thirty, please, if possible.'

As she turned away I felt Rachel's hand slide through my jacket vents. A fingernail poked my vertebra, making me jerk. Rachel stifled a snort of laughter. The assistant looked up. I met her eye. And my voice was husky when I spoke:

'Better make that a two-pack, lady.'

'I beg your pardon?'

'I'm so sorry. May I have two packets, please?'

'Certainly, sir.'

On the way back I entertained Rachel and kept things going with an account of my own sexual history. Now I had had ten girls. I considered doubling, even squaring, this figure. I ended up halving it. All five, I stressed, had been important and serious relationships. I was sorry, but I had no time for the other kind. Excuse me, but I wasn't interested in purely sexual encounters, thank you, although it was true – one hated to say it – that most of the boys I knew were interested ... in precious little else – no, perhaps that wasn't fair. Of course I had tried it, more out of curiosity than anything, I supposed. It was odd, but – I don't know – it seemed that a girl's body was ... empty unless you liked its owner. Sure, the incredibly beautiful girls in these experimental liaisons had got in a bit of a state – what with being so incredibly sexed up at the time. Understandable. (One or two, I didn't mind telling her, had got pretty violent, pretty ugly, about the whole thing.) But I had had just to explain myself, as tactfully as possible. No – hell – they could keep their money; a boy can't fake it.

What was good sex? Well, good sex had nothing to do with expertise, how many French tricks one knew (how convincingly you munched on each other's stools, etc.). No: if there was affection and enthusiasm, that was enough.

With a heart-beat like a drum-roll I led Rachel down the stairs, past the bathroom, to the bedroom.

It smelled to me of every sock I had taken off, all the ear-wax I had pasted under its furniture, each bogey I had swiped across its walls, and the bouquets of cheap talc puffed into the air to disguise these. A Low-legacy, perhaps. Or my own stressed senses.

Rachel generously took off her coat while I subdued the lighting by means of a cotton scarf over the desk-lamp. We sat on the floor next to the fire and sipped the wine I had brought down. The pink glow flattered us. It made Rachel look extra Oriental, softening her features, ironing out the nose, giving her eyes a distant luminousness – you wouldn't call it a twinkle exactly. In strong contrast, my face became even more angular and shadowy, more hollow and ... sinister, my jaw-line more haunting somehow, my mouth – if anything – still more sensual. Let's get it over with, I thought.

'Charles,' said Rachel, 'when I talked about DeForest on the bus, I hope you didn't think I was being callous. I'm really very fond of him. I wasn't just poking fun. It's just that –'

'Ridicule is the only exorcist there is,' I said in a hypnotic voice, 'and laughter the only true deliverance. Don't trick yourself into guilt. – Let's get undressed.'

Balls-aching drivel, unquestionably – and poor tactics, too. One of the troubles with being over-articulate, with having a vocabulary more refined than your emotions, is that every turn in the conversation, every switch of posture, opens up an estate of verbal avenues with a myriad side-turnings and cul-de-sacs – and there are no signposts but your own sincerity and good taste, and I've never had much of either. All I know is that I can go down any one of them and be welcomed as a returning lord.

Here I had gone and played the sage Frenchie, the crack-barrel *artiste de la chambre*; so 'let's get undressed' had seemed obvious, indeed unavoidable. I had pledged myself to stranded, lean nudity. People really ought to stick together at such a time.

Keeping my body well out of the way, I looked on as Rachel methodically revealed hers. She tugged the elasticized bust of the smock over her head, lowered her tights with an electric crackle, bent and turned to unclip her bra. I was still concealed behind the chair when Rachel went over to the bed, pantied, and slipped between the sheets. Leave them on, for Christ's sake; I needed all the vulgar stimulants I could get. For my knob was knee-high to a grasshopper, the size of a tooth-pick, as I skipped across the room and fell to a crouch by the side of the bed.

Only her little brown head was visible. I kissed that for a while, knowing from a variety of sources that this will do more for you than any occult caress. The result was satis-factory. My hands, however, were still behaving like proto-type hands, marketed before certain snags had been dealt with. So when I introduced one beneath the blankets, I gave it time to warm and settle before sending it down her stomach. Panties? Panties. I threw back the top sheet, my head a whirl-pool of notes, directives, memos, hints, pointers, random scrib-blings.

Foreplay included ear-jobs, bronchitic sweet-nuthins, armpit-play (surprisingly good value in this respect), and a high-jinks of arse and thigh work. The big moment came for Rachel when Charles, the runaway robot, sat up, leaned forward, placed a hand flat on either hip-bone, and literally *peeled* off her panties. As soon as she began to show vulnerable self-consciousness (symptomized as usual by raising right knee) I considerately turned my gaze on her face and bunged my fist in the triangle described by thighs and panty-band. Over her knees my reach ran out. Then, in a very superior move, I got hold of an ankle and pulled it towards me, doubling up the legs. In one movement the panties draped her toes. I swung them into the middle of the room.

'Hadn't I better put the thing on now?'

Penex Ultralite come in dull pink flip-top packets of three. On the bed with my back facing Rachel, who stroked it for something to do, I removed a sheath and peered at it: a florin-sized ring of elastic that gathered into an obscene bobble. I undid the elastic with twitchy fingers.

'Won't be a sec.'

But you seemed to need a minimum of three hands to get it on: two to hold it open and one to splint your rig. After thirty seconds my cock was a baby's pinkie and I was trying to put toothpaste back in the tube.

'*Christ* how do you get these things on.' I held it up accusingly. 'Just how, just how are you supposed to get these things *on*.'

Rachel took a look. 'Oh, baby,' she said. 'You don't undo it first.'

So it was more necking, strange and perfunctory necking, and more body patrol.

This time, under Rachel's supervision, I held the nozzle daintily between finger and thumb and pulled the greased wafer down with my other hand.

'Oh, I see,' I said.

After all that sweat and goonery, was there any point in trying to find the blighted hair of passion, a whisper of real desire, submerged in that tub of clotted vaginal fluid?

Supported on elbows, I hoisted myself above her and brought a knobbled knee up between hers, through the thighs. Glancing downwards, my rig, in its pink muff, looked unnatural, absurd, like an overdressed Scottie dog. I watched with approval, though, as the knee bore downwards. Then I got to work on ears, neck and throat, and paid elaborate lip-service to her breasts, on the assumption that they were to be found in the immediate vicinity of her hazel-nut nipples.

'Yes,' said Rachel.

Oh, hi. You still here?

Of course. They have breasts, too. Quite slipped my mind. What have I been missing? I bite a nipple experimentally; she wags her head. I brush the other one with my cheek; she grinds her crotch into my knee. I suck on it with stiff lips; her hands grasp my head.

A definite rhythm was now created in her. Time to consolidate it. My hands taking over from my lips, my lips taking over from my knee, I have swooped downwards. It was too dark there (thank God) for me to be able to see what was right in front of my nose, just some kind of glistening pouch, redolent of oysters. A sniper, through those hairy sights, I watched Rachel's jaw tense.

Finally, once her movements had begun to syncopate and turn in on themselves to produce new and altogether different rhythms, and once the secret shudders that have no rhythm started to superimpose themselves on the regular back-and-forth, side-to-side swing of her body ... then, I wiped my mouth on the napkin of her thighs, and surged upwards, cleverly hooking my elbows round the backs of her knees to bring them along too. My left hand, from underneath, aimed the uncooked sausage on the relevant opening. Rachel's head thrown back? Check. Eyes tight, rictus smile? Check. And, as I entered, she kissed me, no inhibitions, movingly and democratically partook of her own sour gelatine.

At that point – I swear – I honestly did try to get lost in her responses, to engage her motions, to crawl under the blanket of deliberateness between our bodies. No good. It's far, far too sexy. Real sexual abandonment, for the male, equals orgasm, and therefore he is never allowed to feel it except at the end. It exists, for him, only in indolence or in rape. (If this is so, then, surely, I'm in the clear.)

Seconds away, fusing every nerve in my body, I lurched backwards out of her. Rachel subsided, shaking. Eyes wetted by pain and shock, I placed my head on her breasts. For ninety seconds man and sphincter muscle were locked in combat. I won.

Here we go. An old-school repertoire of minimally sexy positions. Examples: I slung her legs over my shoulders; knelt, bending her almost triple; lay straight as an ironing-board; turned her round, did it from behind, did it from the side; I brought my right leg up, kept my left leg straight – I did the hokey-pokey, in fact. But, again, it is change of position that is sexy, not the position itself, and God forbid that I should feel sexy.

By now my head is lodged dourly between her shoulder and the pillow – no flair, no finessing, just cock to the grindstone. Two times two is four. Three times two, moreover, is six. Stop kissing her mouth, work on ears. Let me come. Stop all movement and kiss her meditatively, in slow motion, so that she differentiates it and realizes what is happening: here I am kissing you. Ninety per cent withdrawal, prod her clitoris with my male reproductive organ, feel her contract, smile potently in the half-light. Withdraw to irreducible helmet depth feel her muscles clench and arms tighten pleadingly on my back withdraw till almost out – then – wait – BOOF. She goes stiff then floppy. Pound like an engine, go dog go. Hand on stomach between shuffling webs of pubic hair, take pressure off, pull legs up too sexy slacken calm down. Fast for three strokes then slow for three then fast. Slow and good, then quick and nasty, then slow and good. Suddenly she shouts, lifts and widens her legs, calls from the end of the world, hands knead my buttocks *don't do that*. Two thirteens twenty-six, three thirteens forty-nine, thirteen twenty-sixes forty-two. (As regards the physical aspect, by the way, this is all utterly intolerable.) Industrial accidents, pimples, bee-keeping, pus crapping Tampax exams ... Pick a poet – Because I do not hope to turn the mermaids round from the back singing because I do not hope to keep your hands off me I do not think bloody sheets that they will sing because there can't be anything left I do not hope to turn the pain the pain. Body strung out on a giant whip, the buckled praying mantis soon to be eaten. I grow old I grow old shall I feel her fingernails hear her neigh give me strength O my people affirm before the world no more and deny between the socks not long for the garden where end loves all ten more five more the bathroom in the garden the garden in the desert of drouth, spitting from the mouth the withered apple-seed. (I come now, a token sperm in the rubber nozzle; but that's hardly the point.) Tossed along with the strength of ten men, every second lucid agony, grating thrusts, the crunch of genitals. Then I surfed helplessly on the wave of her climax, pounded and tugged at as it broke by a thousand alien currents. And she came under my dead body.

Rachel's eyes were streaming. She smiled a shamed, apologetic smile. I tried to say something but had breath enough only to mouth it. She saw, though, in the half-light. 'Oh. I love you, too,' she said.

I feel steadier now. Perhaps The Rachel Papers aren't in such a mess after all. With some interleaving of *Conquests and Techniques: A Synthesis*, and an index ... ? When I'm twenty this will be a thing of the past. The teenage boy is entitled to a certain amount of disorder, and, anyway, I'll mellow tomorrow.

'Something particularly revolting gone wrong?'

'Jesus,' said Mr Alistair Dyson, fanning his face with my dental card. 'What did your mother eat when she was having you? Custard and sugar cubes?'

'Bananas and ice-cream?' I joined in.

'No.' He lit a cigarette. 'There's calcium in ice-cream.'

'That bad, eh?'

I knew my dentist quite well. I knew him quite well because I had been coming down from Oxford about six times a year since I was ten so that he could put in and take out all the lousy braces and plates and other crap with which he tried to tame my mouth. Alistair was one of the youngest cosmetic denticians in the Wimpole Street area you know. (At his surgery he had the newest and most awesome equipment, including the retractable white space-ship sofa-chair which had now moulded itself to the contours of my body.) I liked him; he made me laugh. I respected him, too, for being (I imagined) the only British dentist to have exploited the choric, demonic-artificer aspect of the modern dentist, so popular in recent American fiction. Accordingly he poked all his least hideous women patients. But he was pushing thirty-five now.

'Nothing new, no. That front lower might need another support and there's the usual … dozen fillings. No. Nothing new. You've just got crummy teeth, that's all. Fillings don't stay filled. Stay off the hard foods, won't you. Don't try any carrots or apples. Particularly no apples.'

'But isn't an apple a day supposed to –'

'That's all balls. A ginger-beer every other year will keep me away just as effectively as far as vitamins are concerned, and as for hardening them up, you're past all that.'

'Fascinating.'

'Watch the steaks, too. And don't get any ideas about chewing-gum, unless you want it to turn crunchy.'

'When I'm twenty-five,' I said, 'I'll be living off soup.'

'You'll be fed through a straw.'

'Or intravenously.'

'They'll stop decaying soon, though. You just wait till your gums recede.'

'Don't even talk about it.'

We laughed. He sat on a stool by the washbasin and flicked his cigarette out of the window. 'Don't you mind?'

'Not much. Not in the end. Do most people mind much?'

'Yes, and in a solemn kind of way. That's why you make a change. You get tired of telling these trenchy old girls that their mouths are apple-pie when they know as well as you do that the quicker they switch to chompers the better for all concerned. Especially better for me.' He went over to the desk and took out his prescription pad. 'Mandrax?'

'Please.'

'Thirty?'

'If that's okay. And could you fit me in early for those fillings? Just do the more gaping ones. The rest can wait, can't they?'

'It's your mouth.'

'Yes. Well, I've got Oxford Entrance next month.'

'Oh? Watch the Mandrax, in that case. Tell Judy about the appointments. You'll need two, for the time being. Seen the doc about the asthma and things recently?'

'Yes, a couple of hours ago.' We exchanged shrugs. Dr Budrys had simply listened to me breathing, chucked my balls, got me to hawk on to a slide, and delivered a verdict rich in dotard optimism. I never believed him, anyway.

'Nothing spectacular. He winced now and again when he was stethoscoping me. He writes to my mother about it. I think he thinks I'm still about nine.'

Irrelevantly I thought of the time I came down to London for a dental appointment just after I started wearing long trousers. I delayed the visit as long as possible because I thought I would no longer be able to cry there – which I had invariably done, without feeling incongruous, when I wore shorts. I had cried, all the same.

'I'm twenty quite soon. Perhaps he'll level with me then.'

Alistair opened the door for me. 'That'll be nice,' he said.

Twenty past: 'Celia shits' (the Dean of St Patrick's)

Charles looks at the clock out of the corner of his eye. Things start happening faster now.

'Hello? Western 2814? Hello? Is anyone there? Who is this?'

I hung up and redialled.

'937 2814. Hello? Hel*lo*. If this —'

I hung up and redialled.

'Hello? Gordon ...'

'Now look here. I don't care —'

I hung up and redialled.

'If you —'

I hung up and redialled. Engaged. I hung up and redialled.

'This is the operator. We —'

I hung up.

'Well, thank you, Mrs Seth-Smith. And how are you?'

'Very well. Why don't you go on upstairs? Rachel is in her room.'

'Thank you. I shall.'

And on the way there I wondered how Rachel's mother contrived to take so little trouble with her appearance and yet exude so much vanity. The old black party-dresses she always wore looked as though they had been showered in fag ash and dabbed with powder-puffs. Her hair was like my father's in his I'm-not-going-bald period. And what stopped her shaving off that handle-bar moustache? It couldn't possibly have got that way without patient husbandry: pruning, clipping, waxing the ends. Perhaps she thought she was being foreign (hence the equatorial armpits), or perhaps Harry made her do it as a foil to his paunching-gigolo good looks.

Rachel wasn't in her room. I sat on the bed, in between all the crappy gonks and teddy-bears and dolls arrayed there. I had to pretend I liked them, and especially liked Rachel for liking them, so I took the welcome opportunity of doing them over now. 'How's Wollidog den?' I said. 'Where's your mummy, Winstonchester? How would your fwend Munchy like his fucking face –'

To a tuneless hum, Rachel entered the room, brushing her hair, swaying and dipping her head to let it all hang down. I found that in my enthusiasm I had twisted off the ear of a minor golliwog. I put it in my pocket as I stood up. Rachel screamed briefly, quite without alarm, and ran over.

It was more than a week since The Pull, and, for the second Thursday running, I had come on to Rachel's after my class with Bellamy. (Bellamy now tended to be in a stupor of pink gin and sexual excitement by the time I arrived; the class consisted of his pleas that I should not do any work, because I was so brilliant and marvellous, so fucking handsome, etc.) I didn't mind coming here, and Rachel said it solaced her mother. Mrs Seth-Smith was 'very fond' of DeForest and had been 'very upset' when I made Rachel cool him (but, in fairness, not half as upset as DeForest had been).

I took Rachel powerfully in my arms and we kissed, wriggling and shrugging, in the teenage style. On account of the fact that she was wearing a short dress I put my hand under it and applied pressure to her buttocks. Rachel went heavy and breathless, as she always went these days when I did anything like that. We keeled on to the bed, getting many outraged squeaks from the golliwogs.

'Oh, Charles, Charles,' she said, kissing me non-stop. 'Guess what?'

'What?'

'Mummy and Harry are going away. For two weeks.'

'Where?'

'Paris.'

'When?'

'Next Wednesday. My *birth*day. They want me to come.'
I sat up. 'What's going to happen then?'

Excluding the two afternoons at the dentist ('fencing lessons', as far as Rachel was concerned), we had spent every afternoon in bed. Bunk off school at three, meet at the top of Holland Park, and stroll back, sometimes round the park itself, but not often. Then, at home, downstairs, I would come in and draw the curtains, to give the room a warm half-darkness, daylight ready and waiting on the outside. Rachel followed from the bathroom. Between embraces I would carefully undress her, next myself. We pulled off all the bedclothes and would wind ourselves on a deck of smudged sheet. Then she'd stretch out, and I would bring her to her orgasm. Next myself. Then I would bring her to another orgasm with my hand while Rachel told me how nice and safe and good and right that made her feel. Half an hour later: the bathroom, to slip into a fresh contraceptive, cutting the throat of the used one with a razor-blade to ease its passage down the lavatory. Then again.

When Rachel's domestic circumstances permitted it – about every other night – she'd stay on. Come five o'clock we would get dressed and go upstairs. Jenny was more in evidence then, and she and Rachel got on famously. Sometimes, for my part (and later explaining it away to Rachel) I would placate Norman with a few rounds of brag while the girls made tea. At six fifteen or so, as Norman brought out the booze, Rachel and I would calmly and more or less unself-consciously excuse ourselves, go downstairs, and lie in bed, talking. About her life. About my childhood. About our fathers. We'd make love again once or twice, and perhaps I would bring her to another orgasm with my hand (which looked as if it had done two hours of washing-up at Joe's). About midnight, usually, we would dress, have some coffee, and stand like ghosts on the Bayswater Road until a taxi went by.

My one unfallen week.

'I could get my father to ring.'

'Would he?'

'Of course. He'd dive over backwards to do anything like that. He may not worship me but he worships youth. Make him feel sexy and young.'

'Mm. But still.'

'Mm, I suppose your mother would reason that he wouldn't be there to prise us apart. And Norman's hardly ... I suppose they think you want to go because of your father.'

'Eh?'

'Paris. Your father.'

'Yes, I suppose they do.'

'I've got it. Say you don't want to go for just that reason. Painful memories, such a shit, only upset you. All that.'

But Rachel was taking on that look of modest distress customary whenever her father was under discussion.

'Or wouldn't that work? Look, come on, I'll just tell them that you'd rather stay with me. We're living in the 1970s, for Christ's sake. Don't they realize that parents aren't allowed to mind about all that any more?'

Although my tone was rousing enough, I was fairly relieved when Rachel shook her head. You never know, I might have been able to handle it. During my second dinner there I had acquitted myself well, merely by seeming as dull and ugly as possible. Because if there's one thing girls' parents don't want to see in you it's whatever it is their daughters see in you. All my demeanour had had to say, in effect, was: Look folks – no cock! They didn't like me, true, but Harry was far too keen on seeing his name in print on my father's law page, and anyway, for Christ's sake, what did they think when they looked at Archie, who went from catatonia to manic garrulity just as the mood took him, and why –

'There's always Nanny.'

'How do you mean, there's always Nanny,' I asked cautiously. She might have been setting up another visit. I had got out of it twice already.

'I could pretend I was staying with her. She'd back me up.'

'In that one room?'

'I used to stay with her when she had a flat in Bloomsbury. And Mummy's never been to Fulham.'

I wondered how Mummy made it to Putney and Roehampton to see her trendy friends, if not via Fulham.

'*Really?* Then it might just work.'

We planned it all out. Afterwards, I said:

'Think what a lovely time we'll have.'

But, even then, as Memo-pad 3A quite clearly states, part of me wasn't thinking that. Part of me was thinking how well I'd do in my exams with Rachel in France (automatic Fellowship? telegram from the PM?) and what florid letters I could write to her there.

Must have spent too much time alone. For I needed my secret bathroom hours, and I certainly didn't want Rachel to view me pinned and wriggling on its soiled lino. How could I explain my 200-minute baths, my marathon craps? Why, some of my most peaceful afternoons had been spent slumped on the lavatory, fat tears flopping occasionally on to my thighs. (Only there was I possessed by a truly radical vision of life; only there did I really *feel*, in my heart, that, somehow, we were all guilty.) With Rachel there I would no longer be able to go to sleep on a pillow of tissues, or bark into the special coffee-cup beneath my bed, or ever cough the night away, my throat applauding the silent dawn. Ah, those fourteen-hour reads, the vegetable delirium, the drug of exhaustion, the repose of loneliness. And exams in two weeks.

After briefly wanking myself off on top of her (a layer of lav paper tucked down my strides) and after a neat coke with her parents, I left Rachel's early that evening. She said that I had better stay out of sight for a while if she was going to work the Nanny ploy. I was to ask Jenny and Norman if it was all right by them.

And I would have done, too, only they were having a row when I got back.

I was drinking tea in the kitchen. My sister, a swirl of red-checked nightie, flew through the doorway.

'Hi,' I said.

Knocking back tears, splendid with indignation and rectitude, she went to the chest-of-drawers in the breakfast-room and hauled out the folder in which all her documents and certificates were kept. Jenny found what she was looking for. As she turned, Norman entered, a sceptical businessman come to see an appliance he knew wouldn't work and didn't want anyway.

'Hi,' I said.

She ran over to him, seeming very small, and waggled the bit of paper in front of Norman's nose.

'Look. *Look.* It's true. Can't you *see?* You great ... huge *yob*, it's *true.*'

As if on a cinema screen, I watched Norman lean forward, remove the piece of paper, curl it up in his fist, and drop it to the floor. Jenny stared at the crumpled ball for a few seconds in what looked like incredulous grief. Then, in a sudden movement, her palm had come to a deafening halt on Norman's cheek. Oh no, I thought; now he's really going to knock her block off. Jenny froze, hand resting flat on Norman's whitened face. He waited for her to take it away.

'Go to bed, Jennifer.'

After her rapid footfalls came the fading cry, 'You're a *murd*ere-e-e-er.'

Norman picked up the ball of paper with a sigh, put his hands in his pockets, and sank back against the wall.

I wondered if he knew I was there.

'Have a game of brag,' he said.

I was, of course, much too scared to refuse.

'Two down, one up,' he continued monotonously, 'table stakes, black twos wild.'

Your guess would have been as good as mine. However, the teenager's ignorance about such oldster issues encourages an insensitivity to them – and I was resolved, despite my ambivalence, to ask about Rachel that night, to get things fixed up, before some anxiety could put its foot down.

After an hour of brag, I said: 'Hang on. Just going to have a quick crap. Be a sec. Don't fix the cards.'

Upstairs, I knocked on the bedroom door. 'Jenny?'

'I'm here.'

In the sitting-room, aglow as usual with moody street-light, Jenny had turned one of the armchairs round to face the window. I went and crouched by her side. In a soft voice I told my sister about the possibility of Rachel coming to stay for a while. She looked straight ahead, down the square.

'That's okay,' she said.

'I don't think it'll be much extra trouble. She'd help with things.'

'No, that's fine.'

'And you do get on quite well.'

'Mm.'

'And I thought you might actually like having her around, to talk to. Another girl – you know how I'm always going on about girls needing other girls to talk about perms and babies and things. Because you seem a bit low.'

'Have you told him yet?'

'Norman? No.'

'Don't, please, not yet. Tell him before she comes, but not yet.'

'Okay. Why, though?'

'Oh I don't know, but please don't tell him yet.'

I laid my hand on her wrist. I laid my hand on her wrist as a collector might touch a piece of marble to see that it was the required number of degrees below room temperature.

'All right,' I said.

'Fine. She can stay as long as she wants.'

'937 2814? ... Oh God.'

I hung up and redialled.

'Hello? Now look here, this has –'

I hung up and redialled.

Engaged.

I hung up.

The Letter to My Father, onetime the Speech to My Father, was now some thirty foolscap pages. It lay on my desk downstairs, in a manilla envelope, stamped and addressed. Last-minute corrections and revisions kept me from posting it.

I saw Rachel only twice in the six days before she was due to come and stay. Just as well, really : there were still some texts I had to read for the exams, and a good deal of clerking was necessary to keep The Rachel Papers up to date, what with all these new emotions to be catalogued and filed away. First Love, you understand.

I have very little new to say on this subject. And yet, if I may quote from The Rachel Papers? 'As though normal life (Jen + Norm, school) taking place on a parallel dimension in which I can participate or not participate as the whim takes me. Want R. to witness and experience everything I do, looking over my shoulder, want to be permanently in her presence (not the same as with her); but there she always is.'

And I partly realized this by acting as though she were. If she really had been watching me those two weeks I would have had nothing to hide. I felt myself alone only when I closed the bathroom door behind me. I was still at the stage when you feel you are carrying round a barrel of poignancy in your diaphragm; when you feel you could cry at the drop of a hat; when any bugger could show you fear in a handful of dust. But all this is well documented elsewhere.

Lots of whisky and brag on Tuesday night, the eve of Rachel's stay. And I still hadn't told Norman she was coming.

About eight o'clock, accompanied for some reason by his younger brother Tom, Geoffrey floated in. They were hailed with drunken bonhomie by Norman, who immediately convened a seminar on three-card brag.

I was delighted to see Geoffrey, sure that he had long got

176

tired of my disquieting presence and shifty ways. But I was less pleased to see Tom, Geoffrey's analogue of my own Sebastian: sixteen, wealthy in pustules, randy-dog smells, sebum-moist hairline, and other adolescentiana. I looked at him, yawning cluelessly as Norman explained about priles and ack-a-boos.

'How're you, Tom?' I asked.

'I'm cool.'

'Sure, kid.'

Tom (apprentice hippie, second class) fidgeted with the ludicrous bundle of scarves, bandanas and lockets swathed about his boily neck to indicate the sympathetic nature of his views on sex, drugs, Cuba, the fact that he *was* a hippie, despite the contrary evidence of his as yet short hair and unfaded jeans, his conventional though tolerably sweat-stained shirt.

But Tom wasn't paying attention. '*Look*,' said Norman, 'if you get a black two it's … *Far*kin hell.'

Tom looked at his elder brother. 'I can't make this,' he complained.

Norman was drunk enough to be manageable, yet he was also old enough to be wary of and hostile to undiluted youth, inclined to think that there was something inherently scurrilous about it and to feel wet and queer in its company. I became diplomatic, flashing partisan looks at each of them: these-fucking-beatniks for Norman, these-fucking-greymen for Tom, and something rather more natural for Geoffrey. I went up and leaned on Norman's shoulder and helped him clarify the rules, winking at the other two. I shoved round the whisky bottle. Within minutes, Geoffrey started to make an effort, Tom was saying 'yeah' and 'I dig', and Norman was interspersing the lesson with dirty jokes. Then I slipped away.

'Of course, it's your birthday tomorrow. Quite appropriate. How does it feel, about to be twenty?'

'No different to being eighteen or nineteen.'

'But you won't be a teenager any more.'

'So? That doesn't matter.'

'Don't you think? I'm sure it'll make a tremendous difference to me.'

'Why?'

'Beginning of the end. No. Beginning of responsibility. Have to start taking yourself seriously.'

'Well, I don't mind.'

'Christ. I haven't got you anything yet. D'you mind?'

'Of course I don't mind.'

'Is everything okay with your mother?'

'Think so.'

'Well then, I'll see you tomorrow. About six?'

'Okay. I love you.'

'And I love *you*.'

Norman was sitting alone when I returned to the breakfast-room. I asked where the others were. Tom was being sick in the upstairs bathroom. Geoffrey, in bold contrast, was being sick in the downstairs bathroom.

'What for?' I asked.

'The whisky,' said Norman with a judicious air. 'That little sod was bolting it down.'

'Couldn't be only that. Must be sleeping-pills, too.'

Norman shrugged. 'You haven't half got poncy mates. You going to see if they're all right?'

'No. Fuck them. Can't be bothered. They'll be okay, won't they?'

'Yur. Your deal.'

We played in silence. I let Norman win three hands running, then said: 'Rachel's probably coming to stay tomorrow. Her parents are going to ... Cornwall for a couple of weeks.'

'Yeah? Why's she not going?'

'She doesn't want to. I don't want her to.'

'Bloody mad.' Norman poured out more whisky. 'Who was that tart you had round here before?'

'Gloria?'

'Yeah. Tell you what, she's got a right pair on her.'

178

'Yeah, but she's just a bunk-up. Feel different about Rachel. First love and all that.'

Norman raised his non-existent eyebrows. 'Oh, fuck off,' he said.

Then there was the sound of light footsteps. Jenny's head appeared through the sliding doors.

'Has anyone been using the telephone in my bedroom?'

'Me,' I said.

'Well, you left it off the hook.'

'Oh. Sorry.' But she was gone.

'See what I mean?' said Norman. 'Bitch bitch bitch.'

'I know. But you've got to do it in the end. You have to end up with somebody.'

'Woy?'

'Because otherwise,' I found myself saying, 'you go mad, or you start worrying about going mad, which is even worse. You can't go on sleeping alone … Sorry, I'm pissed.'

'Are you now.' He looked at me curiously.

'Anyway, I asked Jenny if it was okay.'

'What she say?'

'Oh, fine.' I folded on a straight. 'Fuck these cards.' I put a fresh ten-pence piece on the table. 'No, it's just that Jennifer seems pretty depressed nowadays. She was always moody, mind. Used to be worse than she is now, in fact. Likes brooding. No, I just wondered whether there was anything in particular she was worrying *about*. Although, knowing her …'

'Yes? Knowing her, what? Cos if you want to know I'll tell you.'

'Well, I mean, don't tell me if you don't want to.'

'*I* don't give a fuck. Just don't start –'

We heard something fall down the stairs. Tom limped into the room.

'You're looking good,' I said.

'Where's Geoff?' Tom asked.

'Puking downstairs.'

'Sorry, man, I can't make it. I'm going to split.'

'Wait. Hang on. I'll get him.' I stood up.

'No, I'm gonna fade.'

I followed Tom as he backed away unhappily into the passage.

'There's nothing to worry about,' I said. 'I'll get him.'

He gestured with his hands, like a comedian quelling applause.

'It's cool,' Tom claimed.

Norman brushed past us as we stood in the hall. He called out: 'Jenny!'

I knelt on the bathroom floor. Geoffrey fluttered his fingertips at me in shy recognition.

'Christ, I'm a drag,' he said.

'No,' I said, helping him into my room. 'It's good to see you.'

'Where's Tom?'

'He buggered off. What did you give him?'

'Half a Mandie, a Seconal – I can't remember – and two Mogadon, I think. Is he gonna be okay?'

'Yeah.' I sat him on my bed. 'How's Sheila?'

'That's the point. She cooled me. The night before last.' He shook his head in disbelief. 'Cooled me. Isn't it a scene?'

'Do you want an apple?'

Apparently what happened was this. Sheila returned from work (she was a sec in an alternative weekly) to find Geoffrey supine on the bedroom floor, a gramophone speaker propped up against either ear, a joint gone out in one hand, an overturned glass quite near the other, tinted saliva oozing from the corners of his mouth. He had been on plonk since breakfast. He had been on plonk since breakfast since September. On rising, Geoffrey found an envelope under his chin. In it was a précis of this state of affairs and a five-pound note.

'And I'm sure I didn't fuck her enough.'

'What makes you think that?'

'Too smashed all the time.' He prodded the ashtray with his cigarette. But it wouldn't go out.

'No hard-ons?'

'No hard-ons. And I kept puking in the bed.'

'How often?'

'More often than not.' He shook his head. 'How're you making out with that Jewish chick?'

I wanted to tell him about it, only I felt this might dash him. 'She wasn't Jewish in the end.'

'Fuck her?'

'Oh yeah. You know, it's not bad, bit boring. You know. Nothing special.'

I'm afraid the next two-and-a-half weeks are rather a blur. The days soon cease to be distinguishable. In my diary several sheets are quite blank, and The Rachel Papers, at this point, are a sorry jumble of cold facts and free-associative prose. However, this prompts me to take a structural view of things – always the very best view of things to take, in my opinion. The dates are there, so are most of my significant thoughts and feelings. And we've only half an hour left.

I sip my wine. I turn the page.

Things start well.

Kneeing impedimenta into the kitchen. Rachel and I were met by Norman and Jenny. They had taken up formal positions before the window; each held a bottle of champagne, and a third stood by on the coffee-table, surrounded by half a dozen Guinnesses for Norman to dilute his with. I was embarrassed to find how much this moved me. But what I felt even more strongly – looking at Rachel's smiles, her adult handbag and dinky suitcases – was a sense of her independence and separateness. Rachel had her own identity, you see – here saluted by Jenny and Norm – her own belongings and her own autonomy. She wasn't just a sum total of my obsessions; she simply chose to be with me.

With fizzy noses we sang 'Happy Birthday To Rachel'.

Champagne: more than a drink, a drug. It seems curious in retrospect, too teenage somehow: like cornering the fat girl after school behind the pavilion, fingertips on navy knickers for me, palmful of inconclusive breast for you, flattering and degrading for her (but who is she to be critical?); or like the friend's elder sister (or mother) glimpsed naked coming from the bathroom; or like the parties knee-deep in duffle-coats and corduroy, beery mouths and sagging bodies conjoin like slow-motion road accidents; or, most obviously, like the endless foursomes of adolescence, when I've got a hand down her shirt, but then again you've got a hand up her skirt, but then again yours is struggling more, who's first? At least, that's how it felt to me, the only teenager in the room, more alive to incongruities.

On all other occasions we had paired off homosexually. Now we have Mr and Mrs Entwistle forming a diagonal truss on the sofa, and Charles Highway with Rachel Noyes across his lap sideways: necking, shouting, laughing, drunk as skunks. Then the shouting and laughing stops. I notice that Norman's hand has started to ride the white billows of Jenny's breasts, and Jenny quails before the all-inclusiveness of Norman's body, the greed of his huge-mouthed kisses. A loud ping follows as Norman frees the top clip of her dress. Jenny, hollow-faced, was being levered on to the floor.

Rachel and I exited.

For a full half an hour after Rachel and I had finished making love directly below, we could hear Norman's bovine heaves and Jenny's cock-a-doodle-doos. Then the joists fell silent.

'Christ,' I said, respectfully.

'Well, it was the first time in nearly a month.'

'Oh, really?'

Some of our pale sobriety disappeared.

'That's what she said.'

'Oh, of course. You're both girls. I keep forgetting. Of course she'd tell you. I suppose she told you why?'

'Ha ha. No, she was going to, actually. But he came in.'

'Could you tell who was doing the withholding?'

'Not really. Him, I think.'

'Seems more likely. Fascinating business. Do you mind, my arm's gone dead.'

'All right?'

'That's better.'

I made love to her again, not to be outdone. She was twenty, after all. I had got my Older Woman.

One good thing about the first week.

I learned the pleasures of cleanliness (Rachel bathed at least twice a day so I had to at least once) and not only of having but actually wanting to have clean clothes and a tidy room. I saw then that I had used to enjoy my disarray; whether – an inference the Low corroborates – this was an attempt to symbolize my internal disorders I wasn't sure. One way or another I spent a fair amount of time in bed, and found that I rested quite well with the brown bundle in my arms. The spanking state of her torso seemed to transmit itself to mine, and, what with the reprieve my chest had given me (demanding only one midnight visit to the bathroom thus far), I received intimations of what it might be to have a body you could look in the eye.

Two not so good things, which (I'll be honest) didn't worry me much at the time.

No frankness. I thought that after I had slept with Rachel, after my sacramental exertions of The Pull, I'd be able to totter up to her and say:

Right then. You're okay, but you're callow and vain and you simper too much and your personality is little more than an aggregate of junior affectations, all charming, only without weight, without *substance*. For example: you wouldn't lie to DeForest about the Blake thing, yet you lied to your mother about the Nanny thing. Fair enough. But does this urge you to restructure your moral thinking? I don't think I need answer that question. Life, dear Rachel, is more of an empirical or *tactical* business than you would perhaps concede.

Me? Me, I'm devious, calculating, self-obsessed – very

nearly mad, in fact. I'm at the other extreme: I will not be placed at the mercy of my spontaneous self. You trust to the twitches and shrugs of the ego; I seek to arrange these. Doubtless we have much to learn from one another. We're in love; we're good-natured types, you and I, not moody or spiteful. We'll get by.

Maybe that would come later. Maybe I could swing it when I was twenty, too.

Meanwhile, it was frantic avowals and wordy mutual praise. We never contradicted or satirized each other. (Once, I affectionately mimicked her pout; she veered away in pained bewilderment, so I changed it to an imitation of rubber-lipped Norman, claiming I had heard him on the stairs.) Neither of us defecated, spat, had bogeys or arses. (I wondered how she was going to explain away her first period, overdue already.) We were beautiful and brilliant and would have doubly beautiful and brilliant children. Our bodies functioned only in orgasm.

Which brings me to my second point.

We weren't all *that* inhibited in bed, though Rachel never went much beyond lying in it and looking nice. Indeed, she was so taken aback by pleasure that it would have seemed ungracious to expect her to do anything more. Her legs went where I put them, her arms flapped about on my back. She toyed with my prick every now and then, certainly, but only toyed with it, nothing positive. Sex was Disneyland to her: an allotment of organized wonders and legal mischief. Highly emotional, for all that: yet emotions of only one kind. Though – come on – did I really want to show her the other side, my place? Dionysian bathroom sex: troop in, tug back the covers, go through the gaping routine, do everything either of you can conceivably think of doing, again, lurch lick squat squirt squelch, again, until it's all over, again. No. And she probably wouldn't let me.

Three important events.

One.

Monday morning, five days later. Rachel intended to go and

184

see Nanny before school, in order to maintain her complicity in the tissue of lies I had woven. (Of course, she played it for maximum mawk-value anyhow.) Rachel rose at about three, giving her time to bath and make up, but she brought me a cup of tea and parted the curtains before kissing me goodbye. So for half an hour I stretched in nubile enjoyment of the bed's warmth and emptiness. Climbing out of it at eight thirty or thereabouts, I noticed a stray pair of panties under the armchair. As I lit the fire I picked them up to kiss and sniff at.

After I had been kissing and sniffing at them for a while I turned them inside out. I saw: (i) three commas of pencil-thick pubic hair, and (ii) a stripe of suede-brown shit, as big as my finger.

'Fair's fair, for Christ's sake,' I said out loud. 'They do it too.'

But all day I fed a perverse desire to confront her with them when she got back. 'Ah, *Rachel*. Come in, please.' (I am sitting in the armchair, arms folded. Exhibit A is pinned out on the desk like a vivisected fieldmouse.) 'Come over here, if you would, and tell me what you see. *Now:* at approximately eight thirty-five this morning ... Have you anything to say? Come come, there's no use denying it; the proof's before you. *You ... shit.*'

With what a ridiculous sense of grief and loss did I drop them into the laundry basket, and with what morose reluctance did I meet her eye when she returned that afternoon. Then I performed a teenage sulk.

It was most illuminating. Our relationship until that moment had been so straightforward and idealized, so utterly without *candour*, that when the first case of honest, rotten moodiness turned up, I (and Rachel, also) discovered that we had no machinery for breaking through it.

That evening, Rachel was too terrified to breathe. I don't think I'll ever forget her face when I said 'Oh really' and returned to my book midway through her how-Nanny-was-and how-sweet-of-me-to-love-her-still speech. A fearful and startled face, as if someone had screamed in the distance or whispered a ghostly obscenity in her ear. I winced at the desk with a thrill of furtive power. To look at *my* face then, you'd have thought I was expecting Rachel to run up from behind and bash me on the head – or tickle me. A very strange expression; most unpleasant, too, I should imagine.

And, at midnight, when Rachel got falteringly into bed beside me, I said 'So tired,' and *turned over*. This would have been the first night we hadn't made love (at least twice). I had a huge erection, of course, and felt quite like it actually. But I had to test my nerve. Stiff five minutes. Then, gradually and painfully, she started to cry.

I whipped round, kissed her, apologized, stroked her breasts, licked away her tears, hugged her, whispered (rather throatily now) that: yes, my mother had rung up crying that afternoon; I didn't know why it upset me so much – but The Shit had taken along another of his fancy women to humiliate her. Would Rachel ever forgive me?

She was still sobbing, with relief more than anything else, when seventy minutes later I brought her to her eighth orgasm and joined her personally in her ninth. It would do anything that night: a truncheon of stupid glands.

She talked me to sleep about her father. Jean-Paul – you've got to laugh – had received a glamorous wound in the Spanish Civil War, fighting (Rachel need hardly have said) for the Trendy Cause.

Two.

Whether The Second Incident was a result of The First Incident is a matter for the psychologists, not for the literary critic.

I woke with my inside buttock in a pool of furry wetness.

'What's going on?' I asked tremulously.

Oh dear God, I naturally thought, *I've* wet the bed. (I shan't pretend that this wasn't a problem of mine in early adolescence. But my father got hold of some vile contraptions. I went to sleep on a gauze blanket with metal coils on my rig – to wake, at three, in a tram station of bells and alarms, flashing lights, buzzing buzzers.)

186

Rachel was steaming shamefully in front of the lighted fire. 'You won't believe it,' she said in a matter-of-fact voice, 'but I've wet the bed.'

I got out and knelt beside her. We were naked.

'Ah, don't worry,' I said. 'Never mind, never mind. Christ, I used to do it every night till I was practically eighteen. Non-stop. Till practically the other week, in fact. No, come on. Don't worry.'

My exams began the next day. During that week she tended me as if invisible. Slid food in front of my nose, laid out my clothes and filled my pens each morning, and at night she was no more than a presence of shadow and oil for me to dip into as I pleased – perhaps not exactly as I pleased; more as it pleased me to think she thought I pleased. I was using the Mandrax my dentist had given me, surreptitiously dropping one at ten thirty, read for half an hour, quick bath, drowsy foreplay, fumble with condom, Rachel's basic two orgasms, starvation-ration endearments, sleep.

I mulled over The Second Incident, when I had nothing more urgent to mull over – on the way to school, while peeing myself. And it seemed to weigh on her, too. She was edgy, nervous and diffident at the same time, as one reasonably might after having bled out all dignity in a series of hot, fetid squirts. What would she feel now as she went to sleep? And I also felt shame: the shame of squiring the girl who farts in a crowded room, the shame of having a mother drunk, the shame of a man whose wife is sick down the dress she's too old for, to veil the tired, freckled breasts. But I tried to imagine her anxiety, after the emotional and sexual drubbing. I tried to imagine what insidious, coaxing little dream she must have had ... waist-high in the sea, crouching behind the bushes, plonked on a convincing lavatory seat, tenseness and panic seeps away. No, too sad, I couldn't bear it.

Three.

Wednesday was Maths and Latin O Level. I sat these at school. No one invigilated. Mrs Tauber herself brought me coffee and a mathematics primer in the morning and tea and a Latin dictionary in the afternoon. I thought I did quite well.

When the Oxford exams began, the next day, so did Rachel's period – harbingered several hours in advance by a festive pimple ... on her nose.

The way things are, boys can afford to look pretty dreadful now and then; they just pretend they're living hard, not sleeping much, heck, being casual and rangy. But the beautiful girl – through no fault of her own – is a perfect girl. I had the odd spot, sure, when Rachel and I were living together. However : boys will be boys; girls shall be girls.

The Third Incident has given me more vestigial doubt than The First or The Second. It was an invitation, no matter how tentative, to candour, and I refused it. (Nothing would have been easier than an adult, left-wing discussion of the other Incidents – nor more detumescing.) Here, though, was a plausible opportunity for me to explain to Rachel that the existence of the body is the only excuse, the only possible reason, for the existence of irony; that some of the body belongs to the bright steel and white porcelain of the bathroom as well as to the muffled, more forgiving warmth of the bedroom : that no one knows what sort of body they'll end up with nor what it will spring on them next. Take, for example, a look at me.

Once again, if her personality had had more bounce and gusto that invitation might have been a firmer one. But to see her pathetic confusion and distress beneath the still chirpy, still as-if-immaculate surface. I think, all the same, that when I opened my eyes to the bubbling big boy inches from my lips, I really should have said : 'Morning, beautiful.' And seeing it half an hour later, matted with make-up, I really should have cried : 'Oh look. You haven't got a spot on your nose!' And, that evening, when Rachel announced : 'The curse is upon me' (misquoting 'The Lady of Shalott'), my answer should really have been : 'Surprise surprise. Listen, you've got it in italics right across your conk.'

(Geoffrey, by the way, once claimed that – second of course to crapping – there was no more intense emotional experience than having your blackheads squeezed by the one you loved. There you go again.)

At Kensington Town Hall, packed down on my desk like a Rugby forward, I had a sequence of (mild) identity crises, a trio of Sir Herberts staring dubiously over my shoulder, handwriting changed beyond recognition in the course of each paragraph. When I looked at the clock I thought: Rachel, Rachel; or alternatively: Who am I? Just *who*, the *hell, am* I?

The Practical Criticism paper. I explicated a Donne sonnet and paid uncomprehending lip-service to a beefy dirge by someone called John Skelton. There was a D. H. Lawrence essay on how passionate and truthful D. H. Lawrence was: a characteristic piece of small-cocked doggerel which I treated with characteristic knowingness. Finally, I belaboured one of Gerard Manley Hopkins's sleazier lyrics, implying (a last-minute reread made clear) that it was high time we burned all extant editions of the little fag's poetry; emendations took the form of replacing some of the 'ands' with 'buts', and of changing the odd 'moreover' to 'however'.

I took a chance on the general English Literature paper, writing for three hours on Blake alone in an attempt to get the erratic-but-oh-so-brilliant ticket. Risky, I know; but my reading was there in bold parentheses: the almost unread Prophetic Books, Milton, Dante, Spenser, Wordsworth, Yeats, Eliot, and, yes, Kafka. 'I like it, I like it,' the dons whispered in my ear.

Throughout, I stabilized myself with lots of examsmanship, in order to depress my fellow-candidates. I would laugh out loud on my first glance at the questions, trot up happily for more paper with only half an hour gone, drift through the crowd afterwards murmuring phrases like ' ... a breeze ... candy from a baby ... I romped home ... bloody pushover ... '

Owing to some professorial caprice, the last paper required from the student a two-hour essay on a single word. There was a choice of three: Spring, Memory, and Experience. I took the last. The Bible, *The Pardoner's Tale*, *Hamlet-Lear-Timon*, Milton again, Blake again, Housman, Hardy, Highway, closing, in semi-delirium, with the exhortation that son of man had fucking better start loving one another, or die.

When I surfaced, dragged along in a tide of fat-legged girls and torpid Pakistanis, cancelled out by fifteen hours of words and months of confused aspiration, born frowning and blinking into the vivid street, there – round-eyed, white-smocked and spotless – was Rachel. I kissed her for a whole minute as the crowd fell apart about us. We went away to the Park in a handicapped shuffle, arms everywhere, to lie in freak autumn weather on cold grass beneath heavy overcoats. In our ears the chant of tired birds who dumbly thought it was summer again, shouting children, and – if we were lucky – the whirr of a pervert's cine-camera. In our noses the smell of trees, soil, and our bodies. O my youth.

Five evenings later, my diary says, the evening before her 'parents' were due back from France, Rachel ran down the stairs and into my room.

'Guess what?' she said.

'What.' The Oxford University candidate was to be seen in T-shirt and khaki strides, his nasal blackheads hovering above the *Evening Standard*'s entertainments guide. I was picking a film for us to see. A going-away treat.

'Jenny's going to have the baby!'

'Which baby?'

'*Her* baby.'

Of course, of course.

'Don't tell me,' I said. 'Norman wanted her to have an abortion. Am I wrong?'

'But now he says it's all right.'

'That's why he was a murderer.'

'What?'

Naturally, them being girls both, Rachel had hardly set foot in the house before Jenny confided in her. She was three months pregnant, pregnant the day I arrived.

'Christ,' I said. 'In six months I'll be an uncle.'

*

'Isn't it wonderful.'

'Yeah. Why didn't you tell me?'

'She told me not to tell anybody.'

'I dare say, but why didn't you tell me?'

'None of my business.'

'Mm. Suppose they'll stay together now. Norman must have come to some kind of decision. Probably didn't want to get tied down. What changed his mind, do you know?'

'No idea. Jenny just rushed up and said he was going to let her have it.'

I reflected that Norman wouldn't have worded it quite so ambiguously, unless he had in fact followed up with a consolation head-butt. Well then. Kevin Entwistle was now poking chauvinistically at the reaches of my sister's womb, combing his hair, smoking fags, planning craps. I would have gone upstairs to offer congratulations, or something, but apparently they had gone out to dinner.

'Well I never. Dash my buttons. He must've decided that the time had come. Guilt, too, probably.'

(Wrong again, by the way. That wasn't why.)

When two couples are living together – no matter how fortuitously – and something like this happens to one of them, something epoch-making, it seems that the other couple is subject to a new kind of self-consciousness, a vague pressure to reinvestigate themselves. It seems also that there need be no logical connection between what has happened to one relationship and what the other couple feel necessary to do to theirs. This, at any rate, was how I rationalized my cumbrous misgivings and uncertainties as I sat next to Rachel in the damp cinema.

I'm fucked (I thought) if I'm going to tool into that bedroom tonight, bung on one of those feelthy heedeous condoms, and complete the hushed, devout routine. I was being at least fifty-per-cent sincere when, prior to The Pull, I said that enthusiasm and affection were enough, that French tricks were unimportant. But then again, then again ... No. Tonight, my lad, *you* are going to get laid. Selfishly. You're going to get gobbled for a kick-off. You gonna bugger her good. You gonna rip out her hair in fistfuls, fuck her like a javelin hurled across ice, zoom through the air, screaming. Then, whether she wants to or not, and especially if she does not want to, she is going to ... let me see ...

Or was all this mere bear-trap credulity? The film, you understand, was *Belle de Jour*. *Belle de Jour* tells the story of a beautiful girl, married to a man so considerate and handsome and successful that she has no choice but to go off to a brothel in the afternoons, there to be fucked by twenty-stone Chinks, snaggle-toothed gangsters, and generally have a good time. Don't forget, also, that I had been reading a lot of American fiction, and that Norman had told me the other night about a girl who used to like gobbling him so much that they found it convenient to sleep one-up one-down, her feet on his pillow.

'Bunuel extends an imaginative sympathy that includes the messiness and arbitrariness of our ... unwanted desires,' I explained, as we made our way down the Bayswater Road. 'And why don't you go on the pill?'

We walk on, our breaths smoky in the November night. This is a mute moot point, never before mentioned. Her hand squirms in mine.

'I don't like to feel – ' Rachel hesitated, then went on – 'that my body's a sort of machine, that I'm a sort of machine ... ' Rachel hesitated, then went on – 'being programmed. Put those in me, and it'll have – ' Rachel hesitated, then went on – 'it'll have a designed effect.'

Ur? What can she mean? She talks as if she's filling in a form. 'What about *me*?' I want to yodel. How do you think *my* body feels, wearing that sliver of bathroom? (It's unpractically pricey, too. A week after The Pull I had to lone up to Soho and buy a gross-pack of 'Sharpshooters' – economy dunkers – three of which I daily transfer to one of those plush Penex three-slots. Knowing, you see, how hurt she'd be if she thought I was fucking her on the cheap. Are there any limits to my sensitivity?)

Apparently not. Instead of saying, You'll get over it, or, Tough, or, Grow up; instead, I halt in front of a lamp-post at the foot of the square, stroke her cheeks with my hands, nuzzle her ear, and whisper:

'I think I understand.'

But that night.

Usually: I slid down over her dull body kissing her breasts, guts, hips, to lodge head between thighs and stir her with my tongue (by now a ham-bone of muscle), already in a contra so that when I loomed upwards my (well-dried) mouth and (nozzled) rig met their respective targets simultaneously.

But that night I station my loins next to her head, sending mine south, and crawl wheezily down the bed, my feet now pressed hard against the wall above the pillow for the necessary purchase. Splendid work. As my tongue lolls inside her I peek up. There it is, thrown in her face. But she takes it between index finger and thumb as though it were a sugar-lump. My eyes bulge as she ferries the foreskin primly back and forth. If you can slash in my bed (I thought) don't tell me you can't suck my cock. So I drive it into her cheek, practically up her nose, and Rachel takes it in her mouth and releases it almost at once. With a croak of disgust. Which says: Even worse than I thought.

And yet I was the one who felt ashamed, dirty, dog-like, in the wrong. To prove it there were tears on her face when I came up for air.

The scene is the main hall at Addison Tutors.

At the near end a group of male students from Rachel's school, in dinner-jackets, stand round drinking champagne and talking to one another. The cleaning lady, Mrs Dawkins – who, though fat and lower-class all right, is invariably in a bad mood and has never called me love – goes about filling their glasses and brushing down their tuxedoes. I am on a straight-backed chair in the middle of the room, predictably dishevelled, with a bottle of brown ale. Rachel is at the far end, on the raised dais. From her posture you would think she is wretchedly uncomfortable, or else deep in yoga meditation: propped up on a cushion against the wall, naked, holding both legs in the air, knees on breasts, cunt splayed. Beside her is a bowler hat, upturned.

I wander over. I nod at Rachel; she grins dead ahead and doesn't see me. I mount the dais and lean on the piano, a few yards away. In the bowler hat, I notice, are some coins: mostly coppers, the odd florin, a single fifty-pence piece. I pull on my beer, and wait.

Now, in twos and threes, Rachel's colleagues begin to detach themselves from the party. They stroll across the hall towards us and come to a halt before the dais. In dubious mutters they assess Rachel the spider-crab. A pair climb the steps; one of them, a small, red-haired young fellow, acknowledges me with a wink – which I return. Rachel beams in the direction of their waists. Then, still sipping champagne, they start to talk more confidentially. The ginger-boy prods her snatch with a patent-leathered foot; the other leans forward to examine her teeth and gums. They come to an agreement. Ginge places his glass on the window-sill, unwraps his cummerbund, folds it, puts it in his pocket, lowers his trousers, stoops, and keels forward on top of her.

I swig my beer.

He bobs away for a few seconds, then goes all weak and amorphous. He veers back, slightly off-balance, and composes his dress. The second boy, much taller and handsomer than his friend, goes through the same routine, but pauses, hand on chin, at the last moment. He has a better idea. Reaching forward he gets a good grip on Rachel's ears and urges her mouth to greet the (massive) rig that cranes from between his shirt-tails. In this fashion, with twelve stiff-elbowed tugs, he has wanked into her head. Rachel murmurs her appreciation. They lob coins at the bowler, and move off. Others take the platform. The process is repeated.

Meanwhile, I pull on my beer, watch, look at the wall, hum popular tunes.

The final group approaches; it is rather drunker than the

first, perhaps. At any rate, the young gentlemen stand be-calmed in front of the dais. Suddenly one of them gasps, looks about in disbelief, and doubles up with a wail of laughter. Soon, of course, everyone joins in. They mill and sway, clutch helplessly at one another, hooting, braying, pointing.

Oh no. Not us, mate. You've got to be joking. You'd be lucky. With her? With that?

Rachel smiles, unblinking.

She's not pretty enough and she wets the bed.

Their laughter is replaced by my own.

'Charles, Charles, Charles,' Rachel was saying. 'Wake up.'

I did.

' ... What sort of dream?'

I lay on my back. The reality of the ceiling closed in. My voice was hoarse.

'Walking down a long, tree-lined path. At night. Above my head the stars were arranged in ... unfamiliar constellations. Pebbles glistened under my feet. I saw your shape in the distance but ... when I tried to move towards you ... '

'Neville Bellamy here. I reng Mrs Tauber yesterday, heard you've been unwell. How are you?'

All right.

'Yes? I gathered it was a touch of esthma. No? It was ... the ... ?'

Yes.

'Ah, the body, the body! One wishes one didn't *hev* one, no? Yug yug yug. Life would be so blissfully simple. Better off without it. Do you not agree? Do you not feel this?'

I do not. (The argument has plenty to recommend it; but then the brain would have nothing to cerebrate about.)

'No? Perhaps not ... mm. Charles! Your papers! How were they?'

Okay.

'Grend. And your interview?'

Monday.

195

'So soon. Well in that case you must certainly come over for a drink, pick up some pointers ... hev-a-chet?'

'Oh. Well.' I couldn't help feeling flattered.

'If you're fully recovered. Why not tomorrow? Usual time?'

'Look, ah, let me think. Shall I see how I feel and give you a ring if I'm *not* coming?'

'Perfect. You hev my number. Goodbye now.'

As Mr Bellamy put down the telephone and picked up his cock, I hurried into the kitchen.

'Then what?'

Jenny placed a stack of handkerchiefs on the table.

'There you are.' She sat down and began to shake her head. 'Well. He said he'd already booked me into the London Clinic and that it was all fixed up. So then I said ... ' She stopped shaking her head in order to stare into space for a while. 'Well, anyway, there was the most ghastly scene and he seemed to have his mind made up.'

'Was that the night I asked if Rachel could come and stay?'

'I ... *think* so. Then, when your friend – Geoffrey? – came and that little boy had been sick all over the lavatory seat in our bathroom, Norman just came in while I was clearing it up and said that he would cancel the London Clinic and that he wanted more time to think about it.'

'Then what?'

'On Wednesday, when Rachel came upstairs to the drawing-room to say goodbye, he said afterwards that it was all right, he didn't mind.' She stretched her arms above her head. 'And that's what happened.'

She looked radiantly happy and so on, but I wanted details. (Not that I wasn't sufficiently embarrassed by what she had told me so far. However, I had made a policy decision about all this and my Jenny pad was not up to date.)

'Why did he change his mind?'

She seemed delighted. 'I don't know!'

'Why didn't he want you to in the first place?' I pressed on. 'Just didn't want to get tied down with kids yet, or what?'

196

'*No*. He said straightway that I could adopt one ... or two ... if I liked.' Jenny frowned, as if the point were occurring to her for the first time. 'I think,' she said, with deliberation, 'I think he was scared something might happen to me.'

'Mm.'

(Correct, by the way. But not quite how she meant it.)

'When's Rachel coming to stay again?'

'Oh. Soon.'

I had figured that I would probably have to cry a bit and was in fact reddening my eyes with my knuckles when Rachel came into the room. She looked more spruce than ever, in the doorway holding her cuboid vanity-case, and dark-spectacled to indicate her own grief. But, even as I was planning the initial burying-of-head-in-hands – my tonsils swelled and my tears gathered, unasked for.

Rachel had to lie on the bed comforting me for fifteen minutes before I would let her leave.

Absurd, really, because all week I had been looking forward to it. Read a book, have a wank, pick my nose, be smelly and alone. When I rang her later that night – Harry answered, his bad manners whetted by a fortnight in Paris – and Rachel did the crying: I felt, well, nothing much, nothing to write home about.

Furthermore, as Mr Bellamy said, I had the asthma to think of. This affliction seemed to collaborate with the other spanners in my respiratory works. It opened up new dimensions to my coughing fits. I would get a tug in the solar-plexus (quite pleasant, actually) and a kind of hollow pressure at the back of my throat (again, not unsexy) which nevertheless I had to lose, and the only way to lose it was to go on coughing: each rasp softened my diaphragm and chipped away at the emptiness in my lungs until I was left with a drunken, emotional, husky resonance deep in the chest and there appeared to be no need to cough any more. One particularly illustrious fit ended when a huge, wriggling blob of gilbert leapt from my mouth and smacked solidly against the bathroom wall – better than *five feet* away. I focused my eyes; it was enormous; it looked like – what are they called? bolasses? – the weighted lassoos employed by South American cowpokes. Soon, I thought, soon, just by coughing in the direction of their legs, I'd be able to trip up old ladies in the street.

It also enriched the texture of my phlegm : I whoofed up goo pretzels, fried slugs, pixie's nylons. And it wouldn't let me sleep and it made me feel old and it left me gasping on the stairs and it cemented my nostrils so that I had to breathe through my mouth, like a yob.

There were good things, too, of course. Some serious work remained to be done, mostly in the form of track-covering – I had referred (abusively) to countless writers I had barely even heard of, let alone read – and there was ample time to percolate anxiety about my interview. The addition of various rhetorical trills to the Letter to My Father gave occasional light relief.

Further, Rachel came to see me every day. She brought presents, a mag or some fruit (bananas and grapes only, after she noticed the apples browning in their dish). She brought me the library books I asked for. She looked marvellously independent and she didn't stay too long. The poems almost wrote themselves.

We talked a lot about the times we'd have when I was well and my interview was out of the way. For I was entering a national under-21 short-story competition, sponsored by one of the colour magazines. With the prize-money we might just have a few days in Paris ourselves.

Twenty to: the dog days

There goes the last of the plonk – and a very nice drop of wine, too. But I'm afraid it hasn't quite done the trick.

My father is alone in the sitting-room, a typescript and a glass of soda water before him.

'Hi,' I said. 'Just thought I'd have … a small whisky.'

'Hi.' He looks up as if trying to catch my eye across a room full of people. 'Why not have one with me?'

'Oh. Well I've got one more thing to write, actually. But how long are you going to be up?'

'Thirty, forty minutes.'

'Then I might well come down later. Valentine's away, isn't he?'

My father cocks his head. 'Yes.'

'Only there's something I want to dig out of his room.'

'Ah. Well then. Hope to see you some time after twelve.'

Valentine's room used to be my room. We switched when I was fifteen. You think I resisted the change? Not at all. I welcomed it. Attics seemed more thoughtful and fair-minded places to be, then. I kneel on the window-seat in the dark and admit the thrillingly cold air. I think about my formative heterosexual experience. It won't take a minute.

Highway's first para-bronchitic summer.

Mother was going through a menopausal introspection-jag, so, by way of therapy, my father persuaded her to throw a tea-party – on the lawn, one Saturday – to make some local friends. After all, Jenny was there to help, and so was … Suki, a friend of hers from Sussex who had come to stay. Suki had a special effect on me at once. I had just finished *The Mill on the Floss* and was achingly in love with Maggie Tulliver (the sexiest heroine in fiction), whose gypsyish, magical good looks

Suki seemed to me to share. Moreover, a girl with a name like Suki – the adolescent thought – would do anything; there was nothing a girl with a name like that wouldn't do.

Mother supervised the preparations in frothy hysteria. Us boys were confined to our rooms for being in the way. 'Who's she invited, for Christ's sake,' my elder brother grumbled, 'Marie Antoinette?' I watched from my window. To ensure a constant flow of hot water a three-point gas-ring was set up outside the dining-room, directly beneath. And a table: cakes like sand-castles, damp strata of bread and ham, crushed-fly biscuits, greying boiled eggs in a marble pyramid.

At four o'clock rowdy hags had grouped on the lawn; some, panting like dogs, formed a tea-queue; others sat on deck-chairs and looked at a pile of gardening tools as if it were a cinema screen. As late as four fifteen, mother flaked out: either the party had aggravated her sense of intraspecific alienation, or her tranqs, all day neutralized by adrenalin, had hit her together in one clammy punch. Someone helped her to her room. Jenny was left to handle the hags. The tea and hot water dispensing fell to Suki.

Suki wore a summer dress of flame-coloured cotton and the summer dress turned out to have a low-cut front. Now if Suki bent forward, which she kept on having to do, and if I simultaneously craned my neck, which I kept on doing, I got to see the lion's share of her hard high brown little breasts and – once – a flash of dark nipple. I sat with a decoy paperback on the window-sill for over an hour. And, as she became more flustered, and sweat surfaced on her forehead and shoulders, and she more frequently palmed the hair from her eyes: to me her movements seemed slower, quieter, and to have less and less to do with filling teapots and lifting kettles and being down there. The flabby blue flame from the gas-ring heat-hazed over her, came shimmering up the outside wall, and breathed thick air into my open mouth. Then her body began to squirm and writhe; I couldn't focus on her, but she was all that was there.

As the party began to end, and Suki went to join the last of the hags, I fell back from the window, dropped the paperback, and swayed about the room actually wringing my hands. I wondered how I had ever played Scrabble, or read a book, or combed my hair, or brushed my teeth, or eaten a meal, when – it was all so clear now – Suki's face was what it was, and her breasts were what they were. I melted on to my bed and lay there trembling, until, with no climax, I started to feel very cold instead of very hot and the voices of the women, at first inaudible, seemed to hail me from the garden.

I was sweaty and feverish the next day and decided to spend it in bed. (Besides, how could I face Suki?) Everyone thought it was the bronch returning, but I knew it wasn't. No. Queer meets right girl, and never looks back.

Up on my knees I can now see from the light in the sitting-room the little patch of grey where the grass never fully re-covered after that swirling, gaseous afternoon. I close the window with an air of self-conscious finality. I think I know how things will turn out. Passing mother's room in the thin passage I hear her call 'Gordon?', but I hesitate, shrug, walk on, and make no noise, having decided to stick to the story.

The night before last, the night before I came up to Oxford for my interview, was the night of my life – an appropriate bas-relief to this my solitary denouement.

The four of us had tea together that afternoon. I was being fussed over in a rather agreeable way: Jen said she'd get up and cook me a 'proper breakfast', Norman offered to drive me to Paddington the next morning, Rachel stressed time and time again that my interview would be a mere formality. Later, she and I popped downstairs and went to bed for half an hour, with something of our former cheekiness. I thought it might possibly be my last teenage fuck, so: our skin was as smooth as mushroom, our breath imperceptible, our demands unso-phisticated, our orgasms coinstantaneous. And when I pulled off the condom and swaddled it in tissue at the bottom of the wastepaper basket, there was no rancour, no sense of being put upon. We dressed in equable silence. I felt strong, walking her down the square in the pale Sunday light.

However, seven o'clock and I was at my desk. A final run through the Interview Folder: sixty foolscap pages of notes and hints, arranged in sections – *Accents, Avoiding Detailed Discussion, Dress, The Female Don* – and sub-heads – 'Blinking', 'Entrances', 'Leg-crossing', 'Flattery, indirect', etc. But I couldn't gather much concentration. At this stage my exam performance either seemed so brilliant as virtually to replace the texts themselves, rendering all previous literary criticism defunct; or else I was at the window, on the look-out for the white-coated male nurses (whom the University had alerted) equipped with chloroform and a net. On my arrival, would I simply be lured into the college lavatories and beaten up by the proctors? Or would I be met at the station by the Vice-Chancellor and Mayor, driven through the town in an open car, waving at the crowds, laughing as I brushed the confetti and streamers from my hair ... ?

'Hel*lo*?' said a busy female voice, 'what number do you want, please?'

'Uh, Western 2814.'

'And your number is ... ?'

I gave it. 'What's up?' I asked. 'Having problems with the bill?'

'The subscriber has asked us to intercept all calls on this line.'

'What's been the trouble? Perverts?'

The girl laughed and her voice relaxed. 'I'm not sure, really. I think just someone's been ringing at all hours of the day and night, then hangs up. And from call-boxes and leaving the receiver off the hook.'

'Maddening. Well, I think they'll talk to me.'

'One moment.'

' ... Gordon Highway speaking.'

'Father? It's Charles.'

'Charles. What can I do for you?'

Nothing much, as it happened. I had rung to see if he had

winkled any information out of Sir Herbert. No luck. My father was reduced, not of course to saying, but to disguising the fact that he was saying, that Herbie knew bugger-all about it and besides he had forgotten to ask him.

'Ah,' I said. 'I tried home, by the way – thought you'd be there.'

'No no. I'm not coming into the office next week so I intended to go up tomorrow. Perhaps I can give you a lift?'

'No, it's all right.'

'Yes. Sorry I couldn't ... wait – hang on. Vanessa would like a word.'

'Hey,' said Vanessa, 'what's your college?'

I told her.

'Right. They've elected a new guy.'

'What sort of new guy?'

'I don't know anything about him. Except that he's shit-hot.'

With featherlight fingertips I skimmed the pages of my Interview Folder. After three-quarters of an hour I had memorized *Sonorous Generalizations*, *Portent but no Content*, and the paragraph on 'Inarticulate sincerity'. I then turned to *Appearance Change Midway*. It ended:

17. Enter without glasses on: put them on *a*) if don over 50, *b*) if don wearing glasses.

18. Jacket unbuttoned: if old turd, do up *middle* one on way in.

19. Hair over ears: if old turd, smooth behind ears on entry?

A footnote referred me to *Accents*, 7. There I read:

Adapt slowly. If wildly out (posh v. regional), cough at beginning of second sentence and say 'Sorry, I'm a bit nervous' in voice identical to don's.

I chewed on my lip ... There must be a common denominator somewhere. Of course! Dons were all queer, weren't they? Perhaps I should just take a chance – leave my clothes in a neat pile outside the door, and go in naked. Or go in wearing transparent trousers and no pants? Or at least go in with my prick dangling out between my fly-buttons. At least. Or –

I heard the telephone ringing. Jen and Norm had gone out to dinner so I put the Folder down and trotted upstairs to answer it. Rachel, possibly.

It was not Rachel. It was Gloria.

'Christ. How are you?' I said.

Gloria wasn't too bad. In fact, she was at a call-box just round the corner and was wondering if she could pop in for half an hour or so. Could she?

'Okay. Yes, by all means. See you in a minute then.'

I stood in the passage, winding my watch for something to do.

'And I got so *bored*. Tel [Terry] wouldn't leave me alone. He wouldn't leave me out of his sight, went spare if I so much as talked to another guy. I mean, you like that at first but it gets on your bloody nerves after a bit.' Gloria gave a scandalized laugh, a hand raised to cover her small, untidy teeth.

'You poor thing. So what did you do then?'

Gloria scrutinized her gin. 'I towed him. Straight.'

'What did he say to that?'

'He belted me. And he said I was a slag. That was it.'

I gave a speech, in idiomatic lower-middle, on the mischievousness of sexual jealousy in all its forms. (Half-way through, Gloria took off her leather jerkin, her eyes intently on mine, to reveal a snug purple T-shirt, which I suppose clashed rather with her tiny brown suede shorts. Although she was obviously wearing panties she was just as obviously not wearing tights, or a bra.) As the speech was about to end, the telephone rang again.

' ... unless you've got your heart *set* on having a bad time. Don't go away.'

I trotted upstairs.

Call-box pips. Terry? No, Rachel.

'Charles? Oh Charles, you'll never guess what's happened.'

'Well?'

'Mummy's found *out*. She found out about Paris.'

'How?'

'She came to see Nanny – and it all came out.'

'How?'

'Oh I don't *know* ... ' She seemed about to cry, but went on wanderingly. 'Mummy came round, saw how small Nanny's room was, asked where I slept ... I don't know.'

'I see. Where are you now?'

'Nanny's. Mummy threw me out of the house.'

'You'd better come round.'

'Right. I'll have to stay here for a while,' she said in a brisk voice, 'because Nanny is in a bit of a state. She thinks it's all her fault and –'

' – Well it *is* all her – '

'What's the time now? Look, I'll be there about nine. All right?'

As I swung my way downstairs I stopped dead for a moment, thinking.

Gloria had taken off her shoes and was lying on the bed. I sat on the edge of it.

'You're so nice to talk to, Charles. You always cheer me up.'

It was eight three precisely.

Eight five. Intricate tangle of bodies. Gloria's fingers were jogging my belt-buckle. Mine trembled between suede and moist cotton. Swampy kisses.

Eight fifteen. Gloria moved clear and pulled at her T-shirt. Blankly I started undoing buttons. Then I stopped undoing them. But Gloria freed her dear little shorts; they fell to the floor and she stepped out of them. Those wonderfully unsubtle, unliterary big breasts. Gloria smiled.

'I'm not on the pill, Charles.'

'Not you too – I mean, not to worry, I've ... '

I hesitated again, and felt a shudder of sobriety. Gloria

looped her thumbs in the band of her panties. And her panties bulged extraordinarily – as if housing a whole cock, if not two.

'I have some contraceptives,' I said.

Eight twenty-five. After some neck-ricking soixante-neuf and a short period inside her unsheathed, I clawed at the little pink holder and took its final trojan. – Not to worry, because this is my equivalent of a flash cigarette-case; the real supply is elsewhere.

Eight thirty-five. 'Yes, it was great for me as well,' I said, truthfully. 'No thanks, I'm trying to give them up. Gloria, the thing is that my sister and her husband are coming back soon. You've never spoken to Norman, have you? No. Well, you see, he's a very puritanical type – stiff-upper-lip, and all that. Very strict upbringing. Anyway, he might –' 'Oh, about five, ten to nine.' 'Oh, that's fine. No panic, really. But he might get in a sweat. You know these posh types. Can't relax about anything. And also I've got my interview tomorrow.' 'At Leeds Polytechnic.'

'I've got to get back, too. I'm glad I could see you for this long.'

'So was I.'

The contraceptive joined its (slightly) heavier twin.

Eight forty-five. Gloria giggled as she worked the T-shirt over her smudged breasts. And I giggled, too, to stop myself crapping all over the floor with anxiety.

Eight fifty-five. 'Goodbye, my sweet. I'll ring you tomorrow.'

'Thanks for being so nice.'

I hurried her out of the front door.

'*Me?* You were the one who was so nice,' I said.

She giggled a second time, and ran down the path.

Draped flaccid over the banisters I treated myself to ten seconds of uninterrupted heavy breathing. Then I was downstairs like a whippet, talc-ing sheets and genitals, checking the pillow for make-up and the dog-ends for lipstick, roping tissues into the wastepaper basket two-handed and sending Gloria's glass beneath the bed with the side of my foot. I thanked the Lord I had slept with Rachel that afternoon: hence oyster smell and churned blankets. Gargling Dettol in the bathroom I looked for post-coital spots. My face was a raspberry purée. I immersed it in a basinful of cold water. If Rachel said anything I'd just have to stutter that I had been terribly worried about everything.

'Do I? No, it's … I've j-j-just been terribly worried about everything. What eck-eck-exactly did your m-mother say?'

'God, it's all so difficult to believe, I know. But you mustn't worry, love. It's not your fault.'

'I feel responsible.'

'Rubbish. My idea in the first place … It was awful, though. She just came into my room and said, quite calmly, "I know you haven't been staying at Nanny's. Would you please tell me where you have been staying, or shall I call the police?"'

'The *police*. Mm, like hell. Who does she think she is? Doesn't she see that none of that's on any more? You're twenty, for fuck's sake, she can't –'

'I told you she was neurotic about some things. I think Daddy …' Rachel knitted her fingers and looked down at her lap.

'What did you tell her?'

'Told her the truth.'

'Couldn't you have sort of made up something? No. I suppose not.'

She sank towards me, shaking and sniffing softly. I put my arm round her shoulders and finished my drink. I noticed that the street-lamps made the dust on the sitting-room windows golden, as if put there for decoration.

On our way downstairs the telephone rang.

'It might be Mummy,' Rachel said.

It wasn't.

'Bellamy here. Charles, is that you?' he asked in a drunken gurgle. 'I suppose you couldn't make it.'

'No. Sorry.'

'I see. Interview tomorrow, then. Well, bonne chance! Perhaps, mm, after it's ... you might – Charles, it would be nice to see you. I want to –'

'No. Sorry. Bye now.' I interrupted him with the dialling tone.

'Who was it?'

'Wrong number.'

You'd have thought that Rachel would be subdued that night, but she was all a-flutter when we got into bed. 'Make me feel safe,' she kept whispering in the dark, 'oh, please, make me feel safe.' Accordingly I furled my limbs about her in a complicated embrace. Yet she kept on whispering. 'Hang on,' I said.

The condom case was empty, of course, so I looked out the box of Sharpshooters. Who needs it, I thought. You'll be coming blood, if anything.

It, too, was empty.

'Damn. None left.'

'No,' said Rachel. 'There was one. I saw it this afternoon. There were two there.'

In a voice that could have been my younger brother's, I asked: 'Are you sure?'

'Positive.'

I turned my back and pretended to fumble in the drawer. 'Ah yes. Here we are. – Whoops! Dropped it in the waste-paper basket! ... damn ... ' My fingers curled round the Gloria-moistened trojan, flicked it aside, and burrowed deeper into the pool of tissue, banana skin and cigarette ash, until it found the one used that afternoon on Rachel herself. I have my standards, thank you. Excuse me, but I do have my principles. True, Gloria's would have been nicer, because Rachel's was much dirtier and danker and *colder* than hers. All the same, that would have been, well, vulgar – and an insult to a fine girl.

Luckily, I had the sort of erection that only familiarity can breed. Wide-eyed with horror, I forced it over the tip, and down.

'There we are.'

Rachel opened the bed to let me in.

Twenty minutes later, next door, I stood gazing into the mirror above the basin. The face there seemed too hollow and disinterested to be my face. As I watched, its expressionlessness became self-conscious, became a smirk, became a smile. Look, kid, the under-twenties do this sort of thing non-stop. Remember: you are only young once. Because the teenager is not designed for guilt but for canine lust; not for regret but for exultation; not for shame but for dismissive, ignorant cynicism. As you yourself have put it, in one of the more hay-fevered passages of 'Only the Serpent Smiles':

> Face full of goo,
> Annotating
> Fuck-lists, mating
> Smells honey-dew;
> Stoked-up heat-haze,
> That guiltless laugh-
> ter in the bath-
> room: the dog days.

The true teenager is a marooned ego but his back is always turned to the new ships; he has a kind of gormless strength that can bear to live with itself. For her, every day, you have been selling your youth. Keep that in mind.

I gave me a wink and reached for the razor-blade. Now: to slit the condom's throat, so that it would flush down the lavatory; a delicate business, since in most moods the bathroom was big enough only for my prick or a cutting edge, not for both, and I was presently to juxtapose the two. Eyes shut, I groped for the teat – stretch it outwards, glance down, and lop the nozzle. It felt rather tight (contraction due to over-use?), but I elongated it (oddly painful), positioned the razor, and looked. Instead of elastic, pinched between finger and thumb, was my foreskin.

My first thought, as the blade tinkled to the floor, was how near I had come to auto-circumcision. My second was: *where had it all gone?*

I found the rubber-band, half buried in hair, shrivelled round my root.

It had broken. Rachel was pregnant.

But the night was young, even if I wasn't.

Rachel sat propped up against the pillow, like a guy, smoking.

'Where've you been?'

'Just freshening up.'

She made room for me.

'Rachel. Would you want me to tell you something that would really worry you even though there might turn out to be no need to worry? Even though it might be quite unnecessary?'

'Of course. And you'll have to tell me now, anyway.'

'Even though I could probably tell you later, when there'd be no need to worry?'

She kissed my cheek. 'Yes. Because I've got something I must tell you, too.'

'Really? What?'

'Tell me first, then I'll tell you.'

'No, you first. Go on. I promise I won't mind, whatever it is.' I couldn't keep the eagerness from my voice.

She drew on the cigarette. The smoke flowed from her mouth and nostrils as she said:

'You know all the things I've told you about my father. All lies. I've never seen him or spoken to him or heard from him in my life.'

I watched the ceiling. 'What, all the stuff about Paris ... ?' She shook her head.

'What, he never even used to telephone you or anything?'

'All lies.'

'Not even a letter?'

'Nothing. Ever.'

My legs stirred.

'Christ.'

She kissed me hurriedly. 'It's so silly, I always do it. I don't know why. I don't mean to.'

'Why do you?'

'I don't know. I just feel it makes me more ... '

'What? More ... substantial? More ... *definite* about your-self?'

'Suppose so. No. It's not that. It just makes me feel less pathetic.'

Her voice sounded altogether different.

'Less pathetic,' she said.

' ... oh, baby, come on, don't worry. I honestly couldn't care less.'

While Rachel cried on my shoulder I reviewed the fiction that was Jean-Paul d'Erlanger. There were one or two felici-tous touches, certainly. I liked the irate telephone calls, for example. And it was impressive that she had covered her tracks so well: those finely gauged remarks about how tactful everyone was, how good they were at not bringing it up. Pre-sumably DeForest was in the dark even now. But the Passion-ate Parisian Painter – and all that catchpenny nonsense about the Spanish Civil War: I mean ... *really*, I ask you.

With fresh curiosity, with a revived sense of the mysterious in her, I kissed the damp corners of Rachel's eyes. Because, come on, she must be mad, mustn't she. I lied and fantasized and deceived; my existence, too, was a prismatic web of mendacity – but for me it was far more – what? – far more ludic, literary, answering an intellectual rather than an emo-tional need. Yes, that was the difference. I hugged her again. What an unknown little thing she was. It felt like being in bed with someone else.

An hour later Rachel was pretty well won round to the opinion that I liked her and found her not entirely contempt-ible. She then asked:

'What was the thing you were going to tell me?'

Some of my mind must have been ticking over on this. When I spoke it was without any mental hesitation.

'Oh, that. Well – seems silly really. No, it's just that I think I've ... ballsed up my papers and won't get into Oxford. I feel I've misjudged it all, in a quite fundamental way.'

As Rachel gushed reassurances, the wind outside, which had been strong all evening, started to make cornily portentous noises, cooed from behind the cellar door, fidgeted with the window-frames.

Midnight: coming of age

So I am nineteen years old and don't usually know what I'm doing, snap my thoughts out of the printed page, get my looks from other eyes, do not overtake dotards and cripples in the street for fear I will depress them with my agility, love watching children and animals at play but wouldn't mind seeing a beggar kicked or a little girl run over because it's all experience, dislike myself and sneer at a world less nice and less intelligent than me. I take it this is fairly routine?

Now I tap The Rachel Papers into a trim pile. The hands of the alarm-clock form a narrowing off-centre V-sign. In seven minutes they will be one.

Of course, I was absolutely delirious the next morning. (I feel the effects still, forty hours later; it occurs to me that exhaustion is the cheapest and most accessible drug on the market.)

Rachel, normally wide-awake at the slightest twitch from me, slept through my hot-lidded fumbling with clothes and Interview literature. At three o'clock, five hours earlier, I promised I would say goodbye before I left. But there seemed little point.

On an impulse, I decided to take The Rachel Papers with me, instead.

Norman sat alone in the kitchen, poring over the *Sun* glamour section. Jen had evidently ceased to concern herself with the propriety of my breakfast.

'When's your train?'

'Nine five.'

(You went along to the college to find out the time of your interview. However, I was a mid-alphabet man and didn't reckon on it being before ten thirty.)

'Ages,' said Norman.

In silence we had some tea and bread-and-butter – again, coffee was the breakfast of queers, toast that of left-wingers. My tongue felt hirsute and my teeth itched.

Twenty to nine: 'Come on, let's go. You look fucking chronic in that suit. Where'd you get it? Army surplus? Here, there's a letter for you. Foreign.'

Norman revved his Lotus Cortina at the top of the square, blue serge jacket on the rear hook. The car smelled of oil, new plastic, see-through Bri-nylon shirts, and essence of old man's sweat. I glanced at the envelope and put it in my pocket. Coco.

'Ready?'

Five seconds of juddering wheel-spin and we catapulted down the hill.

'*Jenny tired?*' I yelped, as Norman ground us into a four-wheel skidding turn up the Bayswater Road.

'*Yeah.*' He decelerated from fifty to nought miles per hour at the traffic-lights. 'Shouldn't get up early now.'

At the first hint of amber Norman hurled the car forward, threading through the traffic like a skier.

'*How long to go then?*'

'*Late May.*'

'*Pleased about it?*'

He shrugged, crunched down into second gear, parped his horn (a fruity yob's Klaxon, which played the first four notes of 'Here Comes the Bride'), and screamed past a lorry on the left, causing a nearby pedestrian to drop humbly to his knees in our wake.

More lights.

'Why were you in two minds about having it?' Norman revved challengingly and murmured threats at the driver of an adjacent milkfloat. 'Didn't want to get tied down, or what?' We were off again, flattened into our seats by the *g*'s.

'Have you, *have you ever fucked a tart who's had a kid?*'

'*No.*' He didn't hear and turned to me, mouth ajar. I shook my head.

214

'*Well I –*' he zig-zagged crazily, squeezed between a taxi and a newspaper van, and drifted two-wheeled up Queensway – '*well I fucking have. And it's no joke. Don't know you're there.*'

Norman squalled to a roasted halt broadside a zebra-crossing, allowed a dumpy blonde to swank past, and whipped the car forward again, snicking the overcoat buttons and ironing the toecaps of two siamese dotards.

'*Like waving a flag in space.*'

More lights. I wanted to ask Norman if he had read Swinburne, but he continued: 'Their guts flop too. Jen'll be okay for one, maybe more. No, fuck, I said she could adopt some, but – *tarts like having babies!* Their cunts', he flicked off the heater, 'turn to mush. Tits' – we pulled away – '*smell of bad milk. And they hang. Pancake tits.*'

'Really?'

'Yur. *Jungle tits. But I thought, fuck it. Jen's all right. Firm.* And I don't fuck her that much now. Drop you here. When'll you be back?'

'I don't know,' I said, sounding surprised. 'Probably tonight. Tell Rachel tonight. And thanks for the lift.'

The door-handle was wrenched from my fingers. I watched Norman accelerate determinedly, torso hunched over the wheel, as a checker-board of nuns streamed into the road ahead.

During the one-hour train journey the Interview Folder lay unread upon my lap. I was shaking studiedly – and twice had to go to the lavatory to have some convulsions. Could that be the only reason he had? I had often entertained this as a foul-minded possibility; I never dreamed that it could actually be *true*. And Norman – so vehement, unreflecting, and free. Are we all such emotional Yahoos? Was it strange that Norman should show a reluctance to dunk his rig into a blood-heat steak-and-kidney pudding for the rest of his life? Wouldn't you?

Going through my pockets for handkerchiefs I came across

the letter from Coco. I could hardly remember who she was supposed to be. Anyhow, she apologized for confusing me with her reference to 'Maybe Land'; it was an expression Coco and her friends used, roughly denoting the area of fantasy or human desire; in fact, the place didn't exist. As regards my other inquiry (whether or not I'd get to fuck her when she came to England), '... I'm not sure that perhaps I'm ready too ...' By way of reply – first draft – I dashed off a prose paraphrase of Marvell's 'To His Coy Mistress': 'If we had all the time in the world, your becoming "modesty" would be quite acceptable. We could relax, and consider,' etc., etc. Normally this exercise would have both calmed and stimulated me. Now, it did neither.

I walked up and down the train, smacked like a pat-ball from side to side as the carriages rocked and swayed. Discarded newspapers, bacterial cakes and rigid sandwiches, swindle-cups half full of grey tea, children, small Harry Secombes with grimed mouths and cheeks, tended by women you might mistake for retired footballers, expressionless men, alone.

I knocked and entered Dr Charles Knowd's rooms, not even partially naked, and with my Adam's apple on the tip of my tongue. According to the lodge notice-board the interview had begun ten minutes ago; the blazered, unsettlingly handsome porter (whom I addressed variously as 'sir', 'your serene highness', etc., like a Yank) himself escorted me to the correct staircase and told me which study to go to. I came in shouting apologies.

Opposite each other, facing an unlit electric fire, sat a pair of hippies. One of them, presumably the doctor, waved his hand at me and said, without looking up:

'The room across the corridor. Five minutes.'

There was a further hippie in the room across the corridor.

'Hi,' I said. 'What's going on around here? Are you next?'

'What's your name?'

'Highway.' What's yours? Manson?

'Right. I'm after you.'

'Is Dr Knowd the one in there with the longer hair?'

He looked straight ahead and nodded. 'I hear he's quite a cool guy. About the coolest guy in Oxford. Around now.' He went on nodding. 'Seminars on Berryman. Snodgrass. Sexton. Guys like that.'

'Christ. What will you be telling him about?'

He bunched his fist and swirled it in the air, as if making some lazy threat. 'If I can just get into Robert Duncan. Or Hecht, maybe ... '

Who *were* these people? I had studied neither the Extremists nor the Liverpudlians.

While I undid my top four shirt-buttons, took off my tie and noosed my forehead with it, put on my jacket inside out (the lining, thank heaven, was slightly torn), and tucked my trousers into my boots, the hippie asked, 'Hey. What are you doing?'

'Bit hot,' I said.

'Yeah?'

'Hey look, just how old is he, do you know?'

'Twenty-five. Six. He's very active.'

'Active?'

'For reform.'

'What do you mean?' Letting girls stay in until midnight rather than eleven thirty? Serving breakfast ten minutes later? 'What sort of reform? Political?'

'Yeah. *Political* reform.'

'Oh shit.'

The door opened.

'Highway?' The second hippie gestured with his beard.

I raced towards him. 'That's me.'

'You're next.'

'Hey, how did it go?' I whispered.

Gatty, it must have been, paused on the stairs. 'Okay, I think. Don't worry, he's pretty friendly. Nice cat.'

'What did you talk about?'

'The Russian neo-symbolists.'

*

Dr Knowd had moved to a cushionless window-seat in the far corner of the room where the December breeze playfully tangled the errant curls of his hair.

'Does the air bother you?' he asked, in a voice without much in the way of accent; rather like my own.

'Not at all. Do you mind if I take my jacket off, actually?'

'Not at all.'

I could see my exam-papers resting on his thighs. They were marked in red ink.

'Sit,' the man said.

On the floor. No: too obvious – too *simplistic*. From a choice of sofa, two armchairs and a stool, I took the last. For Knowd, who continued to sift unemphatically through my papers, was in urban-guerrilla dress: variegated, camouflage-conscious green and khaki canvas suit; beetle-crusher, pig-stomper boots; beret. Jack-Christ face and hair. Softly I hummed the Internationale, in order to stop my teeth chattering.

'Mr Highway ... do you like literature?'

Oh come *on*. What kind of question is that? What novels have you been reading recently? What are your problems?

I smiled. 'What kind of question is that?'

'I beg your pardon.' He glanced up at me. 'But if I've read your papers correctly ... '

Sweat flushed my face and armpits. I took out a handkerchief.

Knowd spoke. 'For example. In the Literature paper you complain that Yeats and Eliot ... "in their later phases opted for the cold certainties that can work only outside the messiness of life. They prudently repaired to the artifice of eternity, etc., etc." This then gives you a grand-sounding line on the "faked inhumanity" of the seduction of the typist in *The Waste Land* – a point you owe to W. W. Clarke – which, it seems, is just a bit *too* messy all of a sudden. Again, in the Criticism paper you jeer at Lawrence's "unreal sexual grandiosity", using Middleton Murry on *Women in Love*, also without acknowledgment. In the very next *line* you scold his "over-facile equation of art and life".'

He sighed. 'On Blake you seem quite happy to paraphrase the "Fearful Symmetry" stuff about "autonomous verbal constructs, necessarily unconnected with life", but in your Essay paper you come on all excited about the "urgency ... with which Blake educates and refines our emotions, side-stepping the props and splints of artifice". Ever tried side-stepping a splint, by the way? Or educating someone urgently, for that matter?

'Donne is okay one minute because of his "emotional courage", the way he seems to "stretch out his emotions in the very fabric of the verse", and not okay the next because you detect ... what *is* it you detect? – ah yes, a "meretricious exaltation of verbal play over real feeling, tailoring his emotion to suit his metrics". Now which is it to be? I really wouldn't carp, but these remarks come from the same paragraph and are about the same stanza.

'I won't go on ... Literature has a kind of life of its own, you know. You can't just use it ... ruthlessly, for your own ends. I'm sorry, am I being unfair?'

There was a knock at the door.

'We'll be just a minute,' he called.

I hawked richly into my handkerchief and studied its contents. Knowd stood up and so I did, too.

'Is it really as ... ?' I shrugged and looked at the floor.

He held out my papers. 'Would you like these? I've included a break-down of one of your more pageant-like essays, it may interest you to see it. Would you like to take another look at them, see if you agree?'

I shook my head.

'All right. Now. I want you to do a great deal of hard thinking in the next nine or ten months – I'm going to take you anyway; if I don't, somebody else will and you'll only get worse. Stop reading critics, and for Christ's sake stop reading all this structuralist stuff. Just read the poems and work out whether you like them, and why. Okay? The rest comes later – hopefully. You'll get the letter in a few days. Tell Leigh to come in, would you?'

*

Oxford skylines offered spurious serenity in the form of gold stone against sharp blue, which I of course refused. I wondered what made this town think it was so different. Keep your eyes level and your feet on the ground and I don't see how you can miss the ugly, normal, tooling, random street-life of record-shops, dry-cleaners, banks. Once you stop following the architectural lines upwards, then it's just like anywhere else. But Oxford doesn't think so; never known a place so full of itself. And not a single person looked at me as I walked to the station.

In George Street, though, I stopped, put down my case, and straightened my tie. Then I did what I suppose I had been intending to do all along. I turned right into Gloucester Green and asked the time of the next bus to the village. There was one in fifteen minutes. I felt hungry, something I couldn't remember ever having felt before, so I had some liquid fudge in the cafeteria, and also a tapeworm omelette (or a 'bacon' omelette, to use the menu's phrase). Then I went home.

Mother and her youngest son were in the passage by the back door. She was polishing Valentine's shoes, while he picked his nose, with both hands, paying elaborate justice to either nostril. They greeted me as if I had nipped down to the shop and back.

'Hello,' I said. 'I've been for my interview – and I got in! ... I've been accepted. To Oxford.'

It appeared to make few odds to Valentine, who was anyway nibbling on a rather complicated bogey. But mother said:

'That's rather super, isn't it?'

'Yes.'

'Your father – Valentine, darling, *don't* do that – will be pleased.'

'When's he coming?'

'About six, he said. Um. Charles, there isn't much lunch, because I'm afraid I –'

'Doesn't matter. I'll help myself.'

Upstairs I began the Letter to Rachel. Three hours' work and the fair copy was written out. I have the carbon before me now. It reads:

My dearest Rachel,

I don't know how anyone has ever managed to write this kind of letter – anyone who does is a coward and a shit and used to dishonesty, so I can only minimize all three of these by being as candid as possible. I got a feeling some weeks ago that what I felt for you was changing. I wasn't sure what the feeling was, but it wouldn't go away and it wouldn't change into anything else. I don't know how or why it happens; I know that it's the saddest thing in the world when it does.

But it is I who have changed, not you. So let me hope you feel (as I do) that it has been worth it, or that it will turn out to have been worth it, and let me beg your forgiveness. You are the most important thing that has ever happened to me. C.

There was a pleasingly unrehearsed air about the repetition of 'feeling' and 'feel' and of 'changing' and 'changed'. That 'it is I' seemed rather prissy; perhaps 'it's me' would have been a bit beefier and ... more modest. And I still can't decide whether all the 'it's' and 'don'ts' are nastily groovy or nicely Robert Frost. But, so far as I know, Rachel is not a fastidious reader.

I wrote it out once more, altering accidentals. Coco's letter would have to do as it was.

On the way to the front door, the telephone rang. It was for me. I put the envelopes down on the hall table, not wishing to smudge them.

'So how did it go?'

'Mm? Oh fine. I got in.'

' ... You don't sound very pleased.'

'Oh, I am really.'

' ... Why didn't you come home?'

'Dunno really. Felt a bit shattered.'

' … When will you be?'

I clenched my teeth. 'Not really sure. I feel a bit, I don't know, strange.'

Rachel gulped. 'Charles, what is it?'

'I'm sorry. The interview was a bit harrowing. Not a bit what I expected.'

'But you did get in?'

'Oh yeah. Have you heard from your mother yet?'

'Yes, she rang this morning. She almost apologized. Archie's coming round to get me this afternoon. I suppose I'd better go back. Shall I?'

'Oh, yes, definitely. Far the best thing. Look, sorry I'm being so awful. Don't worry about anything, I'll most likely be back tomorrow. Ring you if I'm not. Okay? I love you. Right. Bye!'

And I felt next to nothing as I walked to the village; I paid my respects to the countryside yet was unable to detect solemn sympathy in its quiet or reproach in its stillness. Usually that road brought me miles of footage from the past: the bright-faced ten-year-old running for the Oxford bus; the lardy pubescent, out on soul-rambles (i.e. sulks), or off for a wank in the woods; the youth, handsomely reading Tennyson on summer evenings, or trying to kill birds with feeble, rusted slug-guns, or behind the hedge smoking fags with Geoffrey, then hawking in the ditch. But now I strode it vacantly, my childhood nowhere to be found.

The drinks were on Mr Bladderby when he heard the happy news, and I stayed chatting to him and his wife for twenty minutes with the letters still in my pocket. That landlord had imploded a few more blood-vessels, Mrs Bladderby had lost her mother, two front teeth, and about a third of her hair, but all in all I was surprised how little they had changed. It seemed I had been away for years. No, not years. Days? No, nor days. It seemed I had been away for three months.

On my return, however, after a visit to the post office, the hollow feeling began to be displaced. So the trees obliged me by wringing their hands when I approached the lane, and the wind booed me as I made my way to the house, slowly, in frightened tears.

The Letter to My Father – what a remarkable document it is. Lucid yet subtle, persistent without being querulous, sensible but not unimaginative, elegant? yes, florid? no. Ah, if Knowd-all could have read this. The only question is: what do I do with it?

The old rogue didn't in fact turn up until Tuesday, this morn-ing. I took the Letter along when I went to see him in his study, on the off-chance.

'I've been for the interview. I got in.'

My father appeared to be genuinely delighted. He came up and cuffed me on the shoulder. It was the first time we had touched for years. It made me blush.

'Pity we're too early for a drink,' he said.

'Yes. The thing is – not all that important – but I wondered whether I couldn't go to my second-choice college. I know it's not as good, but I didn't much like the don who interviewed me. He's got a lot of crappy ideas. And he says "hopefully".'

'Hopefully? But –'

'No, he says the *word* "hopefully". I'm in all right.'

He smiled, as he had smiled on Norman's stairs, and in the bathroom passage here, and a hundred times before: at my moods, my opinions, the letters I made him sign explaining my unwillingness to do PT, at each show of eccentricity. I didn't care now.

'*Well*,' he said. 'Is he giving you a scholarship?'

I said I wasn't sure.

'If he is it may well mean another college is after you and he wants to get you before they do, so to speak.' My father laughed, so I thought I might as well laugh.

'He did say that if he didn't take me someone else would.'

'Then perhaps he is going to give you an award, in which case I'll ring old Sir Herbert and see what he suggests. Yes?'

'Yes, fine.'

There followed a silence, quite a relaxed one.

'Uh, father, don't think I'm getting hostile again – I'm not asking this petulantly – but what do you think's going to happen with you and mother? I'm not challenging – just want to know. I realize I've been ... but I think I understand these things better now.'

My father sat down and motioned me to do the same. He crossed his little legs and stitched his fingers; he looked alert, as if trying to evaluate my sincerity. Then, throwing his head back, Gordon Highway said:

'I expect I shall stay with your mother at least until Valentine is grown up, possibly ... probably longer. It's highly likely that we'll never separate.'

'You're not considering divorce?'

'Not at this moment in time. As you know, it's an extremely expensive and ... messy business, not to be undertaken without desperately serious thought. As you know. And marriage is always something of a compromise, as I'm sure you're now aware. Any long-term relationship is – and one does *have* to see it in the long term, Charles. No, I expect your mother and myself will never divorce.' He shrugged his self-effacement. 'It's uneconomic and, at my age, usually unnecessary.'

This may be bluffing, but I think that one of the dowdiest things about being young is the vague pressure you feel to be constantly subversive, to sneer at oldster evasions, to shun compromise, to seek the hard way out, etc., when really you know that idealism is worse than useless without example, and that you're no better. The teenager can normally detach his own behaviour from his views on the behaviour of others; but I had no moral energy left.

And besides. Twenty tomorrow. Get my hair cut, get my trousers taken out and turn-ups put on them, buy some fawn cardigans, wool socks, brogues.

'I see,' I said, 'Well, that seems reasonable.'

'And what about you?'

'Eh?'

'How are you getting on with your young lady?'

224

There was a pause between 'with' and 'your'; even so I was surprised, almost moved, not by his question but by the fact that he had asked it.

'It's all over. I lost interest. For a number of reasons.'

He rubbed his cheeks. 'Yes, that's always a shame, of course, but don't be got down by it. These things come and go. It's all experience.'

'You're telling me. It's experience all right. And why—' I felt the uneasiness of a good actor with bad lines – 'why does it take so long coming and so little time going?'

My father laughed wealthily. 'My dear boy, if I knew the answer to that question I should be a happy man.' He slapped his hands on his thighs. 'Well! I'm glad we've had this chat. It's cleared the air. See you at dinner?'

'Possibly. I might have something early. Letters to write, and so on.'

'Of course.'

My penultimate teenage experience occurred at 6.30 p.m., nearly five and a half hours ago. I had been to the pub and was struggling with the front door, a bottle of plonk in both pockets. I waited. Gradually, as though it were the least I could expect, I heard the sound of wheels on gravel. I turned : headlights at the corner of the drive.

The red Jaguar pulled up. Rachel's dark glasses stared straight at me. DeForest was so keen not to stare straight at me that he scraped against one of the stone urns in the porch.

'Hello,' I said.

DeForest chose to stay in the car.

I led Rachel to my room in businesslike silence. She sat on the bed and dug a cigarette from the handbag on her lap, taking her eyes off me for a moment. I found I was unsurprised and unfrightened. I pretended to be both.

'Did you get my letter?'

'Yes, I did.' She was trying to be officious, as if my letter had threatened imminent legal proceedings and she wasn't about to be fucked with. 'Yes, I did, and that's why I've come here to see you. Do you think you can –'

But she soon faltered. Her head dipped and she lifted a hand with a crumpled Kleenex in it to steady her sunglasses. Her shape seemed to recede before my eyes.

Now I go over and pick out the single cigarette-end from the wastepaper basket. It has a brown smudge. In an experimental spirit I lick the brown smudge. It tastes of ashtrays and I chuck it back. All the same, I think that that was quite a sensual and adventurous thing to have done.

I waited patiently for her to start crying, so that I could move in out of the painful, full-on gaze.

'Why ... ' She swallowed. 'Why do you want to?'

Her nose shone.

'I don't know. But I do. I'm sorry.'

'And that –' She flicked off her sunglasses to get at her eyes. She was crying. I closed in. Rachel cried into her tissue, then on my shoulder, then into her tissue again. 'That *horrible letter*.' She shuddered.

And I stirred.

'What was so horrible about it? It wasn't meant to be horrible. What was it?'

She shook her head.

'The content or the style? I realize it might have seemed a bit short, even brusque perhaps. But that was because it made me very unhappy to write it.'

'So *cold*,' she said, as if recalling an Icelandic holiday.

I resumed: 'Well, probably anything would have seemed "cold" after' – I coughed – 'what we've had.'

Three minutes to go. I return to the wastepaper basket and find Rachel's mascara-ed ball beneath the layers of tissue steeped in my own snot and tears. I examine it, then let it fall

226

noiselessly from my hand. I cover it now with the Letter to My Father.

'But, Rachel. I've been thinking and I'm sure that I can't give you what you want and need. I don't know, perhaps DeForest can.'

If only he didn't have quite such a preposterous name.

Rachel gave me a fierce glance over her tissue, and it occurred to me that I had better start crying too. But that would create more problems than it would solve.

'What can I say?' I asked.

I wished she would go. I couldn't feel anything with her there. I wished she would go and let me mourn in peace.

Five minutes later, she did. She left without telling me a thing or two about myself, without asking if I knew what my trouble was, without providing any sort of come-uppance at all. She left a present, though, and a fairly significant one. The Annotated Blake.

Which reminds me – I never did give her anything, did I?

Six fifty to six fifty-five I had convulsions and I saw stars: vomitless retching, tearless heaves; I thought, I'm having convulsions and I'm watching stars.

By seven I felt fine. I considered Oxford, and I began to give the short-story competition some thought.

Now I go over to my desk and take a fresh quarto pad from the drawer. I wonder what sort of person I can be. I write:

In the dressing-table mirror Ruth saw her idiot teddybear and her idiot golliwog propped against the pillows, staring from behind. She put the letter back in the envelope and put the envelope back in the drawer. She looked down at the rubble of hopeless, pointless make-up, and up again. She leaned forward, fingering the barely perceptible lump on her chin. She smiled. If that wasn't a pre-menstrual spot, she thought ... what was?

227

I read the paragraph through. Twice. It isn't really convincing.

I walk towards the window and I notice that it has gone twelve. I sit on the chair and dangle a leg over the arm. I refill my pen.